ABOUT THE AUTHOR

Colin Bostock-Smith was raised in a remote Devonshire village but made his way to London where he was first a journalist on the London Evening Standard, then turned to writing comedy scripts for the likes of the Two Ronnies, Rowan Atkinson, Tim Brooke-Taylor, Basil Brush and President Ronald Reagan.

Today he lives in deepest East Sussex with his partner Ruth, and writes novels about crime and passion in a remote Devonshire village.

Published in Great Britain in 2024
By Diamond Crime

ISBN 978-1-915649-45-4

Copyright © 2025 Colin Bostock-Smith

The right of Colin Bostock-Smith to be identified as the author of this work has been asserted in accordance with the Copyright, Designs and Patents Act 1998.

All rights reserved.

No part of this publication may be reproduced, stored in a retrieval system, or transmitted in any form or by any means without the prior permission in writing of the publisher, nor be circulated in any form of binding or cover other than that in which it is published.

All characters appearing in this work are fictitious. Any resemblance to real persons, living or dead, is purely coincidental.

Diamond Crime is an imprint of Diamond Books Ltd.

Book Cover design: Jen Rowlands
(https://www.jenrowlandspainting.com)

For information about Diamond Crime authors
and their books, visit:
www.diamondbooks.co.uk

For Ruth. Of course.

STING OF THE NETTLE

Colin Bostock-Smith

CHAPTER ONE

It's an early-summer morning and there's a thin mist shrouding the house and buildings that make up the small West Devon farmstead. The year is 1952, a time when such farms are still integral units, owned by the farmers themselves, and years away from having their hedgerows bulldozed to create vast deserts of agricultural eternity.

The crows in the treetops surrounding the farm may seem to be the only things awake at this time of the morning. But they're not.

The door of the farmhouse opens slowly and silently, and a man perhaps in his early fifties, steps out, closing it quietly behind him. He carries a small single-barrelled 4.10 shotgun. The man is impeccably dressed, as if it was market day in nearby Hatherleigh. His brown shoes are topped by shiny leather gaiters. Tucked into them are a pair of old-fashioned jodhpurs. He wears a neat shirt and tie, a yellow waistcoat, and a check jacket with leather patches at the elbows. A man of the country, looking about as good as a countryman can look.

He walks carefully across the cobbles and trodden earth of the yard, avoiding the cowpats, past the cowshed, the cob barn, and the newish machine shed with its galvanised iron roof, and so on, through a small wooden gate into the orchard.

Once there, he stands with his back to an ancient apple tree, places the single barrel of the gun under his chin, and pulls the trigger.

The crows come clattering out of the trees at the report. But something has gone wrong. The farmer has missed his main target, and merely blown his left ear off.

He leaves a trail of blood as he walks less steadily back to the farm house. He disappears inside, then reappears, ejecting the used cartridge from his shotgun and replacing it with a new one. He regains the orchard, and his position with his back to the tree. This time his aim is true.

The crows, who've just resettled themselves, rise again in furious condemnation.

CHAPTER TWO

While food rationing remained a minor headache for urban-dwelling housewives, even in early 1952, it hardly impinged on the every-day diets of those who lived in the small villages that dotted the West Devon countryside. Take eggs, for instance. Even in wartime there had been a plentiful supply available from the pens and deep-litter sheds that littered the back alleys and lanes of North Tawe.

"Can I have another?" Police Constable Martin looked up from his yolk-smeared plate to his wife Mary as she hovered over the Rayburn.

"You've had two, Derek," she told him with mock severity. "And half that last one is running down your chin."

Nonetheless she ladled one more shining golden example from the heavy iron pan, and Derek attacked it with his usual technique – that is, slicing off all the white and eating that, before plunging a finger of toast into the yolk, and lifting it in the direction of where he hoped his mouth was. Mary fetched a dishcloth and handed to him.

"You can mop yourself up," she told him. "You're twenty-two. Not two."

"Don't move!" he instructed abruptly.

"What?" She froze.

"If you stay quite still, the light from the window means I can see right through your blouse."

"Oh you..." Mary half-tried to be cross but giggles

Sting of the Nettle

overcame her, and Derek pulled her down onto his lap.

"You shouldn't be such a sex-siren," he told her, as he kissed her cheek.

"You'll get egg on me."

"I'll lick it off."

Mary allowed herself a momentary but luxurious morning hug, then escaped his clutches.

"This won't do," she told him. "I've got school. Third year Shakespeare. What about you, what have you got to do today?"

"Sod all."

"Derek!"

"No, really. Nothing."

That was the problem of being a village copper. At least, for being the village copper for North Tawe and its nearby hamlets. Nothing ever happened. Well, not much. The biggest event of the past 10 days had been the vicar backing his Austin Seven into a gate post and demolishing it. But as the gatepost was situated at the entrance to the vicarage, no police action seemed advisable.

"There's always the garden..." Mary hinted.

Derek groaned audibly. "I might have a look at it." 'It' was an awesome green jungle, enjoying years of neglect. He yawned, then burped silently, relishing the taste of fried egg. The prospect of another day of boredom seemed to stretch ahead into infinity...

The distant crash of a bicycle hitting the tarmac, a furious knocking on the front door and Derek just beat Mary in the race to the door, where they found a small boy of about ten apparently having some kind of

Sting of the Nettle

breathless seizure

"He's been shot. Shot dead," the boy screeched.

Derek recognised him as the son of the local builder who ran his business from a barn at the rear of the Green Dragon, the village pub. Shot? Shot dead? My God! Derek felt his heart give a thump. Perhaps, at last, after those long weeks of boredom and inaction, something had finally happened. Perhaps he had a murder on his hands. While the boy was still getting his breath back, the pub landlord, John Jacob himself arrived, with a more measured announcement of the death of Old Tom Williamson. Apparently, Farmer Tom's wife had rung Jacob and transmitted the news that her husband was lying in the orchard with his head spread.

Later, Derek would wonder why on earth Mrs Williamson had chosen to ring the pub, and not him, with her appalling news. But that was village life for you. The pub was seen as the core of the village. Or failing the pub, the grocer's shop. Or failing that, the bakery. Not the police house. And certainly not the immature young constable who some said didn't know his arse from his...

As it turned out, Derek's initial optimism was, well, optimistic. Murder, accident, suicide, or whatever, there was no chance of him being able to deal with a sudden death incident on his own. This was something he had to report in. He thanked John Jacob and the boy, neither of whom showed any intention of leaving the doorstep. Something was happening in the village at last!

He walked back in to the hall, where the telephone sat inconveniently on a small table. He'd applied for it to be moved to his desk, a suggestion which had been received with bewilderment by the authorities in Exeter. God had ordained that telephones in houses must be placed on the hall table. Now his call to the local station went through to the duty constable, who put him through to Sergeant Welbeloved.

Hearing of the sudden demise of Old Tom Williamson, the sergeant said nothing for a moment, but Derek heard a sound that told him the man was taking a swig of tea from his mug marked "Mine". When he did speak, he sounded as if he received news of violent death every half hour.

"Don't panic," he told Derek blandly. "Calm down. No need to panic."

There's nothing more annoying, Derek felt, than being told not to panic when you are not panicking.

"I'm not..." he paused to bring the tone of his voice down a notch or two. "I'm not panicking. I'm just reporting in, before getting out to the farm to check this out."

"All right. I'll meet you there. But if you get there first, for God's sake don't touch anything!"

"Yes, Sergeant." Having given the Sergeant the location of the Williamson farm, which took longer for the Sergeant write down than it would most semi-literates, Derek was tempted to slam down the receiver, but thought better of it, and replaced the thing carefully.

"I'm meeting Welbeloved at the farm," he told Mary.

"How exciting for you!" As a youthful but already seasoned teacher she was fluent in irony.

Sting of the Nettle

* * *

Farmer Tom's farm was only a couple of miles out of the village, at the end of a well-maintained lane. Welbeloved met him at the top of the farmyard, ready to give some sound advice to this inexperienced and raw constable.

"This could be nasty, lad," he muttered confidentially.

"Yes?"

"A shotgun. Makes a mess you see."

"I suppose so."

"Very nasty. Brains and all that. First time you look at something like that, well, it's upsetting. For a young lad. You might not want to get close. Close your eyes. Think of something else. Otherwise, hey - you could lose your breakfast." Sergeant mimed a vomiting motion.

"I'll be okay."

"Don't say I didn't warn you."

Derek did get up close. It was an unpleasant sight, but not as unpleasant as one might have imagined. And what was almost a pleasant sight, almost a sight to savour, was the sight of Sergeant Welbeloved hurling his own breakfast into the long grass.

They sat in the farmhouse kitchen, across an oilskin-covered table from Mrs Williamson. She was taking it as well could be expected – that is calmly, even stolidly, apart from the occasional deep sigh. She offered the men slices of seed cake, which Derek, whose wife had recently become calorie-conscious on his behalf, declined. The Sergeant, perhaps in need of something to

Sting of the Nettle

fill a large and empty stomach, accepted. None of them looked out of the kitchen window to the orchard where a special team of men in overalls, summoned by Welbeloved on the farm phone, were taking all that they could scrape up of Farmer Williamson away in an unmarked van.

The Sergeant was suitably respectful as he asked the widow the necessary questions, while Derek took pointless notes in his notebook. Clearly there was a need to discuss the situation without the possibility of suicide being touched on.

Mrs Williamson had all the right answers.

No, Tom had not seemed anything other than his usual self.

No, he had no particular worries, either financial or personal.

Yes, he always got up early, first light at this time of year, early summer.

Yes, they had rabbits in the orchard. And pigeons. Tom often shot one or the other first thing.

No, she'd be fine, didn't need anyone to come and sit with her. She'd rung Peter at college, and he was getting the first train, be back early afternoon.

The daughter? No, she was long gone, they never talked about her. Useless girl, that Margaret.

A licence for the gun? Course they had a licence. Mrs. Williamson found the document immediately, and with a faint sigh of satisfaction. Derek took a note of the licence number, though for what reason he couldn't think. The interview had been pedestrian, the answers almost automatic. Nobody asked the significant question

– why?

The Sergeant didn't speak as he took his ponderous time to get behind the wheel of his police car. The pause gave Derek another chance to think about that question "why?" There had to be a reason behind the dead man's actions. It would be good to find out what it was. Until he did, Derek knew he'd fret about it. It would be, he realised, a niggle. A niggle in his brain. He wondered if the Sergeant was also wondering, whether he too sought an answer to the question why.

As Derek went to mount his motorbike, the Sergeant reappeared, slightly out of breath from the exertion of squeezing in and out of his vehicle. He laid a fat hand on Derek's arm. It transpired he did indeed have something on his mind.

"Listen. You don't want to get in my bad books, now do you?"

"Sorry?"

"You don't want to get on the wrong side of me. I mean to say, I'll be doing reports on you. Know what I mean?"

"Well, of course. I hope I've been doing all right. No complaints?"

"No, no, nothing like that. Listen. It was a bad bit of bacon."

"What?"

"My breakfast this morning. I told my wife it tasted a bit funny. That's why my guts were upset. In the orchard, early on, you see?"

"Oh, right. Right."

"Nothing to write home about, eh? Nothing to talk

about. Nothing worth mentioning. Not to the other lads."

Good God, Derek thought. The man was pleading with him. It was his vomiting that was on his mind. Not the death of Old Tom Williamson.

"Of course not, Sergeant. None of my business, anyway. "

"Good lad."

CHAPTER THREE

Derek stood at the back of the scruffy little Okehampton courtroom and listened, stunned, to the Coroner as he delivered his verdict on the sudden death of Old Tom Williamson. Derek had not been required to give evidence, even though he had been the first officer called to the scene of the tragedy, because his Sergeant, George Welbeloved, had become the senior officer on site, and it was he who had appointed himself to give the necessary information to the Coroner.

When speaking in normal conversation the Sergeant used a lively, expressive and spittle-flecked tone of voice, but on this serious occasion he modified his style, and instead echoed the sonorous tones of newsreader, Alvar Lidell, as he told the court how Mr Williamson had been found beneath the apple tree, with the shotgun by his side and a couple of crushed windfalls under his body. He might have been going to say more - Derek would never know - but the Coroner, who disliked sharing the limelight on these occasions, had cut him off with a brief "Thank you, Sergeant", and now Welbeloved stood alongside Derek, a large and slightly sweaty presence, oozing confidence, authority and body odour.

"I am returning a verdict of Accidental Death," said the Coroner.

There was the briefest moment of silence in the little

Sting of the Nettle

courtroom, as all those present realised that the man had done it again. Never mind the evidence, even if it stared you in the face. Never mind any obvious conclusions. There would be no taint of suicide surrounding the death of Old Tom. No problem with life insurance claims, no nonsense about burial in consecrated ground, no stigma of shame to descend on his family. "Accidental Death" would be the verdict.

Albert Shaw had been the Coroner for the district for thirty-five years – "Man and boy," as he used to say, "But not necessarily in that order!" It was his joke, he made it frequently, and his hearers laughed dutifully, because Albert Shaw demanded respect. He was a tall, white-haired, slightly frail man, and he admitted to sixty-two.

He saw himself as a father figure to the general populace, a guide, a mentor, and, let's face it, superior to almost all of them. He was also a family solicitor, making an excellent living from the conveyances and land deals which his junior partners took care of. At home he was a martinet who bullied his wife. His three adult children loathed him. He didn't care. Here, in the little courtroom, where all present hung on his every utterance, he occupied the seat of judgement unchallenged.

"It is quite clear what happened," Mr Shaw now expanded. "Mr Tom Williamson, known as Old Tom, ventured out to shoot a rabbit for the family supper, and slipped on a rotten apple, thus discharging his gun with fatal results. I offer my most sincere condolences to Mrs Williamson and her family on this tragic accident," he intoned. Then, with just a little edge to the words, he continued: "And I trust that if they should hear any loose speculation regarding the verdict here today, they will ignore it, and not be mizzled."

"Mizzled"? Derek jerked to attention. Was that what the Coroner had said? Mizzled? Derek glanced around the room. No-one else had reacted.

Mizzled?

* * *

In the farming villages of West Devon, deep in the wet and evergreen fields, few took any notice of the Coroner's fanciful verdict. Almost no-one was overly surprised when they heard that Tom Williamson, known as Old Tom despite being still in his fifties, had shot himself. Some pointed out grimly that farmers were often shooting themselves. Local wits replied that they only did it once, of course. But generally speaking it was accepted as a not-that-unusual way for West Country sons of the soil to take their leave of this life.

Why? Why were farmers so prone to topping themselves? There were many answers given. The long lonely hours sitting on a slow, farting tractor, drive you mad, people said. Or the post-war Labour government with its rules and regulations – "them communist bureaucrats who don't give a bugger about agriculture." Or it was the bloody West Devon weather, rain pissing down and flattening the wheat, which could not be lifted by a binder, and so just lay on the clay and rotted. Or perhaps it was just the sheer bloody hard work of harrowing and hedging and shoving cows around which

Sting of the Nettle

made agricultural existence so intolerable to some. Whatever, something or other caused an unlikely number of farmers to forget the original purpose of their shot-guns – the slaughter of rabbits, pigeons and rats – and instead turned their sights on themselves.

And yet one or two eyebrows were raised in Old Tom's nearest village of North Tawe. When you thought about it, Farmer Williamson was not the obvious candidate for a self-administered brain-full of lead pellets. Not the most likely of local worthies to splatter the back of his skull against an ancient apple tree.

For a start, Tom's farm was in a pretty reasonable state. A nice little herd of fifteen Guernseys. A few sheep. Plenty of arable. If anyone was making a decent living off the land in the windy fields of West Devon, it was Old Tom Williamson.

Nice family, too. Well, for the most part. His wife, Alice, was one of those apple-cheeked Devon women, always with a smile on her face. Not that the apple cheeks were an indication of anything more significant than the result of years of facing the elements before dawn on those bitter February mornings when there were cows to milk and calves to feed and the lambing, all at the same time – conditions that would break the veins in the sallowest of cheeks. But she seemed a careful and contented soul, big in the WI, Sunday school teacher at the Methodist chapel, a cheerful and industrious Devon farmer's wife, the sort who always made a trifle for the kids at the do on VE day.

And the Williamsons had children. There was a girl, Margaret, but she wasn't up to much. A bit of a handful, people said, but she'd gone off out of it more than a year ago now, London it was said, never heard from again. But the couple's son, Peter - he was a child to be proud of. Bright lad. Away at Farming College at this tragic time, learning his trade. Eventually he would be expected to take over the farm when it all became a bit too much for his Dad. That was the kind of arrangement many farming families came to. Of course Old Tom would interfere with whatever Peter was getting up to, and Peter would probably find that intolerable, that was to be expected.

But nothing serious. Not something for Mr Williamson to get too upset about. Certainly not enough to make you grab your shotgun one misty morning, do your wife one last favour and not spread your cranial contents all over the front room with its never-used array of Victorian crockery and its antimacassars and its Chambers Encyclopaedia showcase, but instead trudge out to the orchard and...

But that's obviously what Old Tom did. Even if no-one could think precisely why.

CHAPTER FOUR

"Mizzled"?

Derek couldn't get the baffling word off his mind. Or the baffling verdict. For God's sake, what a farce! All the evidence pointed to suicide. Perhaps he should have said something.

But no. Hardly. Admit it, it would have taken a bold individual to stand up unbidden in that shabby little courtroom, and object to Mr Shaw's scenario, to have declared in ringing tones, and in the presence of one's superior, not to mention the recently widowed Mrs. Williamson and her son, that the verdict was arrant nonsense and that the evidence, minimally related as it had been, pointed in an entirely different direction.

Police Constable Derek Martin, two years in the force, despite considering himself to be a courageous young man, was not that bold an individual.

But afterwards, as he relieved himself in the courtroom Gents, examined his face for any more bloody blackheads, and plonked his helmet back on top of his mop of flaming red hair, he allowed his cynical conclusions full rein.

For heaven's sake! It was blindingly obvious even to a casual observer at the scene that there had been not one but two shots that fatal morning. Even an amateur forensic examination of the body would establish that fact. And then there was the trail of blood that led between Tom's corpse and the hallway cupboard in the farm house. The discarded cartridge case. Accidental death, my helmet!

Finishing his post-inquest ablutions, Derek joined his Sergeant outside the courtroom. The two of them stood for a moment in the early summer sunshine, a pose which allowed the sergeant to puff out his uniformed chest until it almost reached the circumference of his stomach, and smile benevolently at passers-by, most of whom were sufficiently intimidated by the sight of authority that they smiled and nodded in return.

"Um, Sergeant," he began...

"What?"

"The Coroner, he said he didn't want the family to be mizzled."

"Oh. Right. Misled."

"Oh. Oh, Lord. Misled. You mean, he mispronounces it."

"He says it wrong, yes."

"But, does he always get it wrong?"

"Far as I know he's been getting it wrong for the last thirty years."

"Well why doesn't someone tell him?"

"Would you?"

No, thought Derek. No he wouldn't. But, 'mizzled'. He kept a straight face under the Sergeant's severe gaze, and told himself that he must remember to tell Mary about it that night. And they'd both be free to giggle.

* * *

Sting of the Nettle

The Sergeant led the way for the half-mile walk back to the Okehampton police station, where, technically speaking, Derek was based. They didn't talk on the walk, so he could think. They didn't talk because 17-stone Sergeant Welbeloved made him wait while he popped into the bakery and emerged with two cream buns, each of which he ate in succession as they made their way through the town centre.

This gave Derek ample opportunity to contemplate the fate of Old Tom Williamson, perhaps to draw a more accurate picture of what actually came about in that orchard that morning rather than the improbable sketch outlined by the coroner, Mr Shaw.

Derek had a clear picture in his mind of what had transpired. He could almost see the farmer tucking the single barrel under his chin, reaching down to find the trigger, something he must have done with some difficulty, he being of short stature and the gun of normal length, and then at the critical moment flinching, which led to the barrel slipping a little sideways, and blasting Old Tom's left ear to tatters.

The shot should, of course, have been heard. But perhaps, Derek reasoned, Tom's wife Mrs. Williamson, still in bed at what was yet an extremely early hour even for a farming family, would indeed have heard the report, and sleepily registered that it would be rabbit for tea. Or with luck, pigeon.

Derek could then envisage Tom Williamson, streaming blood and suffering agony, making his repeat journey across the yard, probably screaming quietly and hoarsely, before finally blowing himself into what the elderly parish vicar at his funeral described as eternal rest.

Now that took guts. That took steely determination. The farmer was going to do away with himself, come what may. After all, Derek reasoned from his admittedly limited experience, for most failed suicides one go is enough. He who casts himself off a bridge into the foaming torrent below, and is then washed up on a patch of shingle, would, one expects, go home, dry himself off and pour himself a large whisky. And she who drinks half a bottle of vodka to wash down a handful of painkillers, and wakes up eight hours later feeling bloody dreadful, will surely be disinclined to repeat the experience.

But not Farmer Tom Williamson. In pain, traumatised, wounded, horrified by the bloody details of his attempted death, he had tried again. And succeeded.

This version of the tragic event was, Derek decided, an accurate account of what had actually happened. And he was convinced that old Tom Williamson, far from suffering an accidental death, had achieved one of considerable purpose. Which raised again the inevitable question – why? What was so terrible about Tom William's life that he went through hell to achieve its end?

Derek wasn't a detective. He had only been a lowly village constable for two brief years. But now he had a mystery to solve. And it niggled. There was an answer to it somewhere. And he needed to find it. He'd start by airing his thoughts, his suppositions, to a more experienced and wiser police mind.

Unfortunately none was available, and he had to

Sting of the Nettle

make-do with Sergeant Welbeloved.

CHAPTER FIVE

"Accidental death?"

Derek squinted through the cloud of Capstan Full Strength smoke that Sergeant Welbeloved blew thoughtlessly into his face.

"So what?" the Sergeant grunted, and sipped at his big china tea mug. You knew it was the Sergeant's personal mug because he had used his wife's nail varnish to paint the word "MINE" on it in rose-pink.

"But it wasn't, was it?"

"Wasn't what?"

"Accidental. I mean, you were there. So was I."

The Sergeant sighed with weary resignation, an expression he employed regularly when he was dealing with naïve remarks from newly-spawned constables. He took another swig from his mug. His wife had been livid about the nail varnish but Sergeant Welbeloved had been married too long to care.

"You heard the Coroner," he told Derek, congratulating himself on being sufficiently unbending and democratic to have a conversational exchange with a juvenile wooden-top. "And you could look at the official record. Or even read the local paper, if that squirt of a reporter gets it right for a change. Accidental death."

"But..."

No, don't bother, Derek told himself. Drink your tea, try to ignore the fact that it was stewed to a kind of, well, stew, and get out of there.

"There" was the station tea-room, where a Mrs. Weston, the office tea-lad, a position unwarranted in such a small establishment as the Okehampton Police Station, but she also did a bit of cleaning so they got away with it – reluctantly poured hot water on what remained in the huge brown teapot and served it up to them, pointing out as she did so that they were late, never mind the inquest, they couldn't expect her to make fresh tea all morning, she had other things to do. Quite what those things were was unclear.

Derek finished enough of his tea to avoid a tedious conversation with Mrs Weston about wasting her precious time. Mrs Weston's time was always 'precious' though you wouldn't think so from the pittance the police authority paid her.

There was no point in continuing to question the Sergeant. In his short time out of training he had learned that sergeants tell constables things. They do not discuss them. Why would they, when they know everything and constables know nothing?

"I'll be off back then," he told the Sergeant. "Off back" meant collecting his laughable little official police two-stroke motorcycle from the station yard and buzzing along through the heavily-hedged Devon lanes to the village of North Tawe.

He was mildly surprised when the Sergeant replied with his usual grunt, but added: "You settled in all right then?"

"Yes, fine."

"Nice little village, North Tawe," the Sergeant

continued. "And your own little police house. Good start for a lad like you."

"Yes."

"Your wife being a village girl."

"Yes."

"Same village too."

"Yes."

"I fixed that, you know. You ought to thank me. Yes, I insisted you got North Tawe."

Did he? Probably not. But there was no point in discussing it.

No point in insisting the last place he wanted to be posted was a sleepy little dump like North Tawe, with its pretty whitewashed cottages and its pub and its church and its shops and its boringly well-behaved citizenry. Yes, yes, by coincidence it was the village in which his wife had been born and raised, and she loved it there, but like they said in the movies, it was Dullsville. After all, he was an Exeter lad. And if he couldn't get placed in Exeter, then Plymouth would do instead. Somewhere where something might actually happen. Something illegal. That is, really illegal. Not like...

Well, just a couple of days ago, for example, it had been after lighting-up time, and he had stopped a young North Tawe lad called Barry Ware for riding his bicycle without showing a rear light. Barry had dismounted, given his rear light a twist which turned it on, and gone on his way rejoicing. Derek had included the incident in his routine report, and felt very silly doing so.

But now had come this - the death of Farmer Tom. Suicide, plain as day, but now officially Accidental

Sting of the Nettle

Death. At least something had happened.

He turned to go but the Sergeant, unusually talkative, called him back. And again unusually, he seemed not quite so full of himself, not quite so bumptious as he was prone to be. He even seemed almost friendly.

"How is Mary?" he asked.

"Fine, thanks."

"Happy to be back home, as it were?"

"Oh yes." Mary was pleased to be 'back home'.

"Good." Another pause. But something in the Sergeant's attitude told Derek he wasn't quite finished. He waited patiently until the man spoke again.

"When you get back, a word of advice".

"Yes Sergeant?" For heaven's sake. Derek strove to keep the impatience out of his voice.

"Don't go rabbiting on about this business, will you? Eh? This verdict thing. You and I, as officers of the law, we might see it one way, and the Coroner might see it another way, and of course, you and I, we were there, as you say, we know what we know but, well, it doesn't do to call these things into doubt. Not good for morale. Might cause talk. Know what I mean?"

Derek could only say one thing. "Yes, Sergeant."

"Off you go then."

Obediently, if a little confused, Derek went off.

CHAPTER SIX

After a couple of miles on his journey aboard the two-stroke, Derek felt a large burp coming on. He allowed its passage. It tasted of Mrs Weston's tea. What on earth did she put in it? Not bromide, at least. Bromide in tea was an experience he had avoided by opting for the police force instead of National Service in the army. Legend had it that new recruits to the armed forces were dosed with bromide in their tea, which effectively dulled or even extinguished their sexual impulses.

The thought led Derek to consider his own sexual impulses. He wondered if by some lucky chance Mary would be home from school early that day. And if so...

It is not wise for a young healthy male to let his romantic speculation, indeed, expectation, run free while riding a motorcycle. It gets uncomfortable. Even dangerous. Derek tried hard to think of something else. It wasn't easy. But after a minute or so, thinking of Sergeant Welbeloved, did the trick.

The Sergeant had been right about one thing. He and Derek had both been there, in that orchard on Farmer Tom's farm. They had both been the officers at the scene. Derek had written a report, but Welbeloved had re-written it, to include some spectacular spelling and inventive syntax, and to exclude any material suggesting the death was not accidental.

Derek had hoped, indeed at first had assumed, that

the tragedy was going to be his first major case. But no. Not with the inept coroner and his bulky sergeant blocking any reasonable investigation. If anything the whole incident had been a damp squib. Accidental death? Pull the other one.

Derek resumed thinking about his wife and the possibilities of her coming early home from school. But she didn't.

Instead he found himself alone, in what he liked to call his office – actually the front room of the house, with bare wooden floor and peeling wallpaper – sitting at what he liked to call his desk – actually an old kitchen table, complete with a ruler, a stapler and a wire tray. Time for office work, he told himself. Yet another illusion, he realised grimly. There was no office work to do.

At that point Derek remembered that there was actually something that he did have to do. And that, lying forlornly and still hopelessly neglected, was his back garden. Well, it was what an imaginative estate agent would describe as a garden but which was in fact an extensive square of vegetative squalor.

Before it had been bought by the Force, and designated a police house, the cottage in North Tawe had been the home of an elderly couple. They had not been well for a number of years, and even when they could move about easily, they were not interested in gardening. So over time what might have been a pleasant back garden became a place to chuck the rubbish, and otherwise to abandon it to nature. Age and a merciful providence eventually disposed of the old pair, and

Sting of the Nettle

while the police authority agreed to some modernisation, including a new Rayburn, a hot water system and an indoor toilet, their effort did not extend to the rear garden, which by then could only be described, perhaps predictably, as a jungle.

The negotiations to buy the property, and then the time taken to re-furbish it, stretched on for nearly two years. During that period Derek and Mary lodged in a single room with "use of facilities" in Okehampton – cramped but handy for Mary's school, while Derek toddled back and forth on his little motorbike between village and town. When, finally, all was ready for them, and they came to view their new home, one of the first things Mary wanted to see was the garden. Derek was keener on checking that the new indoor flush toilet really did work, but after proving that it did, he walked out through the kitchen and the back door, and joined Mary outside.

Together they contemplated their garden.

Mary said: "Well. We've got a job on here all right."

Derek glanced at her. There was a light of enthusiasm, even fervour, in her eyes.

"We?" He queried.

"We. Especially you."

"How about we get a load of concrete in? Smother the lot?" he teased.

Mary glanced at him sideways. "You should be so lucky. The house will do for now. The garden is going to be our project. Bet you've never even used a spade, right?"

"You'll have to show me how. Like, which end to

hold it." Then, with a more meaningful grin, "After all, you've showed me plenty of other things."

Mary backed away, laughing. "Don't start that," she warned.

Derek laughed with her, and thought once again how lucky he'd been to find her, to catch her and keep her. A village girl who'd made good, gone to the Grammar School, then trained as a teacher, and now bringing in a healthy wage. But more than that, definitely the best looker for miles. Slim, graceful, with long slender legs – not at all your average Devon girl, he thought, remembering a recent village dance where the local "maids", as girls were termed in those rural parts, toughened by work on their fathers' farms and nourished on pasties and cream, sat in long patient rows displaying equally long patient rows of formidable purple thighs.

He gestured at the garden. "How are we going to tackle this then? Tools cost money."

"My dad will lend us some. He's bringing them over later. There's no way out of this, you know. And you can start by clearing that lot."

She pointed at a small mound about four feet square towards the back of the plot upon which sprouted a menacing crop of stinging nettles.

"What, bash them down?"

"No. Dig them out, roots and all. Otherwise they just come back. They're a pain."

Derek looked at the offending growths. "Funny, they just grow there, on that bit."

"There'll be a body underneath."

"What?"

"Don't get excited, Constable. Someone's dog probably. Nettles like that sort of thing."

"Great. A bloody great jungle and a dead dog. Welcome to your new home."

And now, so many months later and with the back garden as formidable a challenge as it had ever been despite Derek's spasmodic efforts, he contemplated the aggressive greenery. Then, before he could even pick up a spade, thank heaven the phone rang.

* * *

There was a job for him. A police job. He could have left the job until tomorrow. Or the next day. But, given the choice between spadework and police work he dutifully, and gratefully, chose police work.

A local man had failed to produce his driving licence on request, and subsequently failed to produce it at Okehampton police station within a stated time. Derek was bidden to follow up this minor infraction. The guilty party was not unknown to him. His name was Beauvoir, but he was known by all and sundry as Bucky, and he lived about two miles out of the village in what had once been a thriving smallholding, but since Bucky had inherited it from his father had now decayed into something of a shambles.

Derek was aware of him. Bucky was one of those characters who lived on the edge of minor criminal behaviour. He'd been in trouble before, nothing too dreadful, poaching, and once causing an affray - in Torquay of all places. Now he scraped a living dealing in scrap metal and spare parts for antiquated farm equipment.

Bucky's establishment wasn't the easiest place to get to on two wheels. Derek drove his bike down the ruts in the long and corroded lane from the main road with hesitant care. The house itself stood in a surprisingly large plot of land. To its front was the remains of a formal garden, but now the space was hopelessly overgrown, and only an old mangle and an oil drum could be seen amongst the scrub.

The house itself was a tumbledown cottage with a thatch roof beginning to slide off its rafters. There had, Derek knew, been a wife, but she'd left some years ago. "Good riddance" Bucky told his friends. To the rear of the building was at least an acre of land, which Bucky's father had used as a depot for his scrap metal dealings. Now, since the old man's death in a flu epidemic, it had degenerated into nothing but overgrown wasteland. Some disused and broken farm machinery stood in rusting glory.

Otherwise the area was given over to impassable mounds, hummocks of nettles and other weeds, ditches and a few stunted and neglected trees. Thanks to his father's efforts, Bucky owned the whole place. But Derek, as he walked through the front 'garden', stepping over a mound of unidentifiable muck and nearly barking his shins on what he thought might have been the shaft of a hand-held seed-drilling machine, felt Bucky was welcome to it. It was, he decided, an offensive and smelly dump.

The door to the cottage was around the side, a rickety

affair with a cracked window, through which Derek could see a kitchen. There was no knocker or bell – no, there wouldn't be, he told himself. Such refinements were quite beyond Bucky. Instead he pounded on the door with a clenched fist, making the thing sway on its hinges. Then he waited, amused to find himself half-hoping that there would be no reply.

"What?"

One word, uttered with derision, contempt, even malice. Derek, startled, turned. Bucky had emerged from behind the building and now stood some eight or ten feet away, facing Derek, in a posture of a proud
and suspicious owner resenting the presence of an unwelcome visitor.

He was a formidable sight – about 30, tall, burly, whiskery, in corduroys, a collarless shirt, and a kind of big leather waistcoat, and he carried a double-barrelled shotgun which, Derek was relieved to see, was broken in the correct manner.

Conversation was brief, a mixture of sneers on Bucky's part and patient requests on Derek's, but in the course of time Bucky produced the necessary paperwork. The visit had been a waste of everyone's time, Derek concluded, as he went back to retrieve his motorcycle.

Glancing over his shoulder he noticed that Bucky had remained standing by the cottage, watching, making sure he'd gone. And there was something else. Way beyond the home, at the far end of the back area, partly hidden in some saplings, was a white object. Derek squinted. Yes, a car. A white sports car. What was it doing there,

Sting of the Nettle

on the other side of the chaotic wasteland? How did it even get there? For a moment Derek was tempted to go back and demand the documents relating to that vehicle. But he felt one tedious conversation with Bucky per day was quite enough.

Nonetheless it had passed the afternoon and filled the time when he should have been gardening. Back home he had just time to pick up the discarded spade and assume an appropriate stance to confront the nettles, before Mary returned home from her school.

"You haven't done much." it was not a promising start to the evening.

"Been busy. The inquest went on a bit."

"Oh yes. The inquest. How did it go?"

"Accidental death."

"What?" Knowing the details as she did, Mary was equally surprised. "That coroner. He's hopeless, isn't he."

"Yes. I mean. Why? Not why the coroner got it so wrong. Probably thought he was doing the right thing, the old fool that he is. But why did Tom Williamson do it? There has to be an answer."

Mary looked sideways at him. "Oh-oh. I know what this is. It's another of your wretched niggles, isn't it.

"Well..."

Mary gave an exaggerated sigh. She knew all about Derek's niggles. That itch that got into his brain, the puzzle that became an obsession. She knew the Williamson affair had now become such a niggle. Something that he wouldn't let go. Something that he couldn't let go.

Sting of the Nettle

"Oh well," she said wistfully sarcastic. "Goodbye to a quiet life.

Derek grinned sheepishly. He knew she was right. He decided to change the subject.

"Oh, another thing about the Coroner. Guess what.

"What?"

"He says mizzled."

"He says what?"

"Mizzled. He means misled. Mizzled! Silly old sausage. No-one dares to correct him."

Mary put on her prim school-teacher face. "You shouldn't laugh. It probably stems from reading too much at an early age, without knowing the pronunciation."

"Yes, but 'mizzled'!"

"And you do it too, you know."

"I do not," Derek was suddenly not so amused. "God, do I? What? What do I say?"

She grinned. "Devasted. You say devasted when you mean to say devastated."

"I don't, you're having me on."

"You do. When your aunt Muriel died you said your mum was devasted. You always say it."

"Oh. Oh Lord. Remind me never to say it ever again. If I do, I'll be, um, devastated."

CHAPTER SEVEN

"What do you think I'm going to do with her? I'm going to shoot her."

"What? Just like that?"

"Just like that."

Derek blinked, even flinched a little at the directness of the big man's words. But Colonel George Critchley was, at least at first sight, a man you didn't argue with. Not unless you were anxious to be told your fortune in no uncertain manner. He was the kind of man who, when you met him, you found yourself standing up a little straighter. At six foot two he himself stood like the ex-military man he was. When he'd first come to the area, and bought himself one of the best farms in the district a rumour had gone round that the Colonel wasn't really a colonel at all, but a major too big for his military boots. Mary, Derek's wife, was of the opinion that the rumour had been started by the vicar, who had previously styled himself Major the Rev., but should by rights have been known as Captain the Rev. Or even the Rev Captain, to put such things in the correct order.

But the Colonel really was a colonel, and now he stood four-square in the large oak door of his farm house, and Derek stood before him, feeling like a squaddie on a fizzer, an expression he'd picked up from army mates. He was there because of a report. Not an official one, just something someone said in the local post office, a centre of village gossip presided over by the formidable Miss Phyllis Parker. Gossip, yes, but a good policeman

Sting of the Nettle

must surely act on such overheard bits of gossip. It was said, by someone who might actually be accurate, that there had been a bad incident of sheep-worrying in the district, and furthermore, that an offending dog had been recognised as one belonging to the Colonel.

Derek had puttered along to the Colonel's place on his two-stroke, wondering if he was heading for a difficult, even intimidating, confrontation. He parked the bike, walked diffidently up the gravel path to the front door and lifted the brass knocker which fell back on its plate with a bang that sounded far too loud and aggressive.

While he waited, a beautifully groomed black and white collie dog rushed up out of nowhere, and frisked merrily around his feet.

And then the Colonel was there. He seemed to know immediately why a policeman was on his doorstep, he himself brought up the subject of sheep-worrying at once, agreed that the suspect dog was apparently his, and announced his intention of shooting the animal forthwith.

"I'll be sorry to do it, of course." He looked down at where the dog, having abandoned its attentions to Derek, was now weaving a dance of ecstatic worship around the Colonel's boots. "She's a promising bitch, but... There we are. She has to go."

Was there a slight tremor in the Colonel's voice as he said those last words? And perhaps Derek was imagining the slightest twitch of the man's left eye.

He knew the Colonel's decision was basically right. It was the country code. If his dog was worrying sheep,

Sting of the Nettle

the owner had to take action. Sheep-worrying was a crime that had few equals in that part of the country. If an owner of a guilty dog refused to take action, the police, in the person of Derek, would bring the case to court, where local magistrates, countrymen themselves, would have no hesitation in fining the owner and ordering the destruction of the dog. As it was, Derek realised with a measure of relief, the Colonel was going to do his job for him.

The collie had now once again transferred her affection from the Colonel to Derek, and was winding herself between his legs wearing an expression of deep submission and whining with anticipated pleasure. Derek reached down to pat her, then thought better of it.

"Is this the...?"

"That's her. That's Sally. I inherited her from the last chap here. Just a puppy then. Come on well, she has. But now this. Still, I'm glad you've turned up. You can witness that I've done the necessary." Again a slight flutter in the voice. But the Colonel then stood up even taller, and said firmly, "For your information, I've already compensated the owner, so when the job's done it'll be case closed. Right? Just hang on here for a moment, I'll be with you..."

He disappeared into the house. Derek waited. The dog moaned at him. He couldn't stop himself, he knelt and fondled her, allowing her to lick his face with exuberance. The dog smelled of dog. It wasn't a bad smell.

The Colonel returned, a double-barrelled shotgun hanging in the broken position in his right hand. Derek could see the rim of two cartridges in the breech.

"Come on then," the man said briskly. "We'll do it behind the barn."

He strode off across the farm house, the dog Sally trotting at his heels, Derek following him, stumbling slightly, needing to say something.

"So, tell me. How many sheep did she kill?"

"Oh, there were no deaths, thank goodness. Would have cost me a fortune. No, one sheep aborted. They do under stress, you know. Otherwise... Well, luckily one of Mason's men – Mason's the owner, got a farm half a mile up the road – anyway, this man was bringing some feed in, and the dog heard the tractor and ran off."

"And he identified Sally?"

"Well he said it was a black and white collie."

"But surely, there must be lots of dogs like Sally, black and white."

"True enough. But Sally's the nearest, if you see what I mean. Come on."

He led Derek around the side of the barn, tramping through some undergrowth, and over a few discarded bricks. Sally frisked ahead, yelping with enthusiasm.

"Look at her," said the Colonel. "She thinks we're going ratting." Then he made another sound, was it a word? More like a sob.

They rounded the back corner of the barn. A stack of hay bales stood against the wall. The view from there was one of the best Derek had seen since moving to the area – a big and wide vista of rolling hills, coombes, woods, and in the distance, the blue of the moors. It looked peaceful and serene. Even beautiful. And of

Sting of the Nettle

course, Derek reminded himself, deadly dull and boring.

The Colonel stopped, and snapped the gun shut. Sally sat almost at his feet, panting.

"Look." Derek knew he sounded soft-hearted, like a despised Townie. But he kept going. "Perhaps it was Sally, but, even if it was, even if we agree she did it, then it was just the once. She'd never done it before, right? Perhaps, probably even, she'll never do it again. You could tie her up, or... or..."

The Colonel took a deep breath. "I know what you're saying. I've had the same conversation with myself. But that's not how it works. You ask around here, they'll all say the same. Once a dog gets a taste for doing it, they'll do it again and again until they're stopped. I'm going to stop it now."

"But all the same. it's hardly fair."

The Colonel stood stock still for a moment. Then he seemed to make up his mind. He turned to look at Derek squarely in the face.

"Fair? Ha!" he scoffed. "Something you should understand, son. The world is not as good and fair as you might think it is. Yes, some of life is good and fair. But some of it is the other thing entirely. I fought my way through the war, from the retreat to Dunkirk, to the desert, to Normandy and the rest. And I have seen things. Murder, rape, worse." The man seemed to shudder for a moment, then continued in a calmer but equally intense tone: "And I have come to the realisation that there is a streak of evil in life. A pit of the devil, if you like. And those who fall into that pit don't climb out. And the evil lives on. And, sometimes, men die. And dogs."

Derek surprised himself by what he tried to say next. "This evil." he began, then stopped. It would be a stupid thing to say, to ask.

"Go on, man."

"Well, this evil." The thought came clearer now, and he pushed on: "This evil you describe, if a man became part of it, might it lead to someone shooting themselves?"

"Do you know of a case where?"

"No, no." Derek said quickly. "It was just a thought."

The Colonel clearly wasn't convinced. "Well. Whoever your 'just a thought' was, the answer is yes. Sometimes, if the thing is too dark, too dreadful, then suicide is the only way out."

Derek knew why he had asked the question. Old Tom Williamson. Had he found no way out of something so dreadful. It remained a question in his mind which he couldn't shake off. That constant niggle.

Sally frisked impatiently, and the Colonel looked down at her, then bent to ruffle her head. "As with men, so with dogs," he said. "Once they start along that evil way, they don't stop. If they can do it once, they will do it over and over again. And I don't mean just in war, either. Here. Now. So this," he meant the shotgun, "is the only way out for her. And perhaps me."

"But here, things are so quiet, so peaceful," Derek couldn't help glancing at the bucolic scene before them. "I've been here a while now; can't say I've found anything really evil."

"Then you haven't looked hard enough. Here. In this valley, these pretty villages, it's there. Repeating. Where do you think serial killers come from? What about that

Sting of the Nettle

chap they've just hanged? Haig? Nice looking well set up chap, gentleman type, home counties - killed again and again. He had to be executed. Otherwise he'd have done it again. Same as Sally here." The Colonel took a deep and resolute breath, and snapped his gun shut. "Now I don't suppose you want to see this, right. So wait back there."

Obediently Derek retreated around the corner. He waited, bracing himself for the sound of the shot. It didn't come. Instead, after perhaps five minutes, the Colonel reappeared, his gun broken open again, and Sally, very much alive, frisking around his feet.

The Colonel had turned pale. He said nothing.

"Sir?" Derek said.

"I can't do it," the man said, his voice cracking with stress. "I can't shoot her. God, what is wrong with me? I've shot men. In the war. Plenty. I even shot one of my own men, poor bastard, a shell took off his legs and opened up his guts and he was still alive and screaming, and I shot him. And now I can't shoot a dog. God help me."

Derek stood silently. Sally rolled over in ecstasy. And the Colonel broke into great wracking sobs. His head sank into his hands, his shoulders slumped, and now he was no longer the proud upstanding military dynamo, now he was just a middle-aged man in despair.

Derek raised a hand, to take the Colonel's arm, to comfort and reassure him. Then he dropped it. No. Any kind of physical intervention would be wrong, would be inappropriate. He, Derek, was too young, too insecure himself. The man had to find his own control, to do it on

Sting of the Nettle

his own.

And he did. After two or three minutes he straightened up, and wiped his face with his hands.

"Sorry about that," said, with a watery grimace. "Nerves. You understand?"

"Of course," Derek assured him. Although he wasn't sure he did. He'd heard about this sort of thing. Shell shock, it was called. This must be a case of it.

Sally whined at his feet. The Colonel looked down at her. "You'll have to do it," he said.

"Um. yes of course. The station will contact the vet we use, and he'll come out here and collect Sally, and..."

"No. I'm not having any of that palaver. Sally hates the smell of vets, she'll be terrified. She'll panic. Look at her. She's happy. Content. And she deserves to die that way, quickly, no terror, no suffering. You'll have to do it."

Derek stared at him. "Me?"

"Yes. You."

"You want me... to shoot Sally?"

"Yes. I do." The Colonel looked at him, agony in his eyes. "You can do it. You can. It has to be done, I know it has to be done, and you're here. In your uniform." He managed the outline of a smile. "Call it Official duty."

"No."

"Yes." It was an order. A semblance of the authoritative Colonel he had first met was back. "You don't know this but I'm a member of the County Constabulary Civilian Advisor Committee. So you're in the clear. I'm instructing you to shoot this dog. At once."

"I can't. You do it "Whatever authority or influence

Sting of the Nettle

the Colonel might wield, he couldn't order him to shoot a dog. Could he?

"Look at the state of me." The Colonel held out his hands. His shoulders might be square again, but the hands trembled like leaves in a breeze. "Even if I could pull the trigger, I'd probably miss the spot, just wound her."

Derek shook his head. "No. No I can't"

"Yes, you can." The Colonel's voice was warm, even passionate. The man might be on the edge of a nervous breakdown but somewhere he had found the quality of command that every military officer must have. Derek found himself automatically slipping into an acceptance of his authority.

"You're a policeman," the Colonel continued. "Sometimes your duties are difficult. This is one of those times. Do it now. You will have done me a favour. You will have done Sally a favour. The barrel against the head. Squeeze the trigger. Do it now." And then a final appeal from two grey and tired eyes:

"Please."

Derek looked down at Sally. The Colonel was right. If the vet came for her, Sally would know terror. He remembered how once he had to visit the local slaughter house. He had seen the bullocks in the holding pen. He had heard their moans and bellows. The execution itself was quick. But the waiting, the agony of the knowledge of impending death... They knew. Each one of those beasts knew. Sally must not know it.

"Give me the shotgun," he muttered.

"You know how to use one of these?"

Sting of the Nettle

"School cadet force. Range. Like you said. Point and squeeze the trigger." A thought. "Sally's not frightened by a pointed gun?"

"No, she's not gun-shy. Thank God."

Derek took the gun. Just do it, he told himself. He could do it. He had the courage to do it. He wasn't shell-shocked. And he wasn't a coward. He would do it.

"Come on, girl."

Sally followed him around the corner of the barn. She sat at Derek's feet and looked up at him. Derek lifted the gun, cocked it, counted to ten to boost his courage... and pulled the trigger. The echo of the blast rang round the farm buildings.

He walked back around the barn corner to the Colonel, who was leaning against the wall, his face a picture of troubled misery. Sally trotted happily at Derek's heels, leaving his legs to nuzzle the Colonel's legs.

Derek handed the shotgun to the Colonel, a wisp of smoke still issuing from the barrel.

"I missed," he told him. And turned to go.

Just for once the motorcycle started first kick. He glanced back at the Colonel. The man was sitting on the bare earth, with Sally in his arms. The dog was ecstatically licking the man's face. Perhaps his tears.

Derek put the machine in gear, and drove off towards North Tawe, and home.

CHAPTER EIGHT

He didn't get there. At least, not immediately. Instead, after five minutes he pulled into a gateway, switched the engine off, and sat looking at a field of sheep. He felt strangely close to tears himself.

He'd funked it, hadn't he? He lacked the courage. He'd been weak. Even afraid.

So had the Colonel, of course. But was that any excuse? He thought of how he often fantasised being in situations which required courage. The sort of bravery that any decent policeman surely must display. Had that been one of those situations? And when it came to it, had he failed?

He ought to go home. But he didn't want to. The schools were on holiday now, the beginning of the six-week summer break, which meant Mary would be home. Which in turn meant he would have to talk to her, tell her about the Colonel and Sally. And he didn't want to, not yet. He wanted to deal with it in his own mind first. No, he'd go home at lunchtime, not before. Which meant, he thought, glancing at his watch, he had an hour and a half to kill.

Another thought struck him. Sally, the sweet dog, was alive. Whatever happened next, she was alive now. He felt pleased. Not regretful. Or ashamed. Get a grip, he told himself. There'd be other times, other chances to prove he wasn't a coward.

Sting of the Nettle

Then he thought of Old Tom Williamson. The niggle returned, full strength.

He tried to shake it off. "You're not a bloody social worker!" he told himself, echoing an ad-lib rant that Sergeant Welbeloved had delivered for his benefit a few weeks back, after he had confessed that during a cold snap in early March, he had helped an elderly village lady who lived alone and had a heating problem. All he had done was blag a few logs off a local forestry worker, and trundled them round to her, only to have some foreman complain.

"All right, you see someone in trouble, you tell the social. That's what they're there for. Interfering wassocks that they are. It's not your job to sort them out. Your job is crime. Your job is to catch criminals. It's social workers who feed the hungry and change their nappies, and if you don't like it, you shouldn't have voted Labour!"

And with that the fat Sergeant had stamped off to his cubicle to do more of whatever it was he did in there. Derek had no chance to reply, to defend himself, or even to protest that at the '45 election he'd been too young to vote.

And now he thought again of Farmer Williamson. Or to be more accurate, Mrs. Williamson. And the son, Peter. He was worried about them both, he told himself. He felt guilty that he'd not done more for them. He had been little or no help to the wife when the Sergeant had interviewed her at the farm on that grim morning. And after the inquest, when perhaps a word of comfort might have helped, she and Peter had hurried away to catch a

Sting of the Nettle

bus back to North Tawe, so there had been no opportunity.

Perhaps they preferred it that way. Perhaps they wanted to deal with their grief in private. If so, fair enough, he'd leave them to it. But if they wanted to talk... Well, you never knew, they might give some hint as to why their husband and father ended his life with such a bloody flourish. Why? Why? The niggle in his mind grew stronger.

He reached the top of the rise in the lane leading to the Williamson's home, and free-wheeled down it, coming to a stop just inside the gate to the yard. He switched off his engine. The boy Peter had evidently heard the bike, and was coming out of a barn, shutting the huge iron door behind him.

But before either of them could say a word. before Derek could even swing his leg off the bike, the front door of the house opened with a bang, and a belligerent-looking Mrs. Williamson strode out onto the step.

"What do you want then?" she demanded, hands on hips.

"Oh, nothing. Nothing official anyway." Derek tried to put some good-neighbourly cheer in his voice, but he could hear he lacked conviction.

"Then what are you doing back here, eh?"

"Well, I just wondered, after the tragedy... Whether there was anything you need. Or anything you need to talk about?"

"We don't need nought, thank you very much. And we've been talked about all round the village and we don't need no more of that either."

Sting of the Nettle

"No, of course. I do see..."

"So you can just turn that machine of yours round and bugger off out of it. All right? Got that, Mr, err... Constable?" Her words were belligerent, her tone less so. She hesitated, then turned and stalked back into the house, again slamming the door.

Derek felt his cheeks burning. He'd been stupid to come. This was no place for him. He jammed his foot down on the kick-starter. The engine turned over but didn't catch. He tried again. Same result. He shook the thing, hearing plenty of petrol swishing in the tank. More kicks, but no comforting chunter from the engine.

Shit. This had happened before. He knew what he had to do. He would have to jump-start the thing. He got off, turned the bike around, and began to push it back the way he'd come. The slope on the other side of the incline would do the trick. But he had barely got out of the farm yard when Peter joined him, putting his hand on the rear seat to help push.

"All right," Derek said grumpily. "Don't worry, I'm going. Sorry I bothered you."

"No, I'm sorry. About my mum. What she said."

"Oh, you don't have to apologise." Though Derek was glad he did.

"She was rude."

"Well, this sort of thing. It takes people different ways."

"Yeh, I know, but..."

"I'm sure she misses your father. Come to that, I suppose you do too."

The boy was silent. A few more steps, and they

Sting of the Nettle

reached the top of the incline.

Derek said, "Thanks for that," and remounted the bike, selecting second gear for the impending jump start. But Peter stopped him, putting his hand on the handlebars.

"I'm not a bloody fool, you know. I know it wasn't accidental death."

Derek looked at him, pulled off his helmet, and ran a hand through his ginger curls. "Do you?" he said.

"Course I do. Everyone knows it. He shot himself. Twice, they say. I mean, it's common knowledge."

"Well. Perhaps. But I think some people think it was an accident, not suicide, because your father had so much to live for."

"You'd think so, wouldn't you?" Peter's face was set in a scowl.

"Well you would. I mean, he had his health, the post mortem report said so. Then there was you, doing well at college. And he was well-liked. I just wonder why he would do it."

"Depends what you mean by well-liked."

"What?"

"Dad was well-liked by some. I'll say that. But... Well, who? That's the thing."

There was a silence, but Peter showed no signs of leaving, of going back down to the farm.

Derek said, carefully, "Peter, is there something you'd like to talk about? To tell me?"

Peter hesitated, then said abruptly: "I think it was the Germans."

"What, in the war, you mean? Was he shell-shocked

or something?"

"No, afterwards. Dad wasn't in the war. Reserved occupation. Farming."

"Of course. I should have known. So, what Germans are we talking about?"

"P.O.W.s. There was this camp, Okehampton way. Prisoner of war camp. They didn't go home straight away, after the war, you know. There was repatriation of course, but it took a long time. And while they were just waiting, hanging about, the prisoners were hired out by the government to work on farms. We got two of them. Hans and Horst." He laughed briefly. "Hans and Horst. Sounds like a double act. Laurel and Hardy. Hans and Horst."

"Yeh? What were they like?"

"Hans was all right. Bit older than the other one. From Bavaria, wherever that is. He used to make us slippers."

"Slippers?"

"No, really. Out of bits of material. He was Mum's favourite. The other one, Horst. He was a lot younger. I think he was a bit of a Nazi. Anyway, as far as I can remember, Hans got sent home first, but Horst was still here, and he and Dad..."

"Peter!"

The loud raucous call startled them both, and they both turned to look down the lane. Mrs. Williamson stood at the entrance to the yard, hands on hips.

"Peter, you come on now!"

It was a bellow, rather than a shout, given an extra edge with the harsh Devonshire accent.

Peter said: "I better go. See you." And he turned and

almost ran back down the lane.

Derek put his helmet back on, and climbed back on his machine, freewheeling it down the slope in front of him, then engaging the clutch. The engine caught at the second attempt and buzzed happily through the lanes and back in time for his lunch.

CHAPTER NINE

"Why do you keep going on about it?"

Derek stabbed at the roots of a particularly vicious-looking nettle, which rewarded him by whipping forward and raking its bright green leaves across his bare forearm.

"Shit! Bloody thing got me."

"Language! Get a dock-leaf," Mary advised him. "There's plenty."

Derek found one of the broad dark weeds, and rubbed it vigorously on his arm. The old remedy worked, the worst pain of the sting lessened, but there remained a rash of little bumps on the skin, and Derek knew they would still be pricking him when he tried to sleep that night.

Picking up his spade again he wreaked a terrible revenge on the offending nettle, then asked: "What were you saying?"

"I was saying, or rather asking, must you keep on going on about Mr Williamson? We've had him and his death all through lunch, and all afternoon when you haven't been swearing at the nettles. I mean, it's over and done with, isn't it?"

"Is it? Is it really?" he asked rudely.

"Oh dear." Mary managed to laugh and sigh at the same time. "I'm slow, aren't I! I was forgetting. Of course. It's your new niggle, isn't it!"

"Well it might be."

Sting of the Nettle

"Oh boy. Look. He died, there was a post mortem, then the inquest, and the verdict, accidental death."

"Accidental death my arse!"

"Derek! Your language gets worse. But you're right, of course. Accidental death my... foot."

He grinned at her. Mary would never swear herself and would always seem rather shocked when he let rip with a few expletives. Yet when they were in bed together, when they made love, she sometimes used expressions that astonished him by their passionate prurience. Astonished him and excited him, and even now, as the memory drifted across his mind, he felt his body stir in anticipation.

Perhaps Mary had a similar recollection. There was certainly a softness in her look when she spoke.

"Listen, that's enough for today. I'll get the supper on, why don't you pop down to the Dragon for a quick one? Talk to your friend John. Might help you forget the niggle. For a while, anyway."

"Sure you don't mind?" Derek dropped the spade, then, after a pointed look, picked it up again and propped it against the fence.

"Bring us back a packet of crisps."

* * *

The Green Dragon was one, almost the only one, factor that made a tedious life in North Tawe slightly less tedious. It was, Derek told himself smugly as he strode down the street to the rather tatty village square, everything a country pub should be. It was comfortable,

Sting of the Nettle

it was quiet, it was warmed in winter by a big open fire, and cool in summer with windows opening onto fragrant window boxes and an ancient rustic wheelbarrow filled to overflowing with geraniums. The beer was good, the cider potent, and the long lines of exotic spirits on the shelves behind the bar gave the place a touch of romance, even though no one could remember when a drink had been ordered from any of them. Entertainment consisted of a dart board, a cribbage board, and a shove halfpenny board.

Food consisted of pickled eggs, crisps, and peanuts; packets of the latter were attached to a large colourful display card. The card had a pin-up girl on it, and as each packet of peanuts was purchased, more of the girl was revealed. Young men of the village were said to order more and more peanuts, hoping that the removal of the packet would reveal that the girl was completely nude. She never was.

Another good thing about the pub was the landlord. John Jacob might have been ten, maybe 15 years older than Derek, but they shared a love of cricket, good beer and the novels of John Steinbeck. And just talking. Derek had suggested to Mary that, metaphorically speaking, he and John spoke the same language. Mary said no, they were singing from the same hymn sheet, which he had to admit was a better line.

Now as he walked into the bar Derek noticed that as usual his arrival didn't cause an uneasy stir. There were pubs in Exeter where, if a copper should enter, in or out of uniform, a certain section of the clientele would abruptly disappear through the back entrance. But not

Sting of the Nettle

here, not in the Green Dragon. He was even greeted by a couple of friendly nods from the locals.

But not from one of the drinkers at the bar. From him Derek received what began as a blank look but soon turned into a sneer, and a mutter to his companion that was undoubtedly a comment about the police in general and Derek in particular. It was Bucky.

Derek faced a choice. He could stand at the bar and find himself in hostile conversation with the man. Or he could retire to a corner table, where an elderly and impoverished man named Jack sat in front of a nearly empty glass hoping that someone would volunteer to refill it.

John, the landlord, greeted Derek with a friendly nod, and Derek remembered to ask about his wife, who'd recently returned from hospital after a cancer operation. The news wasn't good. He ordered two pints of bitter and went to sit with old Jack, who accepted his free drink with a singular lack of grace.

But it seemed Bucky wasn't content to leave their meeting at that, because after a few moments he was suddenly there, standing by the small table, looming over them both, with one of the other men from the bar peering over his shoulder. Was this going to be trouble? Another opportunity to test his courage? It might be. If so, he told himself, be ready for it. And it would be interesting to see if his unarmed combat skills, a product of his police training, would be effective against the bull-like figure of Bucky.

Bucky spoke to old Jack first. "Jack, there's a pint for you at the bar. Go get it, and stay there."

Sting of the Nettle

Jack moved with alacrity, taking with him the drink Derek had bought.

Bucky sat on the bench seat that was now vacant, and the second man drew up a chair and sat down.

"Hello Bucky," Derek said evenly.

"Hello Consta-bule." Bucky made a mockery of the term.

Derek turned to the second man. "Who are you then?"

Bucky answered him. "This is Graham." He pronounced the name as one syllable. "Mate of mine. Does jobs for me, now and then."

"He does jobs for you? Lucky you!" Derek's sardonic tone was massively clear. But Bucky appeared not to notice.

"Now and then, like. "

"Oh right. He's your getaway driver, is he? For bank jobs. Now and then."

"There's no need to be like that." Bucky had realised he was being mocked. "You asked, I told you."

Derek could feel his pleasant hour in the pub slipping away from him.

"All right Bucky. What do you want?"

"Just a friendly chat."

"About what?"

"Well." And now Bucky made an obvious effort to get the threatening tone out of his voice. "It was a shame about old Tom Williamson, wasn't it? Him dying like that."

"Yes. It was. So?"

"So, I mean these things happen, right?"

Sting of the Nettle

"What things?"

"Well, accidents. Old Tom, accidentally shooting himself. It was accidental, right? That's what the coroner said at the inquest. Accidental death."

"My God, Bucky!" Derek feigned excitement. "Are you about to confess?"

"What?"

"Did you go over to his place that morning and shoot poor Tom?"

"Don't be bloody silly."

"'Cos if you're about to cough for it, I need a witness. Someone to take notes. And from the look of him, your mate Graham may have certain intellectual drawbacks. Like, can he write? Come to that, can he read? He clearly can't talk."

At this the silent Graham took a breath, as if he might say something, but again Bucky got there first.

"Will you shut up?" Then louder, laying a broad dirty hand on Derek's wrist: "Or have I got to shut you up?"

"Bucky!" Landlord John called harshly from the bar. "Watch it!"

Bucky released Derek's arm. Derek flicked his fingers at the point of contact, as if to ward off germs.

"Technically, Bucky, you just assaulted a police officer. But never mind that, this is far more interesting. Could you tell me where you were on the morning?" He'd forgotten the date but didn't care "Of Old Tom Williamson's death?"

"I was home, course," said Bucky sulkily. "With someone."

"A woman? Don't tell me, a wife? Got a new one,

Sting of the Nettle

have you? When was the wedding?"

"A mate, if you must know. Listen. Will you stop it? I come over here to have a quiet word, so for Chrissake you can stop your yap and let me speak."

Derek sighed. "All right. Say away. If you must."

"Tom Williamson. Accidental death. We're agreed. Right?"

"Well you seem to be."

"I mean it wasn't suicide."

"Wasn't it?"

"No. And we don't want people thinking it might have been, do we?"

"Don't we?"

"No! Bloody listen.! Anyone who goes around saying Williamson killed himself. Well it would be wrong. Bloody wrong. Anyone. Especially - especially some bloody Pc Plod who thinks he's God's Gift to Law Enforcement."

"Good heavens to Betsy, Bucky." Derek tried but failed to hide a grin. "Could you possibly be referring to... me?"

"Course I bloody mean you. I mean..." Bucky made an effort to calm down his rhetoric. "I mean, if people think it's suicide, just cos people say it might be, well then people start asking why, why would he kill himself? And that could be..." Bucky clearly now remembered a phrase he had been preparing in his head. "That could be deeply distressing to his family and loved ones."

"Well bugger me!" Derek relished the swearword. "Now I've seen it all. Bucky the Social Worker!"

Bucky had clearly had enough. He got up with a jerk,

Sting of the Nettle

bumping into the man Graham and nudging the small table. Beer splashed lightly on the surface.

He glared at Derek, eyes blazing, and for a moment Derek felt an unexpected shiver of something like fear.

"You be bloody told!" Bucky blazed. "Shut up about Old Tom and suicide. Cos if you don't, you'll bloody regret it."

Bucky and friend Graham had clearly had their say – or rather Bucky had had both their says – and they left the pub. Derek drained his pint, then wandered up to the bar to return the empty glass.

"Problems?" John queried.

"Nothing I can't handle."

"Don't be too sure. That Bucky, I ought to bar him. There's something about him. Something evil."

"Evil?"

"Yes. Really. What did he want?"

"I'm not really sure. He seemed worried about the reputation of old Tom Williamson. Told me to stop asking about it. You know, his death."

"I read about that in the Western Morning News. Didn't sound like accidental death to me."

"It wasn't. Suicide plain as day. Bit of a puzzle, really. Personally I think the Coroner was a bit, well, mizzled."

"A bit what?"

"Sorry. Private joke." And Derek explained the Coroner's mis-pronunciation.

He turned to go, then turned back. "Listen, John. If you get a chance, see if you can find out anything about it. You can say I was asking, if you like."

"Will do." John clearly relished the prospect of some

unofficial detection.

At home, Derek walked in to the welcoming smell of rabbit stew.

"Guess what," he told her. "You know you said I keep going on about the Williamson death business."

"Your latest niggle. Yes?"

"Well, I think I better stop. I've just been warned off, by the local mafia. I'm quaking in my boots."

"I'll tell you something else that'll chill your blood."

"What?"

"You forgot my crisps."

CHAPTER TEN

It was a lovely evening. One of those gentle mid-summer twilights which seem to stretch out luxuriously and encourage thoughts of deckchairs, cold beers, and a gentle drift towards a late but welcome bedtime. The day had been warm, and the village cricket eleven had achieved a rare and welcome victory. Derek turned out for the team and was known as a competent bat who, and, this was much more important, also bought his round in the pub afterwards. He should have been with the lads in the Dragon now, enjoying the sensation of weary limbs and warm beer. He should have been relaxed. He should have been happy.

Instead, after a quick bath, he was sitting in the passenger seat of his wife's Austin 7, and cursing his luck. He was uncomfortable and unpleasantly hot. He was in his suit, a charcoal-grey effort that was just that little bit too small these days, especially round the chest and the armpits, and given the option he'd had worn his grey flannels and the sports jacket with the leather elbow patches. Or even his uniform. But Mary had insisted on the suit.

"And the blue tie!"

"A tie? Have I got to?"

"And the waistcoat."

"Jesus Christ. In this heat?"

Now at a few minutes before eight, and with his ginger curls smoothed down with brilliantine, he sat in

Sting of the Nettle

the car and sweated. The Devon lanes the little car rumbled through were lined with foxgloves and dog roses. Gaps in the big banks revealed glimpses of shorn hayfields. Friendly horses poked their heads over fence poles. The odd stoat wriggled nimbly across the tarmac. All was well in this hidden pocket of God's world. And Derek wanted to scream.

"I don't know why I have to go to this, this wretched bunfight?"

Mary replied in a tone which indicated she'd already been asked the question several times, and replied in exactly the same way.

"Because you've been invited."

"Invited? Bloody commanded, more like."

"And don't forget, I've been invited too. On my own account. So if for no other reason, that's why you have to go to this wretched bunfight."

Derek settled into a sulky silence. And he was right, he told himself. It had been a command. It had come at the end of the Monday morning meeting, when the handful of village constables gathered in the Okehampton office to have their fortunes told by Sergeant Welbeloved, and his superior, Inspector Reed. The Inspector was a tall but stooped figure, who was approaching compulsory retirement, looking forward to it like a schoolboy approaching half-term, and quite content to allow the routine of police work to remain just that, routine. The last thing he needed was any boat-rocking, and his sergeant did his best to ensure there was none.

So, at the Monday meeting two weeks previously, the

Sting of the Nettle

Inspector had said little more than a general commendation of his constables, and headed off to the calm security of his office. Derek and the four or five others started towards the door in his wake, but now, not for the first time, Welbeloved called them back.

"Not so fast, not so fast. "

The constables heaved a mutual but silent sigh. Welbeloved liked to do this. He liked to have his own little rant at the end of an otherwise bland and boring meeting. He liked, if possible, to cause consternation among his charges. Of course he did. That's what Sergeants are for. Isn't it?

"Now don't look so worried, laddies. I've got a treat for you. You are today each receiving an invitation. Here, hand these out, constable. They've got your names on 'em. You can remember your names, I hope."

He thrust a handful of square buff envelopes at Derek, who passed them round dutifully, then started, like the others, to open his envelope.

"Wait for it! I didn't say open 'em, did I? Just hold your horses a bit. First, let me ask you this. How many of you have heard of the name Bulstock? To be more precise, General The Honourable Sir Arthur Bulstock?"

He looked around. As in the lower ranks of the army, it was not wise to rise to the fishing hooks skimmed across the surface of the law-enforcement pond like this. But Derek took a chance.

"I've come across him, Sergeant."

"Have you, Constable Martin? Have you indeed? And I should hope so too, seeing as he's on your patch. So kindly inform your fellow officers as to who or what he

Sting of the Nettle

is."

"Well, he's, he's..." Derek found himself struggling for the right words. Mercifully the Sergeant over rode him.

"He's a nob. That's what he is. He's a blue-blooded aristocratic dyed-in-the-wool nose-in-the-air hereditary nob! And the important thing to know is, he's our nob. The biggest nob west of Okey, all right? And guess what? He wants to meet you lot."

A puzzled murmur passed between the constables.

"Yes. Amazing, isn't it. Someone actually wants to meet you. Someone other than your mother. Allow me to explain. You are all invited to a reception. For those of you of lesser brain, who think a reception is a successful pass in rugger, a reception is a nob's party. Every year or so, our nob, the Honourable Arthur, likes to exercise his democratic conscience by saying hello to the people who keep this benighted part of the country going. Nurses, doctors, teachers, midwives, council paper-shufflers, bottom-kissers and, coming in last of course, policemen. He likes to give them all a party. A do. A do for the do-gooders, if you like. Peanuts, sherry, awkward conversation. You'll love it. And, because his country seat is in the middle of nowhere, he's particularly keen to get you lot, the village coppers, along. And in your grubby little hands you have your personal invites. Go on, take a look."

Derek fumbled open his envelope. The card inside was thick, the writing on it gold. There was a space for the name and there it was. General Sir Arthur and Lady Bulstock requested Constable Martin's presence at a

Sting of the Nettle

reception, and gave the date and time, the place Truston Manor, and pointed out, at the bottom, that the dress code was "informal"

The Sergeant anticipated Derek's query. "You'll notice is says 'Dress code informal'" he pointed out. "To you informal means formal. Believe me, if any of you tykes turns up in old corduroys and a windcheater, I'll have his guts for garters."

"Sergeant?" One of the others raised a hand, with an equally crucial question: "Is it compulsory?"

"Compulsory?" Welbeloved had obviously hoped for this question, and he smiled as he prepared to plumb the depths of sarcasm. "Is it compulsory? This isn't Nazi Germany you know. No, Constable, it is not compulsory." He allowed himself a delicious moment of self-congratulation, then. "But you've got to go!"

He paused, then treated them to a sardonic smile. "As I have already indicated, you will be offered alcohol at the party. You may accept one glass of sherry. You may accept two glasses of sherry. But that's it, that's the limit. I don't want to see any tipsy young coppers being sick in the lavender beds. Got it?"

A murmur from the group. They got it.

The date of the voluntary compulsory party had seemed far away then. But now it was here. The little Austin 7 nosed its way to a tree-hung T-junction, and turned into another lane even more narrow and winding than the first.

"You do know where this place is, I hope." Derek found the tight bends and the tall hedges intimidating, but Mary whizzed the little car round the curves with

Sting of the Nettle

insouciance.

"Of course I know where it is," she told him blithely. "I used to come out here every Christmas with the church choir. We'd sing carols at the Manor and a couple of other posh places around here. Five pounds, Sir Arthur used to give us. And some mince pies. Nice old couple, they are. Son's a bit weird, but..."

"Who's the son?"

"Fergus. Snobby little sod, he is. Went to Charterhouse and thinks he's God's gift."

"Oh?" He glanced at her. "Ex-boyfriend, is he?"

Mary snorted with laughter. "Not him. He's at least seven years older than me, for a start. Only met him the once, at a hunt meet. He tried to touch me, I was only sixteen. I thought he was a creep."

"Can't wait to meet him. What does he do, apart from feeling up adolescent girls?"

"I suppose he runs the place for them now. That's what poncey sons of the landed gentry do, isn't it? Estate manager, that's his title. Essential occupation. Got him out of conscription."

"Did it now? Hitler must have been relieved."

Mary swung the car through an entrance flanked by a pair of stone pillars, each topped by a lion's head, and on up a gravel drive lined with small boulders, presumably positioned, Derek guessed, to stop the hoi polloi from driving on the grass. The house itself was all you might imagine it to be. Dartmoor granite walls, three storeys of them, an array of windows, an enormous, pillared porch, and even a mounting block. Derek got out of the car, feeling shabby and unimportant.

Sting of the Nettle

Once inside the manor house he felt a little better, but not much. Fortunately Mary, as always, seemed relaxed and at ease and led the way in past someone who, by his dress, black trousers, a light beige jacket, and a small bow tie, was a servant. The man actually bowed as he waved them forward.

Forward they dutifully went. A few steps into what seemed a limitless hall, then on into what had to be an equally extensive drawing-room. Derek found himself shaking hands with a tall red-faced man in his sixties, with a rather over-large moustache and a genial smile on his face.

"Hello!" said the man, obviously their host, Sir Arthur. "Welcome. I've just met your wife, delightful lady, Mrs Martin, such a success at the Grammar School. And you are?"

With a start, Derek realised he was being asked to describe himself. "Constable Martin, Sir. Stationed at North Tawe."

"Delighted." And in a subtle gesture that Derek could only admire when he recollected it later, his hand was released, and passed on to meet that of Sir Arthur's wife. The two of them exchanged brief hellos, and Derek felt himself wafted on to face a third hurdle, another servant in the same garb as the first, this one holding a large tray on which were several small glasses of what had to be sherry. Derek hesitated. Sherry wasn't his thing. Some of the glasses were dark, some light, and he couldn't remember which was sweet and which was dry. He took a dark one, and sipped it. Damn. Sweet. Or if he was wrong, and this was the dry one, God help any diabetic

Sting of the Nettle

trying the other one.

As he turned away, two large arms came between him and the tray, and two fat hairy hands grasped a glass in each.

"Evening, Constable," said Sergeant Welbeloved. "Glad you could make it."

Derek was tempted to answer that he'd hardly had a choice, but instead replied "Good evening, Sergeant."

For a moment the two men stood wordless, staring at each other. Derek realised to his surprise that Welbeloved looked even more ill at ease and out of place than he did. The man was sweating visibly and his tie had repositioned itself under his left ear. He now disposed of one of the sherry glasses in his hands by swallowing the contents in one gulp, and plonking it back on the waiter's tray.

"Right. Better mingle," he grunted. He turned away, then turned back. "Go on then," he said, making it an order. "Mingle!"

Derek looked around the room. He realised he knew no-one. He couldn't even spot any fellow constables in the crowd. And where was Mary? Oh yes, there she was, as ever totally at her ease. She was deep in animated conversation with a man who, with his bushy hair and round glasses, looked like a dissolute poet, but was in fact a Methodist minister from a nearby parish. He could of course interrupt them, join in whatever they were finding so fascinating, but that would seem weak, almost childish. Only really wet drips would run to their wives for social shelter. He had to find someone else to talk to. He turned, and found himself face to face with, and far

Sting of the Nettle

too close to, a thin sinewy man, and the start he gave caused the sherry in his glass to spill slightly on to his hand.

"You better drink that up." The accent was affectedly stilted public school. "Before you spill it on mummy's carpet. She would not be pleased."

"No, sorry." Derek took a large gulp of his sherry, and the sickly liquid caused him to splutter a little.

"Rot-gut, isn't it! Father only buys it for this do. He's probably got his own bottle tucked away somewhere. I know I have."

The man laughed at his own sally, showing rows of rather yellow teeth, which almost matched his yellow waistcoat under his suede jacket. The references to Mummy and Father, this had to be Fergus, the son and heir, the man Mary had summed up succinctly as a creep. The reason for the yellow teeth became obvious as he first handed his glass to Derek, saying "hold that, lad," then produced a packet of untipped cigarettes and lit one up with a silver lighter. He took back his glass, then hesitated. "Sorry." He offered the packet to Derek. "Like one?"

"I don't, thanks."

Fergus sneered, seeming to interpret Derek's refusal as some kind of weakness. "Oh you don't. Well. Tell me. What do you do?"

"I'm a policeman."

"Where? Okehampton or Scotland Yard!?"

"No, I'm a village copper. Stationed in North Tawe."

"North... Oh. Yes of course. The red hair. I should have known. It's you."

Sting of the Nettle

A strong but subtle change swept through the man, like a sudden breeze on a field of corn. He looked at Derek as if he was seeing him for the first time.

My God," he said quietly. "You're Martin."

"Well yes. You've heard of me?"

"Not really. That is... You know, word gets around." Fergus virtually blurted the words. He still sounded at least two grades of class above Dereck, but the stilted tone had gone. "Look, Constable, now you're here, I wonder if we could have a word. Somewhere quiet. Just you and me."

Jesus, was the man a queer? Surely not. "Of course."

"Right." His voice now assumed some of its earlier assurance. "Walk this way, laddie."

Derek followed him as Fergus pushed his way through the groups of guests without ceremony. They left the room by an interior door, crossed a short passage, and Derek found himself in a small book-lined study, with a desk and a swivel chair. The room smelled of old leather and tobacco.

Fergus turned to face Derek, who waited for him to speak, but when nothing happened, he thought he better go first.

"So, sir, how I can I help."

"Oh, it's nothing really. Just a thought. So. North Tawe, eh? Nice pub there I believe. At least so I'm told"

"The Dragon. Yes."

"Yes." Another long pause, then before Derek again felt obliged to say something, Fergus went on: "Great shame about that farmer chappie."

"Farmer?"

Sting of the Nettle

"Yes. Williamson, wasn't it."

"You mean Tom Williamson."

"Yes, that's him."

"You knew Mr Williamson, sir?"

"Nooo. At least, we'd met. You know how it is."

Derek didn't, but said nothing, allowing Fergus to continue, which he did by suddenly adopting the kind of face, manner and tone of a family mourner at a funeral.

"What a tragic accident." Was there a slight over-emphasis on the world 'accident'?

"It was certainly tragic," Derek said carefully.

"I mean. Just to stroll out to pop a rabbit, eh? And then, damned bad luck, steps on a rotten apple, falls over, bang, dead. I mean, tragic. That's what happened, right?"

"Well, that's one theory."

"No you're wrong," Fergus told him, a strident tone creeping into his voice. "It's what the coroner said happened."

"Well he said it was possible that..."

"No! He said it, and that's what happened. And that's what people should understand. I mean, you can't have people going round saying that he, saying something else. That would be..." He paused, then began again, "That would be deeply distressing to his family and loved ones."

It was an echo. For a moment Derek couldn't remember why. Then he remembered. It was almost an exact repeat of what Bucky had said in the pub. Complete with slightly dodgy syntax. How about that!

"Well, I'm sure that..." Derek began, but Fergus, his

sallow face showing two burning spots on his cheekbones, interrupted him again.

"And that would be wrong because then the plebs around here will start saying why he should have killed himself, and having theories, and... and it's got to stop. All right?" For a second Fergus seemed about to say more, but visibly checked himself. Instead he turned, snapped one more "all right?", and left Derek alone in the room.

Derek stood still, holding his unfinished glass of sherry. What the hell was this? Another warning off? First Bucky. Now Fergus.? He put his hardly tasted glass down on the desk, and returned to the party. As he entered the room Mary noticed him at once, and came to him quickly.

"Hey, where did you get to?"

"Oh. Nowhere. But listen, something funny..."

"Never mind. Tell me later. There's some people I want you to meet. Come on."

There were indeed several people to meet, and Derek met them with as much grace and good manners as he could, and indeed, as the talk went on, he found that he wasn't nearly as tongue-tied as before and was able to chat fairly fluently about things he knew almost nothing about. The new farm subsidies, the state of the school bus service to the villages, where to find the best blackberries. Suitable comments tripped easily off his lips, and he sensed Mary's slight surprise at his loquacity. He even began to enjoy himself, to enjoy the "reception". Not up to the standard of a session with the cricket team in the Dragon, but. It could have been worse.

After a while Derek looked around for Fergus, but he was nowhere to be seen, and the parents too seemed to have left the room. More trays of sherry were circulating. This time he snaffled a dry one, the taste of which made him want to sneeze. The noise, the chatter seemed to get louder. Then there was a crash of breaking glass, a burst of high-pitched laughter, and he saw the two servants move rapidly towards Sergeant Welbeloved, who was staring glassily around the room.

"Time to go, I think," Mary said,

Derek endured a tedious session of goodbyes, and then they went as quickly and quietly as possible. As they reached the open air the heavens opened to release a thunderous summer downpour. Coatless, they ran swiftly to the Austin 7 and scrambled inside. As Mary backed carefully, before accelerating down the drive and into the deluge, Derek looked in the wing mirror and saw amid the raindrops on the glass, two distinct things.

One was Sergeant Welbeloved who, having been escorted out shortly after them, was now vomiting several glasses of sherry mixed with his lunch into the lavender beds.

The second was a brief rain-shrouded glimpse of a car parked by the side of the impressive manor house. It was a smart white sports car. An MG TD.

CHAPTER ELEVEN

On the strength of a sip from a small glass of revolting sweet sherry, and a whole glass of equally unpleasant dry sherry, Derek had a hangover. Well, it couldn't be a hangover, not really, but that's what it felt like. Headache, a thick feeling behind the eyes, and above all a sense that something weird had happened the night before which now in the light of day he had to worry about. He might have worried about it last night, but when they'd reached home it became clear that something more urgent was on Mary's mind. She'd had a stimulating evening, talking to old friends and contacts, making new ones, making the less revolting choice of sherry. She was buzzing with giggles and coy suggestions and little hand-clutching gestures.

Derek picked up her mood with remarkable alacrity. In no time they were clambering up the stairs, Derek leaving his wretched suit hanging on the bannisters as they went. Afterwards, as he dozed, Mary slipped down and made tea and toast, brought it back up, and Derek fell deeply asleep halfway through his second slice.

Now, next morning, reviving cup of tea in hand, standing outside the back door, facing the rear garden in all its jumbled glory. Derek dragged his sleep-drugged mind back to the problem he knew he had to think about. And do something about. What actually lay behind the untimely, or possibly timely, if the Colonel's theories held true, death of Old Tom Williamson? And why had he, for the second time, been warned off the subject? The niggle was back.

Mary came out of the house, and took a quick look at his set face. She then adopted an exaggerated crouch, and circled around him in a pantomime pose before popping up in front of him, her face six inches from his.

"Aha!" She exclaimed. "It's the niggle! Am I right?"

Derek nodded sheepishly.

"Something new?"

"Mmmm."

"Come on." Mary led him inside, sat him down at the breakfast table, and sat opposite him, pushing the Marmite and the Puffed Wheat to one side.

"Right. Tell me."

Derek sighed. "It's the same. The Williamson death. I was going to try to drop it, only..."

"Only what?"

"Well, you remember I disappeared for a while, at the do last night."

"Mmm. I presumed you were in the whatsit."

"I wish I had been. No, that weirdo son of theirs, Fergus, he took me into some sort of study, and warned me off."

"Go on. Warned you off what?"

"Well, he basically told me to stop asking questions about whether Tom Williamson really killed himself intentionally, and if so why. He got quite nasty about it, quite worked up. Is he always like that?"

"They say so. They say he drives like a maniac, and when there's a hunt, he thrashes his horse and takes it over stupid jumps. Someone last night was saying he'll either kill someone or kill himself."

"So, why is he bothered about some old farmer shooting himself in his orchard? And the thing is, that's the second time I've been warned off, by people who apparently have nothing to do with it. First that idiot Bucky blasts his very nasty breath over my fragrant pint in the pub, and now this toffee-nosed twit does it again, and what's more uses almost exactly the same words, the same way of saying what he had to say, as bloody Bucky. Yet neither of them have any real connection with either the farmer or for that matter with each other."

"As far as you know."

"As far as I know, yes."

"You don't think it was murder, do you?"

"Absolutely not. Old Tom killed himself. No doubt about that. But..." he stopped, almost distractedly.

Mary smiled at him. "It's a big niggle, isn't it."

Derek drew a deep breath, then reached across the table and took Mary's hand in his. "D'you think I'm making too much of it?"

"No." She put both hands over his. "No I don't. I know I used to laugh at your niggles, but not anymore. Remember my ring?"

"God yes." They laughed together and then Derek remembered something else.

"There was this white sports car..." he began. The phone rang.

Less than an hour later he was sitting in the office of the town police station with the other constables from both town and villages, waiting patiently to be told what the flap was about. They expected Welbeloved to come

Sting of the Nettle

waddling in to deliver one of his hectoring speeches, or perhaps be anxious to explain what he would probably describe as a slight indisposition owing to another bit of bad bacon deposited amongst the lavender last night. But instead it was the elderly Inspector who entered, followed meekly by Welbeloved. With a little hesitation, the group of constables climbed to their feet respectfully.

"Sit down chaps, please," the Inspector urged. "Sorry to call you all in, on a Sunday too, but we have an emergency. I'm afraid any leave, any days off, that's all cancelled as of now. What I'm going to tell you will soon be public knowledge, and will call for an all-out effort. Top priority, you understand. And this isn't coming from me, or from County. This is from Government. And it's this." There was something of the actor buried deep in the old boy, and he enjoyed the dramatic pause that preceded his next four words:

"Rubber Bones is out!"

He also enjoyed the reaction of his men, who were for the moment shocked into silence, then broke into a confused mumble of words, amongst which the phrase "bloody hell" could be heard more than once.

Derek shared in the general reaction. Rubber Bones. They all knew about Rubber Bones. Harold "Rubber Bones" Webb, the Princetown prisoner who had acquired his nickname through his ability to slip out of handcuffs, on one notorious occasion doing so while on an escorted visit to the dentist in Torquay, remarking to his warder "We don't need these, do we?" as he did so. And now, it appeared, he was out. Escaped. On the run. On the run from the grim granite high security escape-

Sting of the Nettle

proof prison at Princetown, high on the bleak hills of Dartmoor.

"How did he do it, Sir?" one of the constables asked.

The Inspector glanced at his watch. "All right, I'll take a moment to tell you, then we must get cracking. They tell me that Webb was locked in solitary confinement, and they even took his clothes away at night, leaving him just his shirt. But somehow, he got hold of a sort of chisel and knocked his way into a hot air duct. He wriggled through a gap of about 15 inches, God know how, he isn't a small man, and that led to another tunnel, and that got him out through a drain into the exercise yard. He'd have been spotted there, if it wasn't for that rain storm last night. He ran through it to a maintenance shed by the wall, found a pair of overalls to wear with his shirt, and a ladder. You may ask what kind of witless idiot leaves a ladder just inside a prison wall, but anyway, he used it, got over the wall, and disappeared into the moor."

"Fantastic," muttered one of the constables.

"Don't make him out to be a hero, son," the inspector warned, getting into what for him was a flood of heroic oratory. "Webb is a thug. Got done for robbery with violence. A birching and five years. That's why we've got to get him. And, gentlemen, we are going to get him. We are going to throw an impenetrable ring around Dartmoor. Impenetrable! A tight barrier across the county. We're going to be at every road junction, at every track and footpath, lane and bridleway, all round the moor. And no matter how long it takes, how long we're out there, whatever the weather, day and night...

Sting of the Nettle

we're going to get him."

A round of applause! thought Derek sardonically.

At first it wasn't the most unpleasant of duties. Derek was given a Special Constable as a partner, a 19-year-old lad called Barry who was as raw and naïve as they come, but excited to be part of the hunt, even though he was not being paid. And being his partner, Derek conceded, had twin advantages. First, the boy had use of his father's Hillman, so Derek could leave his two-stroke motorbike at the Okehampton police station. And second, the boy's family lived only half a mile from the place assigned to them to patrol; a minor road where it was met by an overgrown concrete track coming off the moor, some five miles west of Okehampton.

This meant that when he needed a toilet break Barry could sprint home. But Derek dare not leave the boy on his own, so used the hedge, and, now, as he stared up the track in the direction the escapee might be expected to come, he blessed his forethought in nicking some loo paper from the station gents. True, the need had not yet arisen, but who knew how long they'd be asked to stay out there on watch?

The pair's one moment of excitement in a day that had begun to drag occurred when Derek popped behind a hedge for a pee, and was in mid-flow when he heard a shout, sounds of a scuffle, and then a cry from Barry of "I got 'im! I got 'im!" Caught between the Scylla of wetting his uniform trousers and the Charybdis of his professional duty, Derek chose the latter and leaped back to the road. There he found Barry flat on the ground face down, with a scantily clad bulky figure sitting on top of him, and swearing. The apparent escapee proved to be one Lance Corporal Harris, of the Royal Artillery, who had been out for his daily cross-country run when Barry brought him down with a flying rugby tackle. Corporal Harris luckily had his ID in his shorts, and left the way he had come muttering loudly about the fucking police. Derek's trousers dried off in no time.

Other passing traffic proved light and equally as innocent. Those travellers who did come through generally found the whole thing amusing. A farm worker on a tractor paused for a noisy chat amid clouds of blue diesel fumes. A mother pulled up politely, and her two pre-teen children in the back seat grew hysterically excited at the sight of the uniforms and the prospect of a desperado on the loose. A cattle feed lorry happily invited them to kick every sack on his truck, which they duly did, and there were 40 sacks and none of them contained Harold 'Rubber Bones' Webb.

The day went on, and the evening came, and with it came a light drizzle. Conversation between Derek and Barry dragged, not least because Barry was a fan of someone called Tennessee Ernie Ford, of whom Derek knew nothing when the boy began talking, but after half an hour he knew more about the man Ford that he would ever need or want to know. So it was an unlikely relief when at six o'clock Sergeant Welbeloved rolled up in the station car, explained to Derek for some minutes about his bilious attack the previous evening, and handed them a thermos of tea and some rounds of ham sandwich. The ham was local and delicious. The tea was stewed. Thank you, Mrs Weston.

Sting of the Nettle

With traffic becoming scarcer, Derek took to wandering short distances up and down the road. He wondered about Rubber-Bones Webb. The man was presumably out there on the moor somewhere, soaking wet in his scanty clothing, with night drawing in. He knew it was illogical to feel sorry for a proven criminal, but he remembered that Webb had been birched once, and might be again when he was captured. The barbaric punishment had been generally discontinued in England by now, but could still be administered for breaking rules in prison. And Webb, with his ingenious escape, had certainly done that.

For a change Derek left the road, and walked a few yards up the concrete lane that led onto the moor. After a minute or so he caught sight of a wire fence and a group of domed buildings. Nissen huts, he decided. He turned back to find Barry.

"You lived round here long, Barry?"

"Yeh, all my life."

"So, what's those huts up there? Army?"

"Yeah." the boy snickered. "But not ours. Theirs."

"What? You mean Americans?"

"No." The lad was clearly enjoying an exchange he'd probably had before. "I told you. Theirs. The Germans."

"Right. Prisoners of war, yeah?"

"Yeah. Hundreds of them when I was young. Course, they're all gone now."

Of course. Peter's Germans. This must have been their camp. The two who worked on the Williamson farm. A nice one who made slippers. And a Nazi. What were their names again? And why had Peter even mentioned them? Could they be a factor in Williamson's despair, as his son had rather wildly suggested? And if so, what?

CHAPTER TWELVE

At around midnight another sergeant turned up to inform Derek and the Tennessee Ernie Ford acolyte that the impenetrable ring that had been thrown around Dartmoor by the police force had been penetrated, and Rubber Bones had already been sighted in Soho. Back at the station Derek's wretched motorbike refused to start until he ran it down the street, jumping on it perilously as he let out the clutch. It fired up finally, and he headed for home. He'd be there by half past midnight. And Mary would be waiting up for him, he was sure of that.

He was perhaps a quarter of a mile from the village when it happened. He was puttering happily through the darkness lit only by his weak headlight, and thinking happily of a bath and bed. And Mary. He felt tired, happy and even hopeful.

Then something rolled out of the dark, across the road in front of him, and he had a moment to see that it was – of all things – a wheelbarrow, before his front wheel crashed into the thing, and he was sent sprawling in a kind of sideways somersault, his left shoulder and the side of his helmet smacking into the tarmac, while the bike itself thankfully spiralled harmlessly away. Instinct of a sort took over, and he rolled with the impact, almost but not quite imitating a tumbler and almost but not quite rising gracefully to his feet again, before actually sitting down rather heavily on the road.

Sting of the Nettle

"Shit," he said loudly, half with relief, the other half with annoyance. A quick check assured him that no bones were broken, and he scrambled to his feet. His face felt wet, something dripping. Must have cut himself. Where was the bike? And what the hell was a wheelbarrow?

Something hard, something terribly hard, hit his knee, and he crashed to the tarmac again. Agony... He screamed. He couldn't stop it. Jesus, it hurt.

There was a black shape looming over him in the starlight.

"Got you, you fucker."

Who the...? Bucky? No. Not that voice. He didn't recognise it. He clutched his knee, almost weeping with pain.

The figure above him swung a leg, and this time a boot crashed into his stomach. All air, every semblance of breath disappeared, leaving a dreadful void, an aching desperation, a foretaste of death. He tried to cry out, but nothing came, nothing worked. He was dead.

"You're getting a lesson, Sonny." The shape was leaning over him. Through the agony he realised that his hearing still worked. If nothing else.

The voice continued, with the calculated menace of a baddie in a B movie. "You were told to shut up. You got to learn to do as you're told. See? That's why you're about to get a good kicking. See? When I'm finished, you'll be a good little copper and do as you're told, see?"

As his lungs started painfully to work again, Derek was grimly aware that, dreadful though he felt now, worse was to come. But he couldn't move, couldn't speak, he could only wait.

"Right." The shape above him muttered. "Think I'll take a bit of a run-up for this next one." He laughed out loud, and a blast of beery breath sprayed into Derek's face.

He moved away, but Derek knew he was coming back. He tried to brace himself, tried to protect his groin, to move his head away, but nothing was going to work. Nothing. Fear rose in him like a black thundercloud.

"Fucking hell!" A jumble of noises, some metallic, some scrabbling, some scuffling, more swearing.

"Fucking motorbike."

And Derek suddenly knew what had happened. The shape, the man, stepping back to give himself room, to give himself his 'run-up', had fallen backwards over the crashed machine.

And it gave Derek a chance.

Afterwards he would remember with wonder how, despite the two crippling blows he'd received, he was able to get to his feet, and run. It was fear that did it, he knew that much. Fear of more pain, fear of crippling injury, fear even of dying.

And that fear made him run. He was slow and awkward at first, managing just a few faltering steps back down the road. Behind him he could hear his assailant struggled wildly, perhaps drunkenly, to free himself from the fallen motorbike. Faster, Derek instructed himself. Get away. And now he was picking up speed, running faster, limping from the kick to his knee, but ignoring the pain, just running to escape, to escape even more pain.

And he could run, too. He'd played on the wing in

his school rugby team, even turned out with the Hendon squad on occasion, and now, on the wings of fear, he ran like a startled three-legged rabbit.

The man was back on his feet, Derek could hear him – or imagined he heard him - running after him. But not fast. Instead the footsteps sound what they were – the ponderous paces of a heavy-set heavy-drinker.

Derek ran on. A hundred yards, two hundred yards. He was failing. The pain in his knee, the desperate breathlessness of the blow to the stomach, they were making themselves felt again. He needed to stop. And if he stopped, then he needed to hide.

The road ran down a short but steep dip, at the bottom of which flowed the river Tawe. More of a stream than a genuine river, it was crossed by a narrow two-arch stone bridge. Staggering, Derek slipped off the road, and through some undergrowth, then stepped off the river bank and into the water. The flow was shin-deep at the most, but cold even in mid-summer. Trying not to splash, he waded a few unsteady steps until he could duck under the first arch of the bridge. There, bent almost double and shivering in the water, aching and terrified, he waited.

His attacker, hadn't gone away. He'd followed Derek down the road, but seemed from the sound of it to have stopped about 20 yards short of the bridge. His panting was loud and hoarse.

Derek wanted to pant. He wanted to moan with the pain too, but he did neither. Fear forced him to be silent. He heard the man grumbling to himself, then spitting copiously. And then, incongruously, relieving himself with a long sizzling hiss onto the road surface.

From nowhere, unbidden, bizarre and totally unexpected, an image came into Derek's head. Hiding under a bridge, terrified, dreading discovery... Jim Hawkins! Jim and his mother, crouching under a bridge, escaping from the murderous Blind Pew and the other pirates... Despite his pain and his dread, Derek almost laughed. He was in Treasure Island! He was living a childhood fantasy adventure.

There were lights. A car, approaching from the village, then stopping presumably where the pissing man was standing. Then a conversation. Derek caught some of what the attacker said. "A good kicking." and "Scared the shit out of him..." and "Christ knows..." but he could only hear a dull mumble from the driver in response.

Then a car door opened, a pause, then it slammed. And the car drove on, over the bridge, and away. Derek waited, waited, waited some more. But they had gone.

Clearly neither of them had read Treasure Island.

* * *

Back on the river bank, Derek sat down – on what he didn't care. His police boots and the lower part of his uniform trousers were soaking wet. His knee throbbed. His throat ached, perhaps from his attempts to breathe after the horrendous body blow. His left hand and arm seemed sore, probably grazed, but he couldn't see in the darkness. And there was still something liquid coming from a pain in his face, which looked black on his hand in the night-time light, and had to be blood. But none of that mattered. The pain would go. The physical damage would be repaired, or repair itself.

But the shame. The shame of his fear, of his panic, of his running away like a frightened child.

That would remain. And it was no use telling himself that he'd done the wise thing – perhaps even the only thing. Fear had taken him over. He had not faced up to his attacker. Christ, he had a weapon, his truncheon, in its pocket. He hadn't used it. He hadn't thought of using it, of fighting back. He'd run.

He got up and climbed the bank to the road. There was no sign of anyone, no evidence of traffic. There wouldn't be, of course. Not in the middle of the night, not on that tiny country road. He realised that he was hugging himself, hunched over, his arms wrapped around his chest. With an effort, he dropped his hands and straightened up. He started walking the quarter of a mile back up towards the village, back to where he'd crashed, where he'd been beaten, where he'd been made afraid. The walk took for ever, and it took no time at all.

Somewhere along that walk he made up his mind. This one, this episode, this appalling experience he would keep to himself. No-one would know what had happened to him. He would never talk about it. He would never write a report about it. No-one would read about it. So no-one would know how he had been so afraid. No-one would know. No-one except himself. And he would never forget it.

At the crash site the wheelbarrow was in pieces in the ditch. Where on earth had it come from? Where did his

Sting of the Nettle

attacker find it? Derek left the thing where it was. There must be some sort of farm yard nearby, but it didn't matter. What mattered was what it had done. Which, he had to admit, was simple but effective. His helmet lay in the middle of the road, somehow untouched by the car that must have passed over it. The metal badge glinted in the semi-darkness. He put it on his head gingerly, and the strap scraped against what must be a cut.

He found the motorbike. The machine lay half on the road, half on the grass verge, and as he painfully pulled the thing back on to its two wheels, he wondered if it would ever go again.

It started first kick.

* * *

He reached the village, then a hundred yards from home he cut the engine and free-wheeled the rest of the way. He tried to enter the front door quietly. Mary came slithering down the stairs in her dressing gown before he had time even to close the door behind him.

"Oh my God!" She stared at him, hand to mouth.

Derek looked down at himself. His boots were dripping on the floor. The trousers were filthy and ripped. There was a button missing from his tunic, which was equally dirty. And there was blood too, on the cloth and on his hands.

"I fell off the bike," he told her.

* * *

Sting of the Nettle

"I fell off the bike," he told Sergeant Welbeloved on the phone next morning.

"Do any damage?"

"Not much. Couple of bruises, a small cut."

"I meant the bike."

* * *

"I fell off the bike" he told John, the landlord at the Green Dragon.

"I'd like to see the other chap," said John, staring at his face. The cut had been less severe than he'd feared, but there was some bruising.

"Very funny. Listen, since we spoke, have you said anything to anyone about me asking about Old Tom Williamson?"

"I mentioned it to a couple of the lads, yes. Said you were looking into it. Anything come of it?"

"Not a lot, no. Another thing, was my friend Bucky in here last night?"

"He was here all right. Loud and unpleasant as ever. Come to think of it, he mentioned you. Joking about how you'd never catch Rubber Bones, 'cos you couldn't catch a cold. You know the sort of thing."

"He knew I was on duty then?"

"Reckon so. Then someone came in and announced that Mr R. Bones been seen in London, that he'd got off the moor okay, and Bucky reckoned that was your fault. You know what he's like. Evil bastard, if you ask me."

"So..." Derek hesitated. He didn't want to ask too much. John might get too interested. But the pub was

Sting of the Nettle

empty at that time of the morning. And it turned out he didn't have to worry. It was John who had to worry.

"So. What time did Bucky leave?"

"Normal time. Chucking out time." John was a bad liar. He fidgeted, blushed.

"John?"

"Oh, all right. If you must know I let the lads have a bit of a lock-in last night." He raised a protesting hand. "I know, I know. I could lose my licence. But Christ, you got to understand, mate. You can't make a living with a place like this, not if you stick to the rules. Do you know how much profit I make on a pint? About threepence. The bloody brewery is putting the rent up. I got to pay someone to come in and look after the wife, sometimes I think I'll go mad. And if you report me..."

"John stop it!" Derek told him coldly. "I don't give a bugger. Just tell me, what time did you finally see the back of Bucky."

"Christ. After twelve. Even later."

It made sense, Derek thought. During the night Bucky would have heard, first, that he was still asking about the Tom Williamson death, and then worked out that he'd be coming back late. Time and opportunity to plan an ambush.

"The lads made one hell of a row when they left," John was saying. "I'll have to apologise to some of the neighbours. And another thing. You know that old barrow I had out the front, full of geraniums?"

"Yes?"

"It's gone."

CHAPTER THIRTEEN

Cuts heal, bruises fade, and invisible menders and dry cleaners do wonders with uniforms. But the memory of the attack, of his fear, his running, stayed raw. To counteract it, Derek set himself to get things done. The warm summer days slid softly into early August, and project garden clearance proceeded, though agonisingly slowly, under Mary's guidance and Derek's spade. The dog days of the season brought with them few new police duties. Village bad-lads seemed reluctant to commit even technical or mild offences, let alone actual crimes.

A local small-holder reported the theft of some gin traps, but one gin trap looks like any other gin trap, and there must have been hundreds owned in the village alone, serving as a defence against the rabbit plague, a necessary source of sustenance and an income from the sale of both rabbit flesh and rabbit skin. Derek's professional enquiry as to the missing items went nowhere. And he didn't much care, either.

The office in town understood, but couldn't abide the thought of constables sitting around at home doing nothing, and instigated a campaign to enforce the purchase of dog licences. Derek did what he could. Almost everyone owned a dog, almost no-one had a licence, almost everyone without a licence undertook to get a licence, and almost everyone who gave that undertaking didn't. Derek reported that his actions in the campaign to enforce the purchase of dog licences had been a success.

Another few dead dry baking days passed. Then one morning, when he was about to get out of bed, Mary put a hand on his arm to stop him.

"Listen. Have you stopped niggling?"

"What? Oh. You mean the Williamson business? Well. Yes."

"Really?"

"God, yes. Yes. I mean, it's stupid. A couple of meaningless remarks from a local thug and some inbred twit. And I mean, what's the point? The man killed himself. People kill themselves all the time. No, I'm finished with it."

He hoped this would convince Mary. The truth was, none of what he had just said could convince him. That niggle was surviving the heatwave. But more than that, stronger than mere curiosity, was his need to redeem himself in his own eyes, to re-establish his faith in his own courage. It was a score he had to settle. As the odd sharp pain from his knee often reminded him.

Mary said nothing for a moment, then: "I was thinking about my ring again. When I lost it?"

"Your engagement ring?"

"Of course my engagement ring."

They'd bought the ring together at a jeweller's in Exeter on a day when he was on leave and she had just graduated from teacher training college. It cost twenty pounds, but Mary insisted on paying half, convincing him of something he had already suspected, that their

Sting of the Nettle

marriage was going to be an equal partnership in all aspects, good and bad. It had been a little loose on her finger, but she was keen to show it to her family and friends, and they'd agreed they'd get it properly fitted in a week or so. Bad decision. Next day they joined some other friends in a trip to Bude. They swam, they splashed through rock pools, they sat on the sand and ate ice-cream, they wandered hand in hand through the rivulets of the incoming tide, and when they climbed back into the mini-bus with the others, and the wagon started chugging up the hill out of Bude, the ring was missing from her finger.

"I cried all the way home, didn't I" Mary remembered.

"You did. Wet my shirt."

"And when we got back, you said something really daft. You said you'd go back and find it. No, I'm wrong, you didn't say that. What you said was it's there to be found."

"Yes. Well. So it was."

Yes, he'd known it was there to be found. A niggle told him so. It took him three days, hiking to Bude each day, scouring the endless beach, the craggy rock pools, the headlands, knowing the ring was there, knowing that he would find it. The constant niggle of its loss told him he would. Because he must. On the third day he did. It was underneath the ice-cream van. Mary had wept again.

"It was your niggle, wasn't it? You had it."

Not long after they first met Derek had tried to explain to her something that had been with him since childhood

Sting of the Nettle

– the thing they had come to call a niggle - a compulsion, a mental hook, which meant that when there was some puzzle, something to find out, some action to take, that niggle wouldn't leave him alone. It would drive him on to reach an answer, a conclusion, however strange or absurd or impossible it might be.

"That's when I realised you were a bit weird," Mary said with a giggle.

"Weird!" he said, mock-offended.

"Nice weird." She kissed him. "What does it feel like, this niggle? Can you describe it?"

"Well. I was thinking about that. You know how it is when those nettles sting you, you rub it with a dock leaf and it goes away...and then when you're trying to sleep at night, it comes back tickling and niggling. Well, it's like that.

"And poor Mr Williamson.? That Is still tickling and niggling, isn't it? I know you said forget it, but..."

"Well. There was something the son, Peter, said. About some German POWs who worked for them, on the farm."

He had remembered their names. Hans, the nice one who made slippers, and Horst, the Nazi. Hans and Horst. The comedy duo. Peter had not actually said much about them. His mother had interrupted him. If he went back again, he'd probably get another earful from her. She might complain officially. But...

Mary swung long legs out of the bed. "Well if you're still niggling, you better get scratching, hadn't you?"

"But the garden?"

"Take the day off. The nettles will still be there

tomorrow. Go scratch your niggle."

* * *

The Williamson fields lay alongside the road leading to the farm, and glancing through a gateway Derek glimpsed two men working with pitch-forks, loading sheaves of corn onto a wagon. One of them was Peter. He parked the bike, making sure he was leaving it on a down slope, climbed over the gate and walked towards them. Peter met him halfway.

Derek raised a hand in peace, as they met. "Look, I don't mean to bother you again."

"No, that's fine." Peter was smiling. "Matter of fact, I'm glad you've come. Mother was in a bit of a state that day. She wouldn't normally shout like that, she's not that sort. Not like some round here. Anyway, she said, if I saw you, I was to say she wants to apologise."

"Oh well. She doesn't have to. But, reason I'm here, I'd like to have a quick chat with you. And with your mum, if possible."

"Why not? Listen, it's lunch now anyway. No time like the present."

For a moment Derek was confused. Lunch? It was only half past ten. Then he remembered. In Devon farming parlance lunch was a mid-morning snack, dinner was at one, and tea at around six. Just one of the things you had to remember when knee-deep in the rural west country.

Peter had a word with his labourer. "He's only temporary. For the harvest," Pete told him, as he and

Sting of the Nettle

Derek walked down the road to the farm.

Derek asked: "How have things been? You coping?"

"Well. Better than you'd think. It was the paperwork I didn't fancy, but Dad had this desk he used, in the sitting room, and when we opened it, there was everything laid out – some bills to pay, not many. Savings account. Bank statement. His will. Insurances. Records. Tax paid. Everything up to date, bloody marvellous really. Meant mother had no worries, and we could just get on with things. No probate yet but they say it's coming."

"Yes." Derek spoke carefully. "It would all seem to indicate that your father, lost his life... intentionally."

"Yes. You mean, it proves it was suicide. Not that there was much doubt about it, to be honest. That verdict, it was just meant to make things easier for me and mum. Nice thought, I suppose."

"Yes. And one or two others seem keen on the verdict, too. Do you know a chap they call Bucky?"

"Christ, yes. Steer clear of him, he's a nutter. What's he got to do with it?"

Derek shrugged. "Nothing, as far as I can see. Seems to have a lot to say for himself."

"He always does," Peter said. "He's a head case, that one. Sometime he seems sort of manic. Almost crazy."

"Mmm. And there's another one, I don't know if you know him..."

He broke off, because they had reached the farm yard, and the farmhouse door opened. Mrs Williamson stood on the step, clearly not the stunned woman Derek had interviewed on the day of the death, or the angry

Sting of the Nettle

woman who had shouted at him on his previous visit. Instead she was smiling shyly, holding out a tentative hand to shake his, and, murmuring a slightly jumbled but graceful apology, inviting him in.

The three of them sat at the kitchen table, but not before Mrs Williamson had disappeared into a larder, and returned with a multitude of split rolls piled high with jam and cream, and even a dish of junket, that Devonian speciality, the curds-and-whey that Little Miss Muffet enjoyed. But, remembering what seemed to him to be its vague scent of stomach contents, Derek now politely declined the junket, but accepted a jam-and-cream roll. It was delicious. Fresh tea was poured from a big Brown Betty tea-pot – a very different brew from Mrs Weston's satanic liquid.

Eventually, after listening politely while mother and son engaged in usual farming talk about the state of the field where Peter was working, Derek summoned up the courage to begin the conversation he'd come to have.

"I gather from Peter that Mr Williamson's business affairs are thankfully in good shape."

"Oh yes," Mrs. Williams agreed. "Our solicitor said everything was in order, I didn't have to worry about anything. Even this year's tax was sorted."

"Yes. Very fortunate. I mean, sometimes, after a sudden death."

"Well it wasn't sudden, was it? Well, it was for us, but not for him."

"Not for us, neither," Peter put in.

"And the inquest verdict?"

"Load of rubbish, that's what that was" said Mrs

Sting of the Nettle

Williamson forcefully. "He meant to do it, course he did. Mind you, I wasn't going to argue with the coroner, was I?" There was an ironic smile on her face, typical, he thought, of the tough enduring quality of the women of west country farming stock. Mrs Williamson may have been stunned by her husband's death, and then initially angered. But now she was facing reality and getting on with life.

"Well look," Derek said slowly, helping himself to another delicious bun, "I don't mean to pry but would you mind if I asked you a few questions about Mr Williamson?"

"You ask me anything you like, Constable, I don't mind, my dear."

"Thanks. And call me Derek."

"All right Derek." She didn't invite him to call her by a given name, and he was pleased she didn't. Somehow it was a question of respect.

"So, was there anything about your husband's behaviour that...well, that might have indicated that he was troubled in any way? Or did it all come out of the blue, as it were?"

"Look dear, it was a shock, yes. But not a surprise, not really. Like Peter said."

Peter, who had been spooning junket into his mouth with rather noisy enjoyment, nodded reluctantly.

"You see," the boy said, when his mouth wasn't too full, "He'd been, well, difficult for some time, thinking back."

"Since not long after the war, really. Just getting worse and worse," said his mother.

Sting of the Nettle

"In what way, could you say?" Derek asked.

Mrs Williamson seemed to ignore the question, settling herself back in her chair and pouring herself a refill from the teapot. Derek waited. He sensed that Mrs Williamson wanted to talk, to do more than answer a few police-style questions.

"The thing you got to understand, Derek my love, is that my Tom was a decent bloke. A good man. I was lucky to get him, or so my friends said. I come from over Hatherleigh way, you see, but one time there was this dance in the village, and a group of us come over, and there he was. All clean and shiny and smiling, not like some of the farm boys round here."

"Mother!" Peter's protest wasn't serious.

"I'm right and you know I am. Scruffy lot, they are. Smell of pigs, half of them. Need a good scrub. Anyway, Derek, that was it. I didn't want no-one else and neither did he. This was his Dad's farm, you see. His mum had passed on a couple of years before, and the old man was getting on a bit, ready really to hand things on to Tom. Which meant, of course that Tom needed a wife. You going to run a farm, you need a woman, you know."

"I can imagine," Derek said, smiling. Mrs Williams pushed the plate of jam-and-cream rolls towards him, and he took one.

"So anyway," she went on, "Tom was ready for me, and I was ready for him. In a manner of speaking. Too ready, I suppose. You know what it's like when you're first together, can't stop yourself, can you? Anyways we got married in the February, and I had our first in the June." She jerked an elbow at Peter. "Him. There was the usual talk, but we didn't care."

Peter had gone a shade of pink. "Mother, the constable doesn't need to know that sort of thing. It's embarrassing."

"Oh go on with you! "Derek doesn't mind. In fact, he's probably the same as me and Tom were." To Derek: "I've known your Mary since she was a little maid. What a pretty girl she turned out to be. Wonder you haven't got kiddies by now. You look capable enough."

"Oh." Derek felt himself turning a similar shade to Peter. "Well, we've talked about it of course."

"You got to do more than talk, you know." A hearty chuckle. "Anyway, I was saying, we had Peter here, old Mr Williamson retired to a sort of home on the south coast, Dawlish if I remember right, and I won't say everything was easy, I mean it was farming and that's never easy, but things seemed pretty good all round, really."

"And then there was Margaret." There was a tinge of bitterness in Peter's tone of voice.

"Now Peter!" Mrs Williamson. "Derek doesn't want to know about Margaret. I know you feel bad about her, but... Well she's gone, she's out of our lives now. Leave her be."

"Good riddance, too."

"Peter!" Then to Derek: "Thing is, Derek, Margaret was a difficult child, in many ways. Some girls are, you know. And boys, I suppose. And, yes, all right, Peter, we probably did pay more attention to her than to you, but that's because you were such an easy child, and she was such a..."

Sting of the Nettle

"Such a pain in the bum. Well she was."

Mrs Williamson didn't contradict him. Instead she said: "She got worse when she was 14. We couldn't control her. Lord knows what she got up to. Running around. Men... And of course this was around the time when Tom started acting funny. I tell you sometimes I was at my wits' end either with her, or with him."

Peter abruptly reached across the table and put his work-scarred hand on hers. "But we're all right now, eh Mum?"

"Yes, my dear, we're all right now. I just hope she is, wherever she is."

There was a moment of silence. Derek took a bite of another jam-and-cream effort, then said through a small spray of crumbs: "What happened to her?"

"She just upped and left. None of us saw her go. One moment she was around. She wasn't working, she couldn't hold a job down and she was useless on the farm. And then next moment, gone. No note or anything. Just gone. But we weren't surprised. Sort of expected it really."

"Someone said they saw her," Peter put in. "With some chap, Exeter St. David's. Probably got a train to London."

"I wanted to report her missing," said Mrs Williamson, wiping a single tear from her eye with the edge of her apron. "But Tom and Peter, they both said let her go. We'd done all we could for her. And they was right."

"Well," Derek chose his words carefully, trying not to sound glib, "Do you think? That is, was her going the

Sting of the Nettle

reason for your husband's strange behaviour?"

"Oh no." She was very positive. "No dear, that started long before she went. Soon after the war, wasn't it, Peter? No of course, you'd have been a bit young to notice then, but. Yes. A year or so after the war. I suppose he got a bit worse after she'd gone, it was difficult to tell really." She gave a brief humourless laugh.

"Tell me about what he did. What he was like." Derek asked her.

She looked at her son. "You tell him, Pete."

"I don't know. I missed a lot of it, what with school and then college. But it was like he was driven by something. He could be, what do they call it? Manic. He'd shout and swear."

"And he never swore before," his mother put in.

"And sometimes he'd be full of beans, full of energy, working like the devil. I remember one harvest he was out in the field in the dead of night, using a Tilly lamp to see, making loads, bringing them in, stacking them up, like he was crazy."

"And he stopped eating," Mrs Williamson said. "Said he wasn't hungry. Threw a whole plateful on the lino one day." She hesitated. "Course, this wasn't all the time. Sometimes he'd be almost normal. He'd apologise. Wouldn't say what the matter was, of course. And then, after a few days, he'd be off on one of his trips."

"Trips?" Derek queried.

"Oh yes. Be gone for three or four hours. No-one knew where. Course, this is the sort of country where you can lose yourself if you like. Then he'd be back, out of nowhere. And he'd be even worse."

Sting of the Nettle

Derek licked a layer of cream around his lips, then said: "All this must have been very trying for you."

"There were other things." The words seemed almost to be forced out of Mrs. Williamson's mouth. "But well, I'm not going to talk about that."

Derek waited, and watched. There was a discernible flush on her already weather-beaten cheeks. She hesitated, looked at her son, then spoke again. "No, I'm not going to talk about that."

Derek felt the embarrassment that suddenly seemed to envelope all three of them. He decided he didn't want to know. Whatever "that" was could remain her secret. Instead he began to get to his feet.

"Mrs Williamson, I want to thank you. I suppose what you've told me does, well, illustrate your husband's frame of mind when he took his life. It doesn't explain why he should have been like that but... Anyway. Thank you very much."

"You're very welcome, my dear." There was a warm Devon smile back on her face. "And Peter, you better get back up that field. Before it rains, eh?"

Derek was back on his feet, when he remembered something, and sat down again.

"Oh. One small thing. Peter mentioned something about some German prisoners, working here after the war."

Her smile became even brighter. "Oh yes, that Hans. Lovely man, he was. Didn't matter he was German, he was like a son to me. He made us slippers, all of us. Look..."

Holding on to the table edge for supper, she raised a

Sting of the Nettle

foot to him. "That's one of his."

Derek looked. It was a comfy-looking slipper, stitched together in several different colours.

"Bit of old carpeting, some raffia. He did it in no time. But you should see the special ones he made for me. Wait there a minute."

She disappeared through a door leading to the hall, and Derek heard her footstep on the stairs, then on the creaking ceiling above. Then she returned, in her hands a second pair of slippers. "Look at these, my lovely," she said, pride in her voice. Derek looked. The slippers were impressive - uniquely crafted, he guessed, with exquisite care. On the upper of each one was a picture – a kind of tapestry, Derek decided – of a small flower. Each design was similar, yet subtly different.

"I love the flowers," he told her.

"Them's edelweiss - least, that's what he said. I don't wear them. I keep them under the bed. Remind me of him, you see. Lovely man, like I said."

"But wasn't there two of them? Prisoners, I mean."

"Yes." Her face darkened. "There was that Horst. I never liked him. Bit too military, to my mind. Acted like he'd won the war. Tom got on with him, though. Thick as two thieves sometimes, them two."

"I liked Hans too," Peter told him. "Horst, not so much. Course, they weren't here that long. Then they all got sent home. What do they call it? Repatriated, yes."

"Well not all of them," said Mrs Williamson. "Not Hans, for one. "

"Oh?" Suddenly, from nowhere, Derek felt the niggle twitch in his mind.

Sting of the Nettle

"No. Hans, he stayed on in England. Lots of them did, you know. If they got no one to go back to over there."

"I never knew that, Mum," said Peter.

"Oh yes. I mean, when the war ended the prisoners were free to come and go as they liked, more or less. Hans met some girl, they got wed, and he got the okay to stay in England."

"And he's still here, is he?" Derek asked.

"Far as I know. He said he'd keep in touch, but you know how it is. He fell out with Tom, which was no surprise, and he just went. Where he is now, Lord knows. He's not round here, I can tell you that. This woman he married, I heard she came from up around Taunton way."

Taunton, he thought. Not that far away. "Um. Just for interest, what was Hans's other name? His surname."

"Lord, I don't know." She shook her head, as if the question was faintly ridiculous. "I did know, I suppose, but I forgot. Something German?"

"Yes. probably. Well it's been good talking to you, Mrs. Williamson," Derek said, getting up to go. "Thank you for your time. And once again, I'm sorry about your husband."

"Thank you my dear." She produced her warmest smile, and then said, with a hint of a tease. "You must come again. I'll make you some more jam-and-cream."

"That would be lovely."

"I should think it would. You've ate that lot."

Derek looked back at the table. She was right. Apart from a few crumbs the plate was empty. He'd eaten the lot.

CHAPTER FOURTEEN

"So you won't want any supper, then." Mary gave him a mock-censorious look.

"Or breakfast tomorrow." He burped. "But they were so nice. How do they make cream like that? It was almost cheese, so thick, even crusty..."

"That's us Devon women's secret," Mary told him, emphasising her West Country accent. "Anyway, apart from overfeeding you with goodies, how was Mrs Williamson? She shouted at you last time, didn't she?"

"She shouted at her son, to be fair. But no, this time she was fine. Out of mourning, certainly. I think she welcomed the company. Wants to get on with life, if you know what I mean."

"She's not missing her hubby, then?"

"Truth be told, I think she's glad to be shot of him." Derek realised what he said. "Oh. Sorry. Wrong word. Sorry."

"I should think so. You should be shot!" They shared a shamed-face giggle. Then Mary asked, "What did she have to say about him? Bit of a bugger, was he?"

"Frankly he sounded sick. Raving at times. Sudden bursts of erratic energy. And, well, some things about him, personal stuff, she wouldn't talk about."

"I can imagine."

"I'm trying not to."

They were silent together, gazing out of the window at the back garden, where it lay glistening in the evening

Sting of the Nettle

sun in all its jungle glory.

Then, in a tone to break the spell, Mary said: "You know, every time you clear a couple of yards, another batch of impenetrable vegetation seems to spring up in front of you."

"Mmm." Derek was lost in thought.

"Still, it's got to be done. Shall we leap into action, spades in hand, rakes at the ready, blood-curdling oaths on our lips?"

"Mmm"

"Is that you leaping into action?"

"What? Sorry."

With a weary sigh: "Doesn't matter." And after another short hiatus: "It's the niggle, right?"

He looked up, and caught her eye. "Yes, well. Okay, let's get on with it. One hour hacking at the undergrowth, then a well-deserved break down the pub. What do you say? Deal?"

"Deal"

* * *

The pub was busy, with a large bunch of younger men at the bar, including Bucky again, Derek noted. He stared at him. Bucky had not been the one who attacked him. He knew that for certain. But he might have driven the car. It might have been one of his friends who did the kicking. Must have been.

Bucky looked up, perhaps sensing that he was being watched. He caught Derek's eye for a moment, then looked past him at Mary. He pursed his lips

Sting of the Nettle

appreciatively then turned back to his companions, saying something that made them all laugh and look at Mary.

Mary herself, perhaps realising she was the object of unpleasant attention, tugged his arm, and led him to a corner table where they could talk without being overheard.

And there, over a pint and a gin and orange served by a genial John, Derek gave her a more detailed account of his time at the Williamson farm house. Mary grew grave when, having heard of the dead farmer's furious and inexplicable behaviour, Derek again mentioned how there were some things, conceivably even worse, that the widow refused to relate or discus.

"That's sex then," Mary said flatly.

"I suppose so."

"No suppose about it. And my guess is, it's dodgy sex. If she won't talk about it, then probably something peculiar, or disgusting."

"You don't know that."

"No. But it's a good bet." Mary took a deep breath. "Something you should know about Devon farming women. They talk about sex freely. They're not coy about it. After all, they live on farms with all kinds of animals, so one way or another they're dealing with sex all the time. Putting bulls to cows, pairing up goats, watching to see they all get it right, witnessing everything all the time. I know there's talk about artificial insemination coming in, but it hasn't got this far, not yet. What I'm saying is, when people live close to the soil, as it were, then sex, talking about it as well as having it, it

Sting of the Nettle

just comes naturally. They go on about it all the time."

He grinned. "Not to me they don't."

"Well you should listen in on a WI meeting, once the visiting speaker has gone and the cups of tea have been handed round."

"Good grief. Hey! you go to those meetings!"

"Now you know why. Honest, the things you hear." Then more soberly: "Anyway, the point I'm making is, If Mrs Williamson wouldn't talk about it, well it might be pretty grim."

Mary stopped as she realised that she'd lost Derek's attention, that he was looking at the bar intently.

"What's up?"

"What's she doing behind the bar?"

Derek pointed. John the landlord, had been in place at the bar. He'd served Derek with his drinks. But now he'd disappeared, and in his place was a girl of about sixteen, tall and leggy in summer shorts and a loose-fitting blouse. She was laughing with the group of men at the bar, and clumsily pouring them drinks.

"You know Sandy," Mary told him. "John's daughter. Grown up a bit lately, hasn't she?"

"That's not the point. She shouldn't be in the bar. She can't be eighteen, surely! It's highly illegal."

"She's sixteen, I think. Or nearly." Mary told him. "Bit of a handful, John says."

"Makes no difference. I don't want to come the heavy policeman, but I'll have to stop it. I'll speak to John."

At that moment the girl turned her back on the men, and reached up high to grasp an item on a top shelf. As she did so, Derek saw Bucky lean athletically across the

Sting of the Nettle

bar, stretch out a long sinewy arm, and goose the girl violently.

The girl shrieked, possibly more in shock than pain. As she did, the door at the back of the bar, which led to the living quarters, banged open, and John Jacob blazed into view.

"Bucky!" he yelled, silencing the whole pub with his fury and coming face to face with Bucky across the bar. "I saw that! Get out! Get out! You're barred!"

Bucky tried a feeble defence. "I paid for this pint. I'm going to."

He didn't finish, because the landlord, roused to a new height of rage by this defiance, strode along the bar to the entry flap, crashed it open, and stormed through and towards Bucky. Bucky ran, clattering out of the door, followed by a couple of his friends.

John turned back, and directed his anger at his daughter, the girl Sandy, who stood looking half outraged, half amused.

"You! Get in the kitchen! Go!" She went.

John, breathing heavily, looked around the bar with the authority of ownership. "All right," he announced. "Show's over."

He started to return behind the bar, then noticed, or perhaps remembered, that Derek and his wife were sitting in the corner. Grimly, he walked over to them, pulled up a low chair, and sat down.

"You had to be here, didn't you! Officer!", he said with heavy but friendly irony.

"Yes," said Derek, picking up the same tone. "I had to be here. The long arm of the law!"

Sting of the Nettle

"That bastard Bucky. Excuse me, Mary, but, well, it's a good job he ran. If I got my hands on him, I'd have killed him."

"I'd have helped you," Mary told him.

"And the long arm of the law would have arrested you both," Derek grinned. Then he said: "All the same, mate, this is serious. Sandy behind the bar. You've broken the law, you know."

"I know, I know. She's 15 still, so it's illegal for her to be even in here, let alone serve behind the bar. But you saw, it was only for a moment. I had to pop to the gents, and the missus is upstairs, she's having a bad day. I just asked Sandy to keep an eye on things, not to do anything, just to call me if someone wanted serving. But I should have known she'd start chatting to those lads, egging them on, not that bloody Bucky needs any encouragement. Listen, are you going to do me?"

Derek sighed. "I could do with a conviction," he said. "Nobody else around here does anything worth being arrested. But I think this time an informal warning will serve the majesty of the law – won't it?"

"Thanks. And I'll make sure Sandy stays out of the bar, at least until she's 18. Though what else I'm going to do with her, I don't know."

The man looked suddenly older. "She's a problem, that one. Not a bad girl at heart, I don't mean that, but... Well there's nothing for her to do in the village, is there? And if she goes into town, she stays late, she has to get a lift back, and it's not safe. I don't know." He managed a smile at them. "Don't have daughters. That's the answer." He got up. "Thanks again. I'll bring a couple of

Sting of the Nettle

refills over."

Derek caught a glance from Mary. "You're okay," he told John. "We were off anyway. See you next time."

It was past eight o'clock, and the village street was deserted, but it was still warm. They walked slowly, hand in hand, talking softly.

"So getting back to Mrs Williamson..." Mary prompted

"Well, I can't think of anything else to tell you."

"But has what she told you cleared things up? You know, the niggle?"

He didn't answer. Instead he sighed, and said: "This whole thing, I mean, what have I got? A suicide, no-one seriously argues about that. A description of the poor bugger having what could very well be a nervous breakdown. All right, a bit odd, you'd expect a depression, not all that charging about the place. And there are a couple of German POWs, and an odd remark from the village idiot, and another from the upper-class idiot, but they could mean anything or mean nothing. Just stupid talk, or trying to get a rise out of the local bobby. Anyway, that's it. If I took that lot to Welbeloved he'd laugh in my face."

"But," Mary looked up at him. "Didn't he tell you to leave it all alone?"

"Well yes. But you can discount that. I know Welbeloved, you see. I've sorted him out. Welbeloved's whole thing in life is telling other people what to do. He just wanted to tell me to do something. He told me to leave the Williamson thing alone for the sake of telling me to leave the Williamson thing alone."

Sting of the Nettle

They were nearly home now, just a few more steps, but Mary had a last question: "So. Let me ask you again. Is it over? Has the niggle gone?"

A reluctant shake of the head. "Worse than ever, I'm afraid. There's something about all this that I don't know. I've got to try and find it, find out what it is."

"And you will." Mary told him. "You always do." She took his hand. "Only, one thing. Remember there's a dead body at the start of all this. So be careful."

"I will, of course, but..."

"After all," she over-rode him with a certain emphasis, "we don't want you falling off your bike again, do we?"

Good God. Derek almost choked. Did she know? Or had guessed? He started to speak but Mary had stopped, and was staring past him, pointing, her face shocked.

"Oh. Look! Look!""

He looked.

"Jesus!"

There was a jagged hole in one of the front windows of the house. "You stay there!" he told her, but she didn't, and together they both raced indoors, through the hall, and onto the bare boards of their front room. The couple hadn't begun to work on that room, living essentially in the kitchen and Andrew's office in the dining room. The front room's only furniture was a brand-new and hideous sofa, a wedding present from Mary's mother, still in its plastic protection. Beside it, having just missed landing on top of it, was half a brick.

CHAPTER FIFTEEN

Getting the window fixed would be no problem. Despite its relatively small size the village boasted, amongst other trades, a builder, a cobbler, a bakery, a butcher, a grocer, a sub post office, and a curious shop run by two elderly sisters that sold everything from socks to clothes pegs but very little of anything. A quick chat with the builder, with a promise of payment from police funds would, Derek knew, result in a few days' time in prompt and efficient service and a new pane of glass, fixed in expertly with putty, shining brilliantly, and probably causing Mary to hurriedly clean the other panes so the difference wasn't too noticeable.

Explaining how the window came to be broken, as he had to, to a more lugubrious than usual Sergeant Welbeloved, proved to be more problematic.

"What kind of brick was it?"

What kind of? Derek stared dumbly at the man.

"Describe it, sonny-boy. Describe it. What was it like? Where did it come from?"

"Well Sergeant, for a start it was only half a brick. I've no idea of its provenance. It was just a sort of dusty red, with bits of cement clinging to it. Thinking about it, I suppose it could have come from our own back garden."

"You got bricks in your back garden?"

"Dozens of them. Plus bits of bicycle, tin cans, broken mouse traps, broken bottles. All of them currently camouflaged amongst beds of vicious bloody stinging

Sting of the Nettle

nettles. But the important thing is, someone threw that particular half brick through our front window."

"Did you observe the incident?"

"No, Sergeant. It occurred when both my wife and myself were absent. Otherwise we might have attempted to foil the felonious act before it occurred, or possibly apprehend the villain what chucked the brick in the first place."

Derek eyed the Sergeant. Had he gone too far? He was aware that he was playing a dangerous game with Welbeloved, but it was a hot day, his uniform was sticking to him, his motorbike had taken ten minutes to start, and the police H.Q. had windows which had been sealed shut in the war, and no-one knew how to open them. So to some extent he didn't care whether the Sergeant took offence or not.

Welbeloved was silent for a few moments, regarding Derek quizzically, but when he did speak, he didn't accuse Derek of taking the mickey or of gross insubordination. Instead a smile spread across his meaty features, and before Derek could dodge back, he reached across and patted him on the cheek.

"Well done, my son. Well done."

"Oh. Well. I didn't actually do anything."

"But you did, Constable. You did. You annoyed someone sufficiently to lob a brick through your window. That shows you're doing your job. You're having an effect on your local community. That's good. Police action. You've got under somebody's skin. That's what you're there for. Congratulations, Constable Martin."

Sting of the Nettle

"Well, thank you, Sergeant. But surely..."

"I know what you're going to say lad, I've heard it all before from you young constables. You think you're here to help the public, not to harass them. That's what they tell you at Hendon, right? And I expect you've heard the Chief Constable blethering on about making friends with the community."

He leaned forward, and Derek could see the flecks of corned beef between the man's teeth.

"It's rubbish, lad. You don't want them to like you. You want them to be scared of you. That way you keep them in order. And when they get stroppy enough to throw a brick through your window, that's when you know you're doing your job."

He paused, while Derek reminded himself that he didn't have to be a policeman, he could have been a teacher, or a probation officer, or a cabin boy on a pirate ship.

"And while I'm on the subject..." the Sergeant continued, "... something you need to know about. Let's get ourselves a cup of tea. Should be some in the pot."

He led the way into the otherwise deserted tea-making passage. There was no sign of the tea lady, Mrs Weston, who was undoubtedly doing something terribly important somewhere else, but Welbeloved found his "mine" mug, rinsed out one for Derek, and poured two cups of heavily stewed lukewarm tea.

"Thing is," he said, sipping thirstily, "There's some changes in the wind."

"Changes?"

"Center... centris... hang on, I've got it...

Sting of the Nettle

centralisation."

"Oh." Derek braced himself for what was coming. "Changes" in the force were rarely to be welcomed. "Centralisation" sounded ominous, not to mention difficult to say.

"Only rumours so far, lad. Straws in the wind, you might say. But the talk is, they're going to reorganise the system. Get what I'm driving at? They're going to abandon the village policeman thing. Everyone will be based in the major centres, here, Exeter, Plymouth, Holesworthy, and so on. More cars, less coppers on the beat, and no more personal coverage in the villages. Mobile units will do the job. There. What do you think of that?"

Derek stared at him. No more boredom in North Tawe. No more chasing up dog licences or examining bicycle rear lights. Instead Exeter, Plymouth, real crime, proper police work.

A couple of months ago it would have been an exciting, no, a thrilling, prospect. But now, somehow, it seemed not quite such a dazzling future. All the same, goodbye boredom!

And then there was Mary. Mary his local girl. Home-grown Mary who'd lived almost all her life in the village. Oh Christ what would she say?

"What do you think, Sarge? Is it a good plan?

"What? What?" The Sergeant's face turned purple above the rim of his mug. "A good plan? No it bloody isn't a good plan. It's a bloody disaster. What do they want to change it for, eh? You know what's happening, don't you! Some new pin-head chief superintendent, straight out of university and staff college,

Got to make his mark, hasn't he! Got to shake things up. Bring in some so-called new ideas. Change for the sake of change, that's what this is."

He stopped for breath, and clearly expected Derek to say something, which he now did.

"I suppose you're right." It was enough.

"Course I'm bloody right. Why try and mend something if it's not bloody broken? Tell me that. We've got it running like clockwork here, haven't we? There's the Inspector, right, sort of does the office work. Then there's me, and my team, that's you lot out in the villages. The six of you."

"Seven." Derek corrected quietly.

"Right, right. Slip of the tongue. Seven of you, two in town here, the rest out there in the villages, doing your jobs, under my leadership. And what's the result? Peace and quiet, that's the result. Guided by me, your superior, your presence keeps our honest citizens in peace and safety, and our criminal element quiet. That's how our system works, that's why the district's almost crime free, that's why, well that's why some bloody idiot throws a brick through your window."

Buzzing back through the lanes, with the motorbike only giving the occasional queasy hiccup, Derek replayed the Sergeant's rant in his mind. One conclusion stood out amongst others – Welbeloved was terrified of losing his little fiefdom, his hands-on control of the village coppers, his sense of command, even power, over them. If the village policeman concept was abandoned, he'd find himself with only a couple of town constables to boss about, with every major issue being controlled from the big centres. It would represent a humiliating loss of authority for the Sergeant. Maybe even retirement. No wonder he'd turned purple at the prospect.

But that's all it is, Derek told himself. A prospect. Probably not even a definite plan yet. Of course it would be a good move for him personally. The pre-war image of the country copper, wobbling around his rural beat on his pushbike – or even on his dodgy motorbike – was nostalgic, yes, but out-dated. Now, in the new vibrant 1950s mobility would be the watchword. Mobility from a central hub. Fast police cars. Radios. Even armed police. That was the future. Let it come, let it come.

And yet, perhaps let it come in a little while. Not quite yet. He rode past the lane that led to the Williamson farm, and once again felt that surge of mental disquiet, the niggle, that told him there was something unfinished there, some work he had yet to do, some conclusion. Not to mention some personal redemption to find. Some freedom from the fear of, well, fear. But there would be time for that, surely. If he got on with it.

And then there was Mary. What to do about telling her she might have to move from her beloved North Tawe? Well the answer to that was simple. Don't tell her. Not yet anyway. After all, as Welbeloved had said, it was still only a rumour.

Mary had opened a can of luncheon meat, and they ate it for lunch, with a neighbour's gift of tomatoes and the first slices from a new crusty loaf from the village bakery. As they were finishing, and Derek was

Sting of the Nettle

reluctantly contemplating another attack on the nettle population, there was a knock on the door. Hoping that whatever the call was it would represent a reason to keep him out of the garden, Derek went to answer it.

Three people stood outside. One was John from the pub, who gave him a cheery smile. One was Miss Phyllis Parker, the feisty and talkative village postmistress. And the third was the Vicar, a frail white-haired old lad of nearly eighty who exuded an air of good-natured saintliness and was clearly hoping to die in office, and in his splendid vicarage, rather than be shuffled off to some crowded home for ancient clerics.

"Hello," Derek said. "Problems?"

"No, no, "John said with a grin. "Quite the reverse."

Miss Parker, clearly thinking she should have been first to speak, now said: "We've come, Constable, to say sorry."

At that moment Mary joined Derek in the doorway. Miss Parker was clearly relieved to see her, and said promptly: "Mrs. Martin, we've come to say sorry."

Derek resisted the temptation to say "Why, what have you done?", leaving Mary to ask: "But why?"

"The attack on your home. Disgraceful."

"Oh." Derek cottoned on. "You mean the brick. Through the window. Well, thank you but, well, you didn't do it, did you!"

"One of us did," said the vicar, a little tremulously. "One of us in the village committed the crime. And it shames us all."

"So we came to apologise. On behalf of the village." Miss Parker had the last word. She frequently did.

Sting of the Nettle

"Oh, there was no need," Mary told them. "Really. We know you. We know none of you would do a thing like that."

"You know that, Mary," John Jacob pointed out. "You've lived here all your life. But he doesn't." Then to Derek. "People think you might think the worse of us, when something like this happens. And we don't want you to be mizzled, do we!"

"Mizzled? Mizzled? What's this 'mizzled'?" Miss Parker demanded, going slightly pink.

"Sorry, private joke," John said.

"I don't think we need any jokes, thank you," Miss Parker said sternly, and John took a step back, grinning at Derek.

"This is for you, Mary." Another voice, this from a woman who had been hanging back, but now came into view bringing a bunch of roses and other blooms, a little dishevelled and uneven in length, clearly cut from someone's garden. She thrust them into Mary's arms, and as she did so Derek realised that several more local people were joining them, all talking at once in a babble of good-natured apology. The crowd even included the builder who had agreed to fix the window.

"I'm picking the glass up s'afternoon," he told Derek. "Do it straight off."

"And don't you go charging him, neither," Miss Parker told him.

"I'm not charging him, Miss Parker. I'm charging the police."

"Oh well. In that case do what you usually do. Charge double."

Sting of the Nettle

This produced a burst of laughter from the whole group, under cover of which John leaned over to mutter in Derek's ear.

"Watch out for more flying bricks. Another one, and you could fall off your motorbike again." And he winked.

Good God, did he know the truth too? Derek was about to say something, though what he would never know, because then a male voice shouted: "Look out!" as a car swung round the bend, swerved to avoid people who were standing in the road, sounded its horn and drove off down the street at speed.

Derek watched it until it disappeared. It was a white sports car, a newish MG TD, and while he couldn't see the driver, he was almost sure that the passenger was Bucky.

CHAPTER SIXTEEN

"So when were you going to tell me?"

"I don't know. Now?"

"So why didn't you tell me yesterday?"

"I was going to but - look what does it matter? I'm telling you now."

"About time too."

Mary adopted a sulky silence, Derek a guilty one. Of course she was right, he should have told her as soon as he got home yesterday, but he'd been dreading the look on her face when she heard the news. Well, a sideways glance at his wife, he'd been right to dread it too. She looked mutinous.

They were in what they sarcastically called their garden, great swards of which remained rich in weeds and nettles, and devoid of anything approaching decorative flowers or harvestable vegetables. They had spent a desultory twenty minutes hacking at it, before Derek's conscience got the better of him, and he called a halt. The news of the possible reorganisation, the end of the village bobby, and inevitably a move away from North Tawe for them, as outlined by Sergeant Welbeloved, came spilling out of him.

Now Mary sat on an upturned bucket, her legs straddled in her corduroy trousers. He half-sat, half-leaned against the kitchen window sill. The silence stretched on, broken only by a maddeningly cheerful blackbird, but eventually Mary decided to speak.

"Well. At least you have finally told me."

"And it's only a rumour."

"Ha. If it is, someone must have started it, and they must have had a reason to start it. No smoke, you know."

"I know," Derek sighed. "The old Sarge may be a bit of a prat, but he's got his ear to the ground. I think he was just giving me an early heads-up. So it won't come as a big shock if they suddenly turn round and say..."

"... and say we've got to move."

"Yes."

"The awful thing is, it makes sense. It's the way things are going these days. You wait. One of these days we'll lose the bakery. And the cobbler. It'll all be done by big companies, in town. Do you know how many pubs there used to be in North Tawe? Four!"

"Happy days."

"You would say that." She grinned at him, and Derek knew he'd been forgiven.

Another silence, a lot more comfortable than the previous one. Then Mary said: "What about my job?"

"Plenty of schools in Exeter."

"But they're going to make me department head when Foster retires."

"If he retires."

"And what about this place? What will they do with it?

"Sell it, I suppose."

"And give us one in Exeter or wherever?"

"Well, they've got those police flats."

"I'm not living in one of them!" Mary was suddenly incandescent with rage and frustration. "Ratholes they

Sting of the Nettle

are. I've seen them. Cracks in the ceiling, water running down the walls. No, never. You'll never get me in one of those."

"Yeah, well. Who knows? We might qualify for a council house."

"What? And live on one of those awful estates they're building, in the middle of nowhere?"

"Or we can think about buying our own place. With two of us earning."

"... And if I don't get pregnant. Which those miserable bloody building societies always assume I will."

"Right." It was an abbreviated version of a discussion they'd had during many a quiet evening, a discussion that always ground to a halt at a dead end. Something they both now realised.

Mary left her bucket, and came to stand by Derek, taking his hand. "Sorry," she said. "I'm being a bit negative. But, well, I like living here. This is my home. I couldn't believe it when you got posted here, it was so incredibly lucky, and now it seems like we've only just got here and we've got to leave. It's not fair."

"I know."

"It's not so bad for you, of course. For a start, you're relatively new here. You don't really know everyone, not yet. And I know you're bored. No criminals to arrest. No robbers, no murderers, not even a decent road accident."

"We've had a brick thrower," Derek put in, but she over-rode him.

"But you'll get all of that in Exeter, or Plymouth, or even Holesworthy, and it will be good for your career, you know. You're bright, you'll probably get promoted

Sting of the Nettle

sooner or later, maybe to CID and..." She laughed at herself, "Oh lord, Scotland Yard Special branch. And you're not going to get any of that stuck out here in North Tawe checking dog licences and rear lights on bikes. Are you?"

"No I'm not. No murders in North Tawe. Not yet. I don't suppose you'd like to go and kill someone for me? That might help."

She giggled, then said: "The thing is, I like it here. The village. And the whole place. It's gentle, you know. Soft. Warm."

"Wet?"

"Yes. Wet. But that means it's green. You sometimes forget, when you live here, to look around, look at the views. Look at, I don't know, the patchwork of the fields, the view across to the moor. I mean, when's the last time you stopped in a gateway, and just looked?"

Derek thought of the day he didn't shoot the dog. He'd stopped then. And looked. "Well..."

"I'm the same," Mary said. "It's like people in London, all those theatres to go to, and they never go. You've got to remind yourself, open your eyes, see that you live in God's country. Oh sorry, I'm going to stop now."

Derek squeezed her hand. "I'm with you, you know. I like it out here. I like the people in the village. And the farms. The locals. There's you for a start, you're a local and I like you."

"Oh yes, those people today, coming to say sorry about the brick, with the flowers – you wouldn't get that on an Exeter council estate, would you? Made me cry,

Sting of the Nettle

they did. And you had a tear in your eye, as well."

"Hay fever," he protested. "From the flowers."

They both laughed, and Mary straightened up. "Well, if we've got to go, we've got to go. And listen – what about the Williamson business? You know, your..." She made quotation marks in the air. "Your Niggle.? You better crack on with that, if you ever hope to sort it out."

"You're right, I better."

"That's if you can get any further with it."

"Funny you should say that. I've thought of one thing I might do. And I'll do it now."

He turned to go back inside, then stopped and glanced back at the garden.

"What about the nettles?"

"Bugger the nettles," Mary told him.

* * *

Inside, at his desk, it took Derek only a few minutes to sort through the folder with the routine general information issued to him by the police authority and find what he wanted – a list of telephone numbers for police stations throughout the west country. Scribbling a number in his notebook, he decamped to the entrance hall and the telephone.

"Taunton Police, how can I help you?" said a disembodied voice.

"Can I speak to Police Constable Tony Grey please."

A pause. "Speaking. That's me. Who's that?"

"Oh hi, Tony. It's Derek Martin. Remember me? From training?"

Sting of the Nettle

"Who?"

Not a good start, he thought. "Derek Martin. I was in your class."

"Oh right. Derek Martin. Yes, course, how are you? You won Best Cadet, didn't you."

"Afraid so."

"I suppose you cheated."

"Of course I cheated." They both laughed.

"So. Where are you operating? Okehampton, wasn't it?"

"I'm out in one of the villages. North Tawe."

"Never heard of it. What's the crime scene like? Cattle rusting? Sheep stealing? Sheep shagging?"

"Nothing that exciting. You're lucky to get Taunton."

"I wouldn't say that. Most of the time I'm stuck at this switchboard. Anyway, it's good to hear from you, Derek. To what do I owe the pleasure?"

"I wondered if you could do me a favour. On the quiet, as it were. Unofficial."

"Fire away."

"I'm trying to track down someone. He's German, was a prisoner of war over here, but stayed on, married a British girl. I heard he settled somewhere near you, and I wondered, if you had a list of aliens. He must still have to register with you."

"Name?"

"I only know his first name. Hans."

"Knees and bumpsidaisy?"

"Very funny." Derek remembered now that Tony had been the joker of their group. Well, it didn't cost anything to laugh.

Sting of the Nettle

"And this is unofficial, right?" Tony checked.

"Very much so."

"Okay. It may take me a while to get my hands on that aliens list, if it exists. I'll get back to you."

Derek gave his number, and put the phone down.

Hans, knees and bumpsidaisy. The German, Hans, he must get that all the time from English wits. Derek felt sorry for him.

CHAPTER SEVENTEEN

Routine police work in a village, if there was such a thing, consisted largely of first dispensing with any fatuous queries or instructions from Sergeant Welbeloved, a task at which Derek was becoming increasingly adept over the months, and second, if no anguished or belligerent phone calls or door-knocking emanated from anyone else, of just wandering around the place talking to people.

And today was a day for doing just that. Mary had driven off that morning, to have lunch with a colleague who lived near Chagford. "Lunch", Derek knew from experience, meant an all-day feminine chat session, and that meant she wouldn't be back until evening, when she had promised she would bring back fish and chips. Which was a brilliant prospect, he had to admit. Before she left Mary had cast a meaningful look through the kitchen window at the nettles where they sat sagging slightly in the heat, but had relented and said nothing. Derek took this as permission to skive. Instead he decided to take a lawman's stroll – a beat, if you like – through the village, to see what he could see.

Not that this was an occupation entirely free of problems or at least difficult decisions. Wearing the thick serge uniform and the ridiculous domed helmet and sweating lightly in the summer heat, Derek was, to some members of the village community, also cloaked in an imaginary threat. When he thought about it, he had to

Sting of the Nettle

admit that the village might appear to be a peaceful rural haven, but truth be told, it had its share of suspect characters, those living on that narrow line between slight culpability and actual crime. He knew who they were, they knew who they were, the village knew who they were.

He knew, the village knew, that Joe Wilson, who lived in a semi-tumbledown cottage on the Hatherleigh road, quietly set his gin traps and his mole traps on other people's land, eking out a living by nailing the hides of his prey on the wooden doors of his outhouse, then selling the dried fur on to a London address. Technically Joe was breaking the law. But no-one complained, not officially, because there was really nothing to complain about. So Derek contented himself with giving Joe the occasional sideways look, and Joe crossed the street when he saw him coming.

Derek knew, the village knew, that Mrs Harrington led Mr Harrington a dog's life, occasionally entertaining the odd road mender or water board man in her bedroom, and easing her conscience by frequently battering Mr Harrington over the head with a saucepan. A charge of assault, husband-battering, might have been brought, but Derek learned from the records that when this had been attempted in the past Mr Harrington refused to follow through and give evidence. When Derek met Mrs Harrington in the shop or the post office, she would say good day with a bright smile. She knew she was safe. So did Derek.

Derek knew, the village knew, that Arthur Smith was a lecher and a peeping tom, who occupied his old age by following young courting couples when they wandered off to find some privacy in the woods and coppices. But the youngsters laughed at him openly, the small boys jeered at him in the street, and everyone else treated him as a pariah, which, Derek concluded, was probably punishment enough.

Knowing all this, coming to terms with the limitations of village life both in and out of the law, would sometimes frustrate Derek if he thought too much about it. Which he did now, as he sauntered down the road towards the village square, seeking shade at the side of the street. Welbeloved was wrong, the police authority was right. North Tawe didn't need policing. It policed itself. He was redundant. Exeter would mean excitement. North Tawe, for a young ambitious man, was a living death. Mary would just have to... but then again... and what about?

Oh God. Such thoughts... It was only twelve thirty, but he needed a drink.

The pub was cool, dark and deserted. Derek took off his helmet, then stood at the bar and waited. He could hear voices, slightly raised, perhaps a family argument. He told himself not to listen. Instead, after waiting a few moments, he took a half-crown from his pocket and tapped it on the bar.

A moment later, John the landlord entered through the door to the living quarters. He seemed slightly out of breath.

"Oh, sorry, Derek. Little domestic kerfuffle." He glanced behind at the door, as if worried that the "kerfuffle" had followed him, then turned back to Derek forcing a landlord's smile onto his face.

"So, what is it? Duty? Or thirst?"

"Well, thirst first." Derek enjoyed the combination of the words. "Or first thirst, if you prefer. But actually thirst first and second. No duty."

"Oh, very good," grinned John, rather wanly. "You should be on Workers' Playtime." He reached for a pint pot, and worked the pump handle.

Derek took a long luxurious pull at the beer. "That's good."

"New barrel this morning."

"Ah." Derek pushed the half-crown coin across the bar. "Have one yourself?"

"Better not." Another glance behind.

Derek took his change, and the two men stood silently for a long minute. Derek wanted to ask John the obvious question – what the trouble was – but he knew the query couldn't come from him. And in any case, he sensed that John was preparing to tell him, perhaps just getting up the courage. He waited.

"Did you hear some of that?" John said abruptly, gesturing towards the door.

"Not really, no."

"Just as well. You know, I will have one." And he poured himself a half-pint glass. "My bloody daughter, she'd drive a man to drink."

Derek struggled for a moment to remember the girl's name. Something modern, American. Sandy, that was it.

"Sandy being difficult?" he suggested.

"Difficult! D'you know what time it is?"

"Well. Twelve thirty. Your clock's a bit slow but..."

Sting of the Nettle

"Twelve thirty!" John said explosively. "Twelve thirty, and she's just got up! Just got up! I ask you!" He drank half his beer in one swallow.

"That's just young people," Derek said soothingly, remember similar accusations from his own parents, when he was Sandy's age. "They're all the same at that age."

"Are they so? Then I pity their poor bloody parents. Anyway this is different. The girl is sleeping this late because she was out half the night. Half past one she came in, I'd been out with a torch looking for her, and I come back and I'm thinking of ringing your mob, and there she is. Looking really scruffy and in one hell of a temper. Screaming at me. Shouting, going berserk. Woke her poor mother. I didn't know what to do with her. She wasn't drunk, I know when someone's drunk, she'd had a drink perhaps, but this was something else. Something... you know, sort of mad. Now this morning she's like a zombie, won't say anything. Had a big breakfast, though. Ate like a horse. "

Derek felt a shock of recognition. Where had he heard something like that before? Yes, Mrs. Williamson. About dead husband Tom. The niggle started up with a vengeance. Don't be daft, he told himself. What on earth could be a connection between a dead middle-aged farmer and a stroppy village kid?

"Did she say where she'd been?"

"Just with some lads. Talking, she said. Talking my arse. Until one in the morning? What does she take me for?"

"Mmm. I could possibly find out which lads. The boys

at the Larkin farm perhaps. Or..."

"Forget it, Derek. I rang them all. Last night. No joy. They all swore their kids were safely tucked up in bed. Got quite nasty about it, some of them. Farmers don't like being roused up at midnight, when they've got to get up at first light. No, I reckon any lads she met up with must have come out of Hatherleigh. Or Okey. Or wherever. Christ, Derek, what am I going to do with her?"

"Does her mother know?"

"No, it's down to me. Lucy is... well, she's not well. Not at all.

"Yes, I heard."

"It's not good. I've been trying to keep it quiet, but, well, it's the cancer. It's come back."

"Shit, has it? Well look, these days they can do wonders."

"Not this time." There was a break in John's voice. "They've sent her home to die, Derek. There's nurses come in to look after her when I can't but..." He gestured hopelessly.

"Jesus. I'm sorry, mate. But, is that what's causing Sandy to..."

"No, no, she doesn't know. And she doesn't want to know either. She's like she is because that's what she's like. We had high hopes for her, you know. She got into the Grammar, got good results, talked of being a nurse. All come to nothing. "

"Listen." Derek tried to stop himself saying the next thing, but it came out anyway. "Would you like me to have a word with her?"

"Would you?"

"Yes, sure. Not that it'll do any good, after all I'm not much older than her as it is, when you think about it, but..."

"Worth a try, worth a try. Anything." John acted quickly to stop Derek changing his mind, lifting the flap in the bar and ushering Derek through the door to the kitchen. He didn't follow him.

* * *

"You did what?" It was some eight hours later, and Mary was staring at Derek across her kitchen table, across a jumble of fish and chips, salt and sauce bottles.

"We thought it was worth a try."

"You twits! You clueless couple of..." Words failed Mary, and she raised her hands in exasperation, causing two sauce-dipped chips to fly haphazardly into the air and land with an audible splat on the kitchen floor.

"Well, I felt sorry for John," Derek attempted to explain, as he scrabbled on the tiles to retrieve the chips. "He was at his wits' end with..."

"Oh I'm sure he was. His wits had come to an end, and so had yours. Not one wit left between the pair of you."

Derek heaved a sigh. "All right. I know. Except I felt I had to do something."

"Can you imagine how that poor girl felt? She's had a big row with her father. No mother to run to. And now into the picture comes this big bloody policeman - you were in uniform, I assume."

Sting of the Nettle

"Well."

"And helmet?"

"No. I'd taken it off."

"Oh well done. How sensitive of you." Derek sucked his teeth at the sarcasm, and Mary continued: "But the uniform would have done the trick. All those big silver buttons, and the insignia, and your number, and your big boots. And I bet you smelled of beer, too."

"I just had the one." A thought. "Never finished it, either. And anyway, the pub smells of beer. Pubs do."

"I just hope you didn't draw your truncheon." Mary's indignant rage was beginning to ease. "So go on. Tell me. What exactly happened?"

"Well."

As Derek had entered the kitchen, he heard John close the door, and realised he was on his own. He took in the room briefly, a large kitchen, with a Rayburn against one wall, a stack of dirty crockery in the sink, a modern kitchen cabinet with the doors hanging open, and a slightly stale smell of frying in the air. There was a big oil-clothed table in the centre of the room. At one end was a jumble of newspapers, catalogues, booklets, accounts and more. At the other end Sandy sat, her head face down on the table surface, her two forearms flat beside her head, her fists clenched. At first Derek thought she was crying, he could hear her moaning softly, but then he noticed that her fists were drumming against the oil cloth, and he sensed instead that she was in a rage.

"Hello Sandy," he said.

The girl looked up, said "Fuck!", and put her head down again.

Sting of the Nettle

He tried again. "Sandy, can we talk?"

"I done nothing wrong. You got nothing on me." Her voice was low, hard and harsh, and he wondered if she was putting it on for effect.

"Of course you've done nothing wrong," he told her, trying to put a light laugh in his voice. "I know that. I'm not here to arrest you, you know."

"Then what the fuck do you want?"

"Well. Your father..."

"Fuck him." A low growl.

"He's worried about you. Worried about your behaviour. He wondered if there's something wrong, if you'd talk to me about it."

"Fuck him. And fuck you."

"Look, it might help if you could tell me where you go, late nights. Who you meet up with, that sort of thing."

At this Sandy sat up, and for a moment Derek thought he might be getting somewhere. Then she looked him in the eyes, and he knew he wasn't. It was an unblinking stare, a cold piercing look that was a denial of any feeling, any emotion other than hate and antagonism.

* * *

"Then she got up," Derek told Mary, "walked over to the sink, picked up a tea-cup, and threw it at me."

"Did she hit you?"

"No, it just bounced harmlessly off the wall. But then she grabbed a plate and threw that, and that time it nearly got me. Hit the wall again, and shattered."

"What did you do?"

Sting of the Nettle

"I did what any sensible man would do. That is, I got back into the bar and slammed the door shut behind me. Thank God the place was still empty apart from John. She smashed some more crockery, then it all got quiet. I told John I was sorry, I couldn't help, and then I came home and killed some nettles. You know, I think there's something seriously wrong with her."

"Oh, I doubt it, I really do. For heaven's sake, she's a teenage girl. And that's not an easy thing to be. She's confused, her body's sending her messages she can't cope with, she feels everyone's against her, she's frightened of the future, she's a mess and she needs understanding and help."

"You know that, do you?" Derek asked a little sceptically.

"Yes, I do. Because I was the same at her age. All right, I didn't break many plates but..."

"Look, I tried to help her."

"And got nowhere, right?"

"You think you could do better?"

"Well I couldn't do worse, could I?"

"Well?"

They stared at each other across the cold fish and chips.

"All right." She checked her watch and got up. "No time like the present." She grabbed her cardigan, and left the house.

She was back ten minutes later.

"She's gone."

"Oh no. Christ."

"John said he'd locked the back door and taken the

Sting of the Nettle

key, so the only way she could get out would be through the bar, give him a chance to stop her. But she climbed out of a window."

"Oh boy. Well that's it, isn't it!"

"Can't you do something?"

"What?"

"I don't know. Report her as a missing person? Organise a search?"

"Sweetheart, you can't report a missing person when it's a fifteen-year-old and they've only been missing for a couple of hours. Couple of days, perhaps."

After a moment, Mary said: "I didn't mean to go on at you. You know, before. At least you tried. Sorry."

Derek grinned at her. "Here, have a cold chip!"

* * *

Tony Grey rang from Taunton the next morning. It was an awkward time to call. Mary had gone to the butcher, and Derek was in the loo and halfway through washing his hands. Still dripping, he practically fell down the stairs, just in time to answer the phone.

"It's Tony. And, hey, I've got your man for you."

"Well done." Derek fumbled for the pad and pencil he kept by the phone. Wet hands dampened the paper. His trousers, not properly fastened, slid down to his knees. He left them there. "Okay, go ahead."

"It wasn't difficult. We've only got two German aliens in the town, and the other one's a woman. You want one Hans Bruckner." He spelled out the name, and gave an address.

"That's brilliant, Tony." He felt his trousers slide down his shins, but ignored them. "Did you have any difficulty?"

"Not really. I got into the files when the rest of them were on tea break. You're not reporting this, are you?"

"No. Just between ourselves. And I owe you one, mate."

He put the phone down. He turned to go back to his desk. He fell face down on the hall carpet. He got up, and pulled his trousers up. Thank heaven Mary had missed the trouser farce. She'd have loved it. She might even have told people about it. He regained his desk, sweating slightly with relief.

So. Hans Bruckner, the POW, the nice German, the slipper maker. He was getting somewhere. He'd picked up the phone to call Directory Enquiries, when a motor pulled up outside the house.

CHAPTER EIGHTEEN

Derek opened the door to find himself looking at a strange vehicle, one he had never seen before. At first it reminded him of a jeep, the zippy little motors in which American soldiers used to drive around the west country roads, sitting casually in their smart uniforms, and occasionally chucking out chocolate bars to the scruffy little Brits standing open-mouthed by the roadside. But this wasn't a jeep. It was bigger, boxier, with large aggressive front mudguards, and a roof – or rather a stretch of canvas draped tent-like over the top of the thing.

"It's called a Land Rover." The driver, now climbing out of his seat, and noting Derek's curious glance, proved to be Colonel Critchley. Derek felt a shiver of anticipation run through him. Colonel Critchley, the sobbing, almost hysterical man who had ordered him to shoot his dog. What did he want now?

"I picked it up yesterday. It goes anywhere. Fields, tracks, bogs, you name it. I've been trying it out this morning."

Derek nodded. He could see streaks of mud on the bodywork, and thick clots of earth clinging to the chunky tires. "And it's called a Land Rover?" he asked.

"That's right. Made by Rover."

"I thought they just made swish cars."

"Well they did. This is new, they call it the Mark 1.

Sting of the Nettle

It's been in development this last couple of years, now it's just coming on the market generally. Couple of years' time, every big farmer will have one, I reckon. Four-wheel drive, you know. As I said, take you anywhere. Like a tank."

"Fantastic."

There was a short and awkward pause. Then the Colonel spoke again.

"Look, I didn't come to take up your time discussing motors. I came because, well, you've been on my conscience. About that day. At my place."

"I see." Derek said lamely, then added "Sir", though quite why he couldn't think. It was just what one did when talking to someone like the Colonel. Even someone as emotionally damaged as the Colonel.

"Yes." The man came up to Derek, looking him squarely in the face. "Firstly, I behaved badly. I put a lot of pressure on you. I know how heavy I can get. I was totally unfair. Sally was my dog, my responsibility. And certainly not yours."

He paused, and the steady gaze wavered. "I was weak. It was a bad moment. And I owe you an apology."

"Really, Sir, but Sally, did you?""

"No. I couldn't then and I can't now. I'm keeping her in, I take her for walks on a lead, she hates it, but I'm going to do nothing until someone makes a formal complaint about her. I hope that's okay with you?"

"Of course, Sir."

"I also feel that I owe you an explanation for my behaviour. If you can spare me the time?"

"Of course, Sir. But," He looked around. "Perhaps it

Sting of the Nettle

would be best if we went inside?"

"Quite right."

Derek led the Colonel into the hall, and into his office, where he found the man a chair, and sat in his own at the desk.

"Now then," the Colonel began. "As you saw, my spirit failed me, with Sally. As I think I may have told you at the time, I shot men in the war, of course I did. But now, in the peace... There have been other moments when I've, well, lost it. Lost my own mental strength, something which, in the past, I could always rely on. Can you understand?"

"Yes, Sir."

"Don't 'Sir' me. My name's George. Call me George."

"Yes, Sir. George." Derek felt himself blushing at his clumsiness.

"I know." The Colonel smiled for the first time. "Awkward, isn't it, especially when I strut around and talk the way I do. Thirty years as an officer does that to you. But recently that hasn't stop me acting like some silly girl, or over-reacting to a quite harmless situation."

As he was speaking, something began to make itself known in Derek's mind. Something that the Colonel had spoken of, at their first meeting. Something that might help him, help with the niggle.

"It's not unusual, apparently," the Colonel was saying. "A sort of shell-shock, it used to be called. My wife said I should see someone about it, there are experts in this sort of thing these days. I said stuff and nonsense. One reason why she up-sticks and left, I suppose. Bit late now. In the meantime, all I can do is to express to you my sincere regrets and apology for putting you in the position as I did with Sally. And thank heaven you didn't do what I asked."

"Well, thank you. But there is really no need. Look, can I offer you a cup of tea?"

"No, no. Thank you but..."

"I wish you would, Sir. George. There's something I'd like to talk to you about, something a bit odd."

"In that case, certainly. I'd love a cup of tea."

Derek led the way into the kitchen. To his surprise, Mary was there, putting some sausages away in the meat safe.

"Oh. You're back."

"Mmm. Came in the back way." And, as she saw the Colonel behind him, "Oh, do we have a visitor?"

"Oh, this is my wife, Colonel. Mary, this is..."

"Oh we've met," the Colonel said heartily. "You're head of English, aren't you, Mrs. Martin? Or at least you're going to be." Then to Derek: "They've put me on the Board of Governors. Heaven knows why. The rank, I suppose." Then back to Mary: "Your husband has kindly offered to make me a cup of tea."

"I better make it," Mary smiled and reached for the tea caddy. "He makes dreadful tea."

"Perhaps he does," the Colonel replied, sitting at the kitchen table and perceptibly relaxing. "But in other respects he's a very fine and admirable young man."

"Oooh!" Mary reacted with an ironic yet pleased response.

"Oh, I mean it, he's a first-rate chap," the Colonel insisted. "And I don't think he quite realises it himself yet. But he will."

"When he does, he'll be unbearable," Mary told him with a laugh.

"Thing is," the Colonel continued, "He did me a big favour."

"Really?" Mary was now genuinely concerned.

"Yes. Didn't he tell you?"

"He never tells me anything. What did he do?"

Derek winced, groaned to himself, waited for it.

"He didn't shoot my dog."

"What?" Mary dropped a spoon and started at Derek.

The Colonel smiled. "Yes, I suppose it does sound a bit strange, put like that, but..."

But Mary over-rode him, and turned on Derek. "You didn't shoot his dog?"

"Well, yes. Or rather, no."

"You, you don't normally shoot people's dogs, do you?"

"No, but, well, the Colonel asked me to."

"But you can't go round shooting people's dogs, for God's sake."

"I don't." Derek suddenly felt a laugh coming on., and struggled to supress it. "I actually go round not shooting dogs."

"Mrs Martin, let me explain." The Colonel held up a pacific hand. "I seem to have put my size elevens in it. I did indeed ask your husband to shoot my Sally. No, more than that, I told him too. Indeed, if you'll forgive the military parlance, I gave him an explicit order. And like the sound man he is, he decided to disobey the order."

Sting of the Nettle

"But why? Why shoot your dog anyway? Oh God, not rabies."

"Sheep worrying. You're a local girl, I'm told. You understand how farmers feel about that sort of thing."

"Yes. And I also know that some farmers are only too liable to blame some poor dog when one of their animals falls into a ditch and dies. Are you sure your dog did something?"

"Well, I was," the Colonel continued. "But now I'm not so sure. Someone said they saw a collie, and she's a collie, but there are plenty of that breed around here. I don't think I was thinking straight. That's why I'm here today, Mrs Martin, To apologise. If Sally had to be shot it was my job to do it. And at the last moment I couldn't do it, and I tried to get someone else had to do it for me. Pathetic, I know. Nerves you see. The war. Fortunately I asked the right man. A man with what we soldiers call bottom. Your husband has bottom, Mrs. Martin."

"Yes, he certainly has." With a steady hand Mary brought the kettle from the Rayburn to the big brown teapot.

Derek looked closely at her. There was a look on her face he couldn't remember seeing before. He wondered what she would say once they were alone together.

But for the next twenty minutes the three of them talked like old friends. Mary and the Colonel did most of the talking, the Colonel giving more details about his state of mind since he'd left the army, and Mary recalling that a colleague on the school staff seemed to be having similar problems. The two of them exchanged telephone numbers, with Mary promising to look into whatever

Sting of the Nettle

help might be available. Derek drank his tea in comparative silence.

Afterwards he followed the Colonel out, and stood by as he climbed into the driver's seat. But the Colonel didn't start the engine. Instead he turned to Derek.

"Now then, young Derek. You said earlier there was something you wanted to talk about, didn't you? I didn't mention it in there, in case..." He left the rest of the sentence unspoken. Then he said: "I've put my foot in it once already, haven't I! But now, perhaps?"

"Yes." Derek took a deep breath. "You remember, something you said back at the farm, about evil. About how you'd seen it in the war, and about how it exists, even somewhere like, well, West Devon."

As he spoke the lorry from the egg packing station rattled by, and across the road he could see a housewife harvesting runner beans from a high wigwam of red flowers. Everything was so normal. Was he making any sense? he wondered.

"I remember," said the Colonel. "It's something I do believe. A kind of black spirit, unseen but always with us."

"Well, the thing is, I think I may have caught a sense of it."

"Ah. You said something before. About a suicide."

"Yes. Nothing I can put my finger on. It's just a feeling that something is wrong. Something around here. And I'm afraid if I do find something definite, and try to report it, I just won't be believed. I mean, some half-baked theories of a village constable. Anyway, there's still nothing concrete. But I might come to you for help when

Sting of the Nettle

there is."

The Colonel held out his hand through the open door of the motor, and Derek took it automatically.

"Of course. Whenever you're ready to talk about it, come and see me. I may be able to help. I will certainly back you with your bosses, and I have some weight in that direction, you know. Or at least I did. I won't let you down. That I can promise you."

For the rest of the day Mary didn't mention the Colonel, his visit, and the shooting of the dog. But in bed that night she abruptly put her book down, and turned to him.

"I'm glad you didn't shoot Sally."

"So am I," he told her. "But..."

"But what?"

"Well. I was going to. Nearly did. But then, I'm not sure whether I stopped because I thought it was the wrong thing to do. Or because I lacked the courage to do it, that I was frightened to do it. Didn't have the guts."

"Doesn't matter. What matters is, you did the right thing."

"Christ, I hope so."

"And listen. You mustn't keep these things to yourself. You must talk to me about them."

"I'll try."

"No. Say 'I will'"

"I will."

She felt for his hand and squeezed it. "And now, at least I know you've got bottom. But then," she giggled, "I've always known that. It's here somewhere, isn't it?"

CHAPTER NINETEEN

"Hello."

"What?"

The voice was quite guttural, but was that a 'V' instead of a 'W' in the 'What?"

"Um, yes, can I speak to Hans Bruckner please?"

"What you want?"

The words were blunt, even harsh, but there was something hesitant in the voice, and Derek sensed a weakness behind the bluster. Doubt, perhaps. Even fear. But the accent was unmistakeably German. He'd got his man all right.

"If that's you, Mr Bruckner, I just wish to talk to you. About your time as a prisoner of war."

He paused. There was silence on the other end of the line.

He tried again: "I understand you worked on a farm. The farm belonging to and Mrs. Williamson."

"Nein... No."

"Tom Williamson...didn't you help them out, when the war ended?"

"I do not want to talk!" The words came more fluently now. "Please go."

"But Bruckner, I just wish to ask you..."

"I am legal. I apply for..." A pause, then "...for naturalisation. I just a soldier. Not Nazi. Please. No more questions." He was pleading now.

Sting of the Nettle

"But..."

Before Derek say more there was a confused rustle on the phone, and then a woman's voice broke in, sounding even more desperate than the man's.

"Please! Leave us alone! He's a good man, not a Nazi. Just go away."

With an abrupt click the call disconnected. At his end, Derek slowly replaced the receiver, and leaned against the wall of the hall. "Christ!" he said.

Mary was at the kitchen table, working on some papers that had come from her school in the post.

"Coffee?" Derek asked.

"Mmm."

He opened the kitchen cabinet and took down the bottle of Camp coffee. It was a simple routine. Two cups, a spoonful of Camp in each, hot water from the kettle on the Rayburn, and milk from the bottle delivered faithfully to the doorstep every morning.

"Thanks." They both sipped the hot drink. Rationing had long ago obliterated any craving for sugar.

"So." Mary put down her cup on the oilcloth. "You rang your German then?"

"Yeh. Bloody farce." He told her of the conversation with Bruckner, as much of it as he could recall. "He was bloody rude. And so was his wife, if that was her."

"Well what did you expect?"

He shrugged. "I don't know. Normal civility?"

"You think so? Look, imagine what life's like if you're German in England today. It can't be easy. You'd probably get hate calls, make you scared to answer the phone. Then there'll be kids shouting at you in the street, calling you "Hitler" or "Achtung Spitfire!", doing the goose-step."

"That's just kids."

"'Just kids'? Ha! We had a German boy in school last year, a Jewish refugee of all things, and the little sods made his life hell. Oh, we jumped on it when we could. And anyway, it's not just kids you know. There are plenty of adults happy to join in the fun. Plenty to make your Hans and his wife suffer. Anything from calling him Fritz, to calling his wife a German prostitute, to shoving shit through their letterbox."

Derek started to speak but she held up a hand.

"Yes, all right, I know what you're going to say. Perhaps people, some people, do have cause to resent the Germans. After Plymouth, and Exeter. You were in Exeter then. You must remember the raids."

Derek remembered. Those months in 1942, April and May. April wasn't too bad, but bad enough. They said seventy-odd people were killed. But in May the bastards came back and it was much worse. High Street, Sidwell Street, Paris Street flattened. Even the Cathedral had been hit. Thousands of houses destroyed, hundreds dead.

"It was bad," he told Mary. "I was scared to death."

"And, of course, it was nothing to what we did to them. You've heard about Berlin and Dresden."

"Of course. Just as bad, I suppose."

"Worse. Much worse. But that was war. It's peace now. We should be pleased that your German has chosen to stay here. People should leave him and his wife alone."

"You mean people like me? That I should leave them

Sting of the Nettle

alone"

"Perhaps you should."

Perhaps he should. But no, he didn't want to. And he wasn't going to.

There wasn't too much time to think about Germans or anything else other than police work. After a constable in Plymouth was savagely beaten by a couple of sailors, Derek and his fellow constables were called to Exeter for a one-day special training session in unarmed combat.

Sergeant Welbeloved came with them, herding them around like a school outing, and several of the group, including Derek, had the pleasure of facing the Sergeant in man-to-man struggles during which the big man was thumped to the matting frequently and painfully. The Sergeant took it well, though after a while his professions of appreciation and good fun became slightly strained. And Derek himself wondered why he could cheerfully tackle the Sergeant, but had fled from the boots of his mystery attacker, the man with the wheelbarrow and the beery breath.

That evening, a quiet Thursday night, and with his limbs aching in places after the rough-and-tumble of the training session, Derek persuaded Mary that they deserved some relaxation. Together they popped into the Dragon, and found John Jacob in a mood of restrained desperation mingled with tenuous hope. His wife had had a bad night. "Bloody painkillers don't work half the time", but she was okay this evening. Even listening to the radio, not something she could usually bring herself to do.

"There's that new programme they're talking about,"

Derek mentioned. He quoted: "An everyday story of country folk. Specially for farmers and the like."

John managed a smile as he gestured at his near-empty bar. "Must be where they all are then."

Mary asked: "How's Sandy?"

"Oh." John pulled a face. "Came home with the milk yesterday. Terrible state. But then she slept for 24 hours, couldn't wake her up. She's okay now, though. In the kitchen, eating like a horse. I don't know what to make of her."

"I missed her last time," Mary told him. "Okay if I go back and try again?"

"Good idea." John lifted the bar flap, and Mary disappeared into the kitchen.

"How about a drink then?" Derek suggested.

"Sorry. Pint, is it?"

Derek watched the beer pouring into the glass, noting as ever that the pleasure of watching the drink being prepared even exceeded that of drinking it. He took a sip, then remembered what he needed to ask.

"Any idea where she goes yet?"

"Sandy? No, not really. But I got my suspicions."

"Yeah?"

"Mmm. Nothing concrete but, well, I was wondering if maybe Bucky and his friends?"

"Oh come on John. Not Bucky. She wouldn't be with him. He's years older than she is for a start. And let's face it, he's a, well, he's what the Americans call a douchebag. I mean, he's hardly a young girl's dream, is he?"

"I know. But, listen, I popped into Holesworthy. day before yesterday to pick up some crisps and stuff the

Sting of the Nettle

brewery had missed out, and I forgot it was market day, and would be packed out. Anyway, he was there. Bucky. I think he might have been booted out of another pub, the way he was going on, shouting at someone, kicking the side of a car. And then he saw me, and started on me."

"What did he say"

"Oh, something like, 'How's that little girl of yours, Jacobs? Tell her I got a treat for her next time!' And then he did this, thing, with his hips, sort of pushing them out, know what I mean?"

"Yes, but that was probably just talk. You know. Trying to get your goat."

"You think so? I'm not so sure. But if he is trying to mess with her, I'll tell you now, Policeman, if he is, I'll kill him. And that's not a threat, it's a promise."

Mary came back into the bar, and John let her through the flap. She looked pale and worried.

"No luck then?" Derek asked.

She shook her head. "I'm sorry, John. I couldn't get a word out of her. She's, I hate to say it, but she's like a zombie. All she's doing is sitting there eating bread and butter. She must have had at least half a loaf, judging from the crumbs. There's something very wrong here, you know. Can't you get her to a doctor?"

"She won't hear of it. I tried. She said she don't need no doctor cos there's nothing wrong with her. I tried to get that new young doctor they got in Okehampton to come out and see her here, but they don't do much home visiting now, not with this new National Health Service. Not like before, when you could just pay and they'd come."

None of the three said anything for the moment. Then John said: "Well thanks for trying, Mary. You too, Derek. But who knows, perhaps it's just a phase, perhaps she'll grow out of it. And I'll get my lovely daughter Sandy back again."

The hope hung in the air like dust specks lit by the evening sun.

* * *

Two days later Mary walked into the bedroom, to find Derek folding his police tunic and packing it into an open hold-all on the bed, even tucking his helmet in.

"You're definitely going then, are you?"

"I've got to." He looked at her with a helpless apology. "It's all I've got."

Mary sat down on the bed, and made him sit beside her.

"You don't think, do you," she said gently, "You don't think that this time you're taking this thing too far?"

"But it's the..."

"Yes, yes, I know. It's the niggle. But sometimes it almost frightens me. Especially now. You don't know what you're getting into. You can't know."

"No, true. But I know it's... something."

"Mmm." She looked at the hold-all. "Why are you taking your uniform and that silly helmet? Won't that frighten your German?"

"That's the idea. He got stroppy on the phone. If I turn up looking official, and on duty, he'll talk. They always

Sting of the Nettle

do when they see the uniform."

"But the truth is, you're not on duty, in fact you're breaking all the rules, as far as I can see. Operating on your own like this. Out of your area, too. Have you told Welbeloved what you're doing?"

"God no. He'd laugh, he'd sneer, and he'd order me to stop being a silly bloody fool."

"And what if I ordered you to stop being a silly bloody fool?"

"But you wouldn't, would you?"

Mary put her hand on his, lifted it, kissed it.

"No. I think, if I tried to change you, to stop you doing what you need to do, well, then I'd be the silly bloody fool."

CHAPTER TWENTY

The local rail halt was some two miles outside the village. This morning Derek was the only passenger waiting for the London-bound train. That's if you didn't count two boxes of day-old chicks. The train was 10 minutes late, but Derek didn't mind. Trains were always late. Waiting for a train was part of the fun, part of the experience. Derek loved trains. He loved everything about trains.

He loved looking down the long straight line in the direction the train would come, he loved searching for the first sign of steam in the distance, and then the little black shape of the engine as it poked its way into view. He loved to stand close, but not too close, to the platform edge as the huge machine huffed past him, enveloping him in great clouds of harmless steam; and then came the equally enthralling wrenching open of the great swinging doors, the shuffling down the corridor searching for an empty compartment, and then the joy of finding one completely vacant, and gleefully moving in, sliding the door shut behind him, making it all his, his place, his own little kingdom.

And then came the ritual of settling in. The heaving of his hold-all up and onto the netted luggage rack, the memory of how once, on an incredibly overcrowded Christmas train out of Paddington, packed with demobbed squaddies and half-demented Londoners

Sting of the Nettle

headed for seasonal get-togethers, he had actually climbed up into a similar rack and slept his way down to Exeter, his head on some posh woman's suitcase and his feet on her fur coat. And now, with hold-all safely stowed, there came the selection of the seat; always, if available, the window seat facing the direction of travel. A glance around the compartment to check that it was clean. No left-over bottles or wax paper wrappings, the detritus of previous interlopers into his kingdom. And a swift check on the travel pictures above the seats advertising Bude and Tintagel with unlikely-looking families cavorting on golden sands and quite possibly losing their engagement rings. And finally, sitting back with his head inclined against the side headrest. A position which, if you were lucky, you could spot a train zooming towards you on the other line and brace yourself for that teeth-rattling moment when it roared past banging and screaming like a mechanical banshee. But that would come later.

First came the silence, with just a gentle hiss from the engine, as if it was taking a deep breath. Then the bang of the last door, the whistle, the very gentle jerk preceding the first sensation of movement, and we were off!

"I'm a child," Derek told himself. He knew it. But no-one else did.

He kept his head down at the Okehampton stop. There was always the possibility that someone he knew might see him, even join him, wanting to talk, asking what he was doing, out of uniform, on the London train. But no-one did.

Sting of the Nettle

At Taunton, reluctantly reaching the end of the journey, he retrieved his holdall, climbed out, approached the station book stall, and bought a copy of the town map. The address he sought was simple enough to find, and a twenty-minute walk took him to a small terraced street which led off from the town centre. Here he found an alleyway containing little but a couple of metal dustbins. He ducked in out of sight, opened the holdall, and quickly put on his police tunic and helmet.

The house he sought was the last in the street, on the right-hand side. Beyond it was a patch of rough ground strewn with rubble. Bomb damage possibly. As he came closer to the house, he noticed that the far side of it was propped up by a huge wooden buttress. The building itself was in general and urgent need of repair and renovation. The paint on the window frames had long peeled off, leaving exposed and cracked grey wood. One window pane was replaced by a square of cardboard. There had once been a doorbell on the door frame, but the wire from it was hanging loose and leading nowhere. Luckily a stout knocker still hung on the door itself.

Derek knocked, firmly, indeed almost aggressively. The knock of a confident and determined police officer.

The door was opened by a youngish woman, short and thin, with mousy brown hair tied back in a bun and a pale face devoid of make-up. She wore a shapeless dress, mostly covered by a spotless white apron.

"Good morning, Madam," Derek said, before she could speak, and using his most official voice. "I wish to speak to Mr Hans Bruckner."

"Oh." A sigh, as if she was expecting nothing less.

Sting of the Nettle

She turned and called over her shoulder: "Hans, it's the police." And then to Derek: "You better come in."

The front door led straight into what was clearly a living room, with a further door through which Derek could glimpse a small kitchen. The furniture was minimal – a table, some chairs, a sideboard, all "utility", the grim government-sponsored and rationed furniture that now was disappearing from most households as fast as it could be replaced. There was a small gas fire in what had once been a proper fireplace. The room spoke of grinding poverty, but he noted that it was nonetheless clean and tidy, and on the table, there was a jam jar with a small bunch of wild flowers in it.

A man, clearly Bruckner himself, sat at the table. Derek had the impression of someone big but soft, even pudding-y. He had a long face and his hair had been cut extremely short and rather inexpertly. He had been in the process of rolling himself a hand-made cigarette, but now his hands were still, and his startlingly blue eyes held Derek's with a hostile stare.

Derek met his gaze with equal severity. "Hans Bruckner?"

When Bruckner spoke it was with, as Derek had expected, a heavy German accent. "I have done nothing wrong."

Odd, Derek thought. Those were more or less Sandy's first words, in the pub kitchen.

"My name is Police Officer..." A moment of inspiration "Welbeloved. You can help us with our enquiries, Sir," Derek said, maintaining his official approach. "We wish to establish first that you were the

Sting of the Nettle

Hans Bruckner, German prisoner of war, who in 1947 worked on the farm belonging to..." And now he produced his notebook and pretended to consult it. "...belonging to a Mr Tom Williamson, North Tawe, in the county of Devonshire. Is that correct?"

"No."

Derek was so surprised at the answer he said nothing, but stared at Bruckner.

"No. No more questions. I don't answer no more of your questions." The German half rose from his chair, but his wife, who had pulled up a chair to sit beside him, laid a hand on his arm to settle him back.

"Mr Bruckner."

"Nein!" It was said with more force. "No. I have to answer questions, questions, I have to fill forms, and people spit at me in street, and I cannot work. My wife, she clean in office, no other money. Send me back. If you not want me, send me back! War not my fault, you know? I just soldier, not Nazi. England not want me, send me back. Mr Policeman!"

And he slammed a hand flat on the table, making the flowers shake.

"Why can't you leave us alone?" His wife's tone was taut and cold. "We only came up here because my home is here, and yet it's like we're, what are they called? Lepers! My mum won't speak to me. The kids shout at us. And look." she pointed at the window. "They threw a stone through that last week. Just leave us be. Leave us alone."

She turned her face into her husband's broad shoulder, weeping. Derek looked at the couple, the man defiant yet defeated, the woman crushed by the prejudice of her own people. A small world of sadness.

And he felt ashamed of himself. What the hell did he think he was doing? He was treating these people like criminals. He was the heartless bully. He was the Nazi.

Shame flushed over him. Abruptly, he stood up, threw off his helmet. It landed with a crash on the floor and rolled under the table. Then he shrugged out of his uniform tunic, rolled it into a bundle, and chucked it into a corner.

He sat down and looked at the couple, who were now looking back at him with mild astonishment.

"Mr Bruckner, Mrs Bruckner, I apologise. I am deeply sorry. I'm not here as a policeman. My name's Derek, Derek Martin. I mean, I am a policeman, but not today. I'm just here to, well, to try and help Mrs Williamson."

He searched their faces for some sign that they were believing him, but saw nothing but puzzlement and rejection. Then abruptly Bruckner spoke.

"You say you know Mrs Williamson. I not believe you."

"But I do. I've talked to her. She told me about you. She liked you, she said..." a moment of inspiration, "... she said you made slippers for her."

A dismissive shrug. "I make many slippers, prisoners do that. Make money." He looked away.

"Yes, but you made a special pair for her. She got them out, she doesn't wear them, they're too nice to wear, she says."

The man looked back at him, with a flicker of interest.

Derek produced his trump card. "There's a design on

Sting of the Nettle

them. A picture. Of a flower." He searched his mind. "Edel something."

"Edelweiss." Bruckner's face lit up with a sudden and devastating smile. "Yes. I make special for Mrs. Williamson. She nice woman. Like a mother."

"That's her. And I'm here partly on her behalf."

"Okay. I believe now." Bruckner put an arm round his wife and hugged her, and she responded with a watery smile. "I like Mrs Williamson very much."

"And she liked you. She speaks very well of you. I think she'd love it if you got in touch, perhaps write to her?"

He shook his big head: "I speak English now. But not write it."

"Perhaps your wife would?"

Mrs Bruckner gave a wet self-deprecating simper. "I don't do the reading and writing," she explained. "Never did."

Derek felt a little silly. "Well," he went on, "I agree, she's a very nice woman. I have come to know her well since the death of her husband Tom. I've been trying to find out..."

"He dead? Old Tom dead?" The man was genuinely shocked.

"I'm afraid so."

"How?"

"Well, I'm afraid it looks as if he took his own life."

"Ahh." The sensation of shock faded, to be replaced by more a feeling of understanding, of the inevitably of life and death, of fate.

"This doesn't surprise you then?"

Sting of the Nettle

A big sigh. "Poor Mr Williamson. He good man to work for first. Then things go wrong, he go strange. Crazy sometime" He shrugged. "I leave."

"Go on."

"I do not know. I meet Hannah, you see. We get married, move here, apply for citizenship. But it sad about Mr Williamson."

"Yes. What I can't understand is, why he should have become so, difficult, as you put it. And then to take his own life. There must have been a reason, but..."

He stopped talking, realising that Bruckner was now looking at him intensely, his face working. Then he spoke, one word, one harsh syllable.

"Horst."

"Horst?" For a moment Derek thought that the man's thick accent was mispronouncing an English world. Then he remembered. "Right, of course, the other prisoner, the one working with you. Horst. What about him?"

"He give it to him."

"I'm sorry?"

"Horst, he give it to Mr Williamson. I not sure. But I think. "

"Yes, but, give him what exactly."

"He give him Pervitin."

CHAPTER TWENTY-ONE

"Pervitin? Well well."

The Colonel's face displayed a faintly quizzical look, as if he was reacting to a reminder of his far-off school days. Derek waited. As soon as he'd mentioned the words the Colonel, while admirably controlling his facial expression, had frozen in mid-stride across his kitchen, his coffee cup slurping in his hand, the hot drink spilling onto the kitchen lino.

"Yes. Does it mean anything to you, Sir?"

"George, please, call me George. And yes, Derek, yes. Pervitin. It certainly does mean something to me. Wait a sec, I better mop this up, or my wife will be, well she would be, if she were here."

While the Colonel fussed around, Derek waited patiently but with mounting anticipation. He reflected that compared to the home of the Bruckners in Taunton, he could hardly be in a more contrasting household. Here, in Critchley's farmhouse, he sat in an extensive kitchen, which was both functional and yet elegant.

An oak table that would seat ten stretched across the centre of the parquet floor. A massive range stood in what had once been an inglenook fireplace. An array of burnished copper pans dangled from shelves along one wall. A series of ornamental lights hung from the ceiling. And an arrangement of paintings, picturing Dartmoor scenes and with the look of having been created by a

Sting of the Nettle

gifted amateur, enlivened a second wall. Leaded light windows looked out across a lawn bordered by ranks of carefully tended rose bushes. The whole place spoke of rural class, money, taste and comfort.

Afraid that it might seem rude, Derek stopped gazing around him. Instead he took a first sip of the mug of coffee the Colonel had handed to him. Good God, what was this? Not coffee as he knew it. Not Camp coffee from the bottle Mary kept in the kitchen cupboard. Instead it was a rich, heady and utterly gorgeous brew that infused his head with its smell and its taste. He took a second sip. Heavenly...

"So." The Colonel sat down opposite him. "Actually I've come across Pervitin in my time. Several times. But first, would you like to tell me what you know about it?"

* * *

In the mean little cottage in Taunton Mrs. Bruckner had given Derek Camp coffee, once the ice between them had been broken, and Hans had begun to explain what he meant by Pervitin. He had broken off to apologise for the drink.

"In Bavaria before the war we have real coffee. From Africa. Then, when the war go bad, no more coffee. Instead, ersatz. Coffee made from... from..." He searched for the word.

"Acorns," Mrs Bruckner put in, as she put a blue china cup in front of Derek. "I ask you. How can you make coffee from acorns?"

"War," her husband said darkly. "Allies blockade."

Sting of the Nettle

Derek wondered for a moment whether he should apologise for the British war effort, but decided against it. "This is fine," he told them. "This is what we have at home. But getting back to this Pervitin..."

"Pervitin" Hans corrected his pronunciation. Derek couldn't detect any difference between his version of the word and the German's, so pressed on.

"What exactly is it?"

"Pill," Hans told him. "Pill to make you feel good."

"Really? Well, sounds okay to..."

"Make you feel strong, brave." Hans overrode him. "Make you fight. Stay awake, one, two, even three days. Fight. Kill. Don't care. So they give it to us, to Wehrmacht, to Luftwaffe. Then we fight like devils."

"It's a sort of drug then? Wasn't it illegal. Against the law?"

"No. Plenty Pervitin before war. You buy it in shop. And in army, they give it to us free. Everyone take tablets. Even they say Rommel. They say he took it every day! That's how he beat the British." Hans laughed at the thought.

"Did you take it?" Derek asked.

"One time, two time. But no. No more. It make me do things I not want to do." He glanced sideways at his wife who gave him a reassuring smile.

"But other soldiers."

"All the time. Pilots. Tank crews. Especially tank crews. You remember Blitzkrieg? When we drive the British into the sea? Allies not understand how we were so strong, so quick. Ha! Pervitin! Keep going all day, all night. Not care."

Sting of the Nettle

There was a hint of triumph in the German's voice – understandable, Derek thought. After all, they lost the war. Total surrender. Perhaps they need to remember small victories. As when a football team loses by several goals, but gets a consolation goal in extra time. Dunkirk, the Ardennes – German consolation goals.

"And you were saying before; Horst, he gave Pervitin to Mr Williamson. Are you sure?"

"Of course. I remember. I saw it. Harvest time, Mr Williamson very tired. Horst give him tablet. He work all night."

This rang a strong bell. Hadn't Mrs Williamson said something, about her husband working in the fields for twenty four hours?

"But that was after the war had finished. How did Horst get the stuff?"

"Parcels. From home. He write, his family send. They say it still simple to get in Germany, even now. But more expensive now, he say."

"So how did he afford it? You POWs weren't exactly well off, were you? And if it's expensive..."

"Horst clever bugger." The swear word sounded funny in Hans's German voice. "He make friends here, soon as we allowed out of camp. Like me I meet my Hannah!"

He smiled at his wife, who said to Derek: "Actually my name's Anne. But he likes to call me Hannah, like in Germany."

Derek returned her smile. Then said to Hans: "So, Horst made some friends, you say."

"Ja. Not good friends. Two I think, but one had

money. Rich boy. He pay Horst to get Pervitin. From home. In post service."

It made sense, Derek concluded. A logical bit of drug-running. By post.

"But then they sent Horst home, didn't they? That must have been the end of that."

"No, no." Hans shook his head vehemently. "Now they send money to Horst in Germany, he send Pervitin back. He happy. Things bad in Germany. Worse than here. Money very, what is word?"

"Scarce," his wife prompted.

"Ja. Scarce."

"And what about Mr Williamson. Did he go on taking it? With these friends?"

"I think he try not to. But he had to. Pervitin very, what is the word, when you have to go on doing something?"

"Addictive?"

"Yes. Addictive. I tell Mr Williamson. Please stop. But he go mad at me, he curse me, try to hit me. That is what it does. So I leave. I know it is no good to say anything. He must go on taking it. He need it."

Derek drew a deep breath. "Listen, Hans, these friends of Horst, do you know who they were? Did you meet them?"

Hans shook his head. "Horst not tell me. He keep them to himself."

* * *

"I expect he did," said the Colonel, as Derek finished his

account of his Taunton meeting. "Refill?"

Derek eagerly pushed his mug across the table, and the Colonel poured them two more from a pot on the range.

"He'd keep it to himself because I'm pretty sure that sort of thing is highly illegal in this country. Or if not, it should be. And the reason I say that is, it is one of the most dangerous, perverse and destructive drugs on this earth."

He resumed his seat, and Derek had another pull at the coffee. It tasted even better.

"Curious that you should come to me with this, because I happen to be something of, well, not an expert, but I've had some experience of this sort of thing. End of my service, really. I was based on the Rhine, which is where we began to realise how significant these damn Pervitin pills had been during the years of conflict."

Derek asked: "What exactly is it, then?"

The Colonel smiled: "It is exactly Methamphetamine. Sorry, hate to be clever-clever, but that's its technical name. Basically it's a performance-enhancing drug. It gives you amazing drive and endurance, it dispenses with any need to sleep, it relieves you of any self-doubt, of conscience even, and will make you sexually compulsive and over-active. Ha! The look on your face, young man!"

Derek felt himself blushing. "And it's a German thing, is it?"

"Well not exactly. It's been around in one way or another for some years. But, typically enough, the Germans were the ones who refined it and put it to positive use. It was synthesised by a Berlin pharmaceutical company in the thirties, and marketed as Pervitin, a sort of pick-me-up. It was a big seller."

"But if it did all those dreadful things to you."

"Well it seems the odd pill now and then didn't do much harm. Just gave your German hausfraus a kick up the bottom. But then in 1938 a certain Nazi doctor, name of Ranke, suitable name if you ask me, he experimented with more concentrated doses, and came to the conclusion that it was going to win the war for Germany. Quite literally."

"But it didn't. We won." Derek's voice trailed off as he realised he was stating the obvious, but the Colonel didn't seem to notice.

"It very nearly did, actually. The Nazis were quick to see the potential of the stuff, and dished it out to the troops willy-nilly, and in enormous quantities. Literally millions of Pervitin tables were produced, and orders issued that the troops must take their ration. Sometimes it was even put in chocolate for the soldiers. Ironic when you think about it. Hitler had pushed the image of the ideal Aryan German as clean-cut, pure and unsullied, but actually its tank crews and its infantry, and its pilots, all went into action with their brains sodden with the filthy stuff. My God, think of the blitzkrieg, the way the panzers smashed their way through Belgium and Northern France."

"So, didn't we think we could use it? Against them?"

"Well we thought about it, or so I understand. But wiser heads decided against it. Instead we gave our front-liners Benzedrine. It kept them awake all right, but it

Sting of the Nettle

didn't turn them into sadistic monsters."

He stood, collected the coffee mugs, and began to rinse them off in the sink. Without looking at Derek, he said: "remember when we first met, I was a bit over-emotional that day, a bit, you understand?"

"Yes Sir. George."

"You'll recall I spoke about evil, about a dark force that can be found anywhere, anytime."

"And is that Pervitin?"

"No. I believe that evil exists as an entity. But something like Pervitin, it's a tool of that evil."

The Colonel carefully set the mugs upside down on a draining rack. Derek noticed that his hands were trembling.

He went on: "Tell me, Derek, have you ever heard of a French village called Oradour? No? Or how about Malmedy?"

Derek shook his head. "Sorry."

"Well, let me enlighten you. At Malmedy the SS took 84 captured and disarmed American soldiers, and shot them out of hand."

"I think I heard something about that." Derek began, but the Colonel continued remorselessly.

"At Oradour, the troops of the SS Panzer division known as Das Reich, killed six hundred and forty two of the people in the village, old men, women, babies, and left the place in ruins."

Derek couldn't think of anything sensible to say, so he stayed silent.

"Now, this man you met, this Hans chap, would he have done something like that?"

"No." Derek was emphatic. "Hans is a good man. Not a murderer. And I see what you're driving at. Hans said he did take Pervitin, he was ordered to, everybody did. But he stopped. He said he didn't like what it did to him. He wouldn't go into details. His wife was listening, but..."

"Sensible man. My own wife has listened too much to me and my memories. Which is another reason why you won't notice any trace of femininity around here at the moment. "

"Oh. Yes." There was an awkward silence for a moment.

"That's by the way," the Colonel resumed. "What I'm trying to say is, the men who committed those atrocities, they can't have all been sadistic murderers. Some of them must have been ordinary men, basic decent chaps like your Hans. So what was it that enabled them to gun down defenceless prisoners, to slaughter women and children, to do so without hesitation, or guilt, or mercy, or conscience?"

He waited for Derek to answer.

"Pervitin?"

"Pervitin."

CHAPTER TWENTY-TWO

On his return from Taunton Derek had ridden his motorcycle straight from the station to the Colonel's farm. Now, with images of sadistic cruelty and death in his mind, he rode home to Mary and to tea. And it was pasties for tea.

Exeter born and bred as he was, Derek drew a blank with pasties. Pasties were, he had come to realise, iconic food in more rural Devon, ranking alongside jam-and-cream splits and bloody junket in popularity and presence. But why? He had no answer. After all, what was there about a pasty to like? The filling of gristly meat, overcooked carrot and small chunks of suspiciously green potato? The pastry, which veered between a rock-hard teeth-challenging crimped ridge on the top of the thing, and a bottom layer soggily reminiscent of a baby's blanket? Or perhaps it was the impossibility of eating the thing without it disintegrating under the first pressure of the knife and fork, and scattering much of its constituents to all corners of the table?

Mary loved pasties. She bought them from a village woman, who sold them at a cost of one shilling per pasty. The village woman, Mary frequently told Derek, was famous for her pasties. Derek thought "infamous" would be a more apposite word, but forbear to say so.

Mary knew, of course, that Derek had doubts about pasties. She only produced them once a week, hoping

Sting of the Nettle

that gradual familiarity would change his opinion. So far, no luck, but Mary was the sort of girl who didn't give up easily. And today she had bought and shelled a big bag of green peas, produced by an elderly couple who ran a small holding nearby. Now she piled them on the plate alongside Derek's gold-brown pasty, hot from the Raeburn. Derek took his knife, made a clear separation between peas and pasty, then took the appropriate bottle from the kitchen cabinet and smothered the latter in a thick layer of brown sauce. Mary watched him do this. Neither of them said anything.

Instead, when he had reached the stage of chasing the last few peas around his plate, he began to tell her about what he had heard that day, first from Hans, and subsequently from the Colonel. It was an edited version, leaving out some of the more horrific aspects, but as he continued Mary's eyes widened with shock.

When he had finished, she reached across the table, and took his hand. "You're getting in too deep," she told him. "This is dreadful. It's dangerous. I mean, drugs!"

"You're getting brown sauce on your sleeve," he told her, trying to lighten the atmosphere, but Mary was having none of it.

"You're just a constable," she told him. "You're not Sherlock Holmes, or Biggles, or, I mean, you can't handle this on your own."

"Handle what?" he asked her. "I've got no real evidence of anything. Yes, I believe what Hans told me, about the drug and Mr Williamson, but there's no evidence. I'm not even sure any crime has been committed. Certainly nothing to stand up in court.

Sting of the Nettle

Rumours at best. If I took this to Welbeloved he'd laugh at me."

"He wouldn't laugh at Colonel Critchley."

"No. But think about it. The Colonel knows less than I do. And anyway, I like him, I do, but he's only helping me 'cos I helped him. He's not in a good way, you know. Like he told you, he's shell-shocked. And I think, from what he said, if I've got it right, his wife's left him. No, before I try to drag him or anyone else into the firing line, I've got to find out what if anything's going on now, and if so, who's involved. For definite. You must see that."

Mary grimaced. "What I see is Constable Derek Martin, stubborn, focussed, obsessive, and bloody-minded. Yes, yes, I know, it's your niggle, you've got to chase it down, but... It's time you started being careful."

She was flushed, and her eyes glistened. Derek forgot about the brown sauce and squeezed her hand. "Okay," he said. "I will. I promise."

Mary got up and began to clear the table. "You might not get the chance, anyway." She said after a moment. "Not if this police reorganisation takes place like they say."

"Like who says?"

"There was a piece in the Western Morning News apparently. The butcher was telling me about it. Some county councillor banging on about modern conditions requiring modern policing. Just think, you might be out of here sooner than you think. Exeter here we come. No more rear lights and rabbit traps. Real villains to catch. What you've always wanted."

"Yeah. But not you, eh?" Derek got up to help her.

Sting of the Nettle

"Mind you, after today, I'm not sure what I want."

"Hard life, isn't it." She threw him a tea-towel. "So, what are we doing after this? Nettle bashing? Or pub? You choose."

* * *

On the way to the pub, Mary said: "I've had a thought. About your Hans chap and his wife."

"What about them?"

"Well, you said Mrs. Williamson was fond of Hans."

"Like a son to her, I think she said."

"And he liked her."

"Oh yes. Made her special slippers, didn't he."

"And they're not doing well at Taunton, he can't get work, she's slaving away as a cleaner..."

Derek stopped abruptly, turning to Mary, grinning.

"Of course! Clever girl! They must need help on the farm, with Tom gone. And they can stay in the farmhouse until they find somewhere, it's big enough. Brilliant. I'll suggest it. No, better still. Your idea. You suggest it."

"We could go together. Help talk her into it."

"Fair enough. But I think they'll both jump at it, her and Peter."

There was immense pleasure, Derek reflected, in thinking of something that's going to make someone else happy, and he led Mary into the pub with a contented grin on his face.

They walked into a loud and aggressive row. A thin man in shabby clothes was clutching a one-time army knapsack on the bar, and arguing hotly across the surface

Sting of the Nettle

with John Jacob.

John was repeating, in a world-weary tone, a simple sentence. "You've had enough, Simon. You've had enough."

The customer was saying "No. Listen. Listen, you." his voice rising ever higher to what was almost a screech. Then abruptly it changed to a more supplicant whine: "Well, fill me bottle then. Go on. I got the money." He produced an empty lemonade bottle from the bag.

Jacob looked at him for a long moment, then with evident reluctance took the bottle and proceeded to fill it from one of the barrels that were stacked in a row behind him. The man scrabbled some coins onto the bar, then grabbed the filled bottle, and shambled out of the bar.

Derek and Mary found seats at their usual corner table, waved at Jacob, and mouthed "the usual". Jacob poured a pint and a half of bitter, checked that no-one else needed serving, then brought the drinks across and sat down to join them.

"See that?" he asked. "Bloody nuisance. Cider-man."

"A what?" Mary queried.

"Cider-man. That's what I call them. There's more than one around here. All they drink is this rotgut cider. And it's a killer."

Mary said sententiously: "Well. Any alcohol taken in excess is bad for your health."

"No, love. You don't understand. Cider's different. At least this rough stuff from the barrel is. It's like they can't get enough of it. Look at him, taking it off in a bottle, and he'll be in first thing for more. You can always tell a

Sting of the Nettle

cider-man. He stinks of it, for a start. But it's in the face, it's very acid, rough cider. It eats away at them. You look next time you see him. The stuff's addictive, I tell you. I wouldn't sell it, only the brewery say I got to, and anyway, money's money."

"Was that a hint?" Derek asked jokingly, as he felt for his wallet.

"My round," Mary said, producing a ten-shilling note, and John returned to the bar and his till. Derek sipped his beer silently.

"You're very quiet suddenly." Mary said.

"Sorry. I was just thinking. Addictive, he said. That's what this Pervitin stuff is, apparently. You know. I'm going to ask John something when he gets back. Don't stop me, will you."

"Why should I?"

"Well, it could be a bit, you know, intrusive."

"Well don't upset him. I like John. And I like coming here. And..." with a chuckle, "if I have to stop coming here so do you!"

John returned with Mary's change.

"John, got a minute?" Derek asked.

The landlord looked around the bar. "Yes, sure."

"First, how is Sandy."

"Oh Christ, same as ever." He sat down heavily. "Up and going at it all day and all night, then sleeping for hours and hours, not eating, staying out, rowing, just the same."

"Look, I don't mean to pry, but do you think it might be drugs?"

"What, round here? Never. And anyway, I'd know. I

was posted to this American base in '43, up in Lincolnshire. I got to know a bit about drugs. Couple of the guys used to smoke this marijuana. Then they'd just sit and giggle at you. And one of them said he's used heroin in the States, and he said you just pass out on it. Well that's not our Sandy. Quite the opposite."

A shout called him back to the bar. Mary said: "That didn't get you very far, did it?"

"I'm not sure." He took a deep swallow of his beer. "Hang on a bit, he'll be back. I think he likes talking to us. Well, to you probably, but..."

"Oh go on with you!"

John returned after five minutes, with two more glasses of beer. "Refills," he told them. And quietly so no-one else in the bar could hear, "On the house"

He sat down. "No, it's not drugs, I'm certain of that. Wish it was, she might be a bit quieter."

Derek said: "I take what you're saying but, well, I don't suppose Sandy's ever been addicted to anything."

"No, course she hasn't." John's initial dismissiveness changed to something more thoughtful. "Well. There was the cough mixture."

"Cough mixture?"

"Yeah. Quite bad, that was. It's the codeine in it, so the doc told me. Sandy would have been about twelve, I suppose."

"Where did she get cough mixture from?"

"From my Dad, actually. You know this was his place, only he got ill at the end of the War, I got early demob to take over from him. Anyway he used to cough something dreadful, so we got him plenty of cough mixture, and it always seemed to be running out or go missing. Turned out Sandy was drinking the stuff. Found empty bottles under her bed. We were able to deal with that, her mother was very good with her. God, I wish she could be now."

Lost in thought, John automatically picked up Derek's glass and drained it, then realised what he had done.

"Ooops. Sorry mate. I'll get you another."

* * *

At home, Derek sat himself and Mary down at the kitchen table.

"Serious talk coming up?" Mary asked.

"Yes. Look, Sandy's an addictive personality, we've established that, I think. The cough mixture, right?"

"Well yes."

"And her behaviour sounds like what I've been told about Pervitin, you'll agree."

"If you say so."

"I do. So. I've made a decision."

"On three pints of beer?"

"Two and a half, remember? John had the other half. And anyway. I think I've taken this whole business as far as I can on my own."

"I told you that."

"Yes, I know you did. And you're right. When you think of it. There were those warnings I got, from that Bucky bloke and the chinless wonder at the reception."

"Fergus"

"Right. And what Mrs Williamson and Peter had to

Sting of the Nettle

say about Tom Williamson's behaviour, and what Hans told me, and what the Colonel told me..."

"And the brick through the window."

He nodded: "And the brick through the window."

"And falling off your motorbike."

"And. Look." He stared at her. How much did she really know?

"Never mind." Mary made a dismissive gesture. "Go on with what you were saying.

"Anyway I think that's enough. I think I can take all that, and tell it all to Sergeant Welbeloved, and even the Inspector, and then there can be a proper investigation."

"Well done. And you think they'll take you seriously?"

"Yes. They'll take me seriously."

CHAPTER TWENTY-THREE

They didn't take him seriously.

Thinking about it afterwards, going over the humiliating episode that he endured at the Okehampton police station, Derek told himself that he had never really expected Welbeloved to take him seriously. It was the Sergeant's personal policy to dismiss any suggestion or proposal from a junior rank with scorn and, if the context allowed, with mocking laughter.

The Sergeant didn't laugh. Possibly because he remembered that Derek had twice witnessed him vomiting into various examples of vegetation, and he was aware that, true to his word, Derek had said nothing about those incidents to any of his colleagues. But that didn't mean he would stay silent, especially if provoked. So the sergeant made sure he didn't upset the young constable more than convention made necessary.

"Hmm," he said with overdone thoughtfulness, when Derek had told him in outline that he had evidence of what might be a sinister drug operation in the quiet district of North Tawe, which might have contributed to a death, and which might be still up and running. A lot of 'mights' in that, Derek admitted to himself. But he wasn't going into any further detail for Welbeloved.

"Quite a story, that, Constable Martin," the Sergeant continued. "More suitable for a Biggles book, eh? Or Bulldog Drummond?" He smiled to take unnecessary

Sting of the Nettle

sting out of his words.

"I wouldn't know, Sergeant. I don't read comics."

The Sergeant's blood pressure moved up a few notches at this. He possessed an extensive library of Biggles books.

"But. Fair enough. I'm sure you're not intentionally wasting your time, or my valuable time, and I'm sure it is equally not your intention to waste the Inspector's very valuable time. He's a good man, our Inspector. A kind man. He doesn't like to stifle the enthusiasm of young constables such as yourself. At the same time, he wouldn't want one such as yourself to blight their career with fantastic tales that waste police time. Which by the way, ha ha, is a criminal offence!"

The sergeant laughed heartily at his own joke. Derek kept a straight face with no difficulty whatsoever.

"I understand, Sergeant. Nonetheless, I would like the opportunity to present my theory to the Inspector."

"And so you shall, laddie. So you shall." The sergeant heaved his bulk out of the most comfortable chair in the station. "You wait there. I'll see if he's got a free moment to see you."

Derek sat alone and waited. He felt he knew exactly what was passing through the sergeant's mind. The theory was rubbish, of course. The sergeant would be sure of that. Drug rings, in deepest West Devon? No no no. But then, you never know. Perhaps at least a small fraction of the Constable's ramblings might have a tenuous link to the truth. In which case he didn't want to be labelled as the sergeant who rubbished a genuine insight into crime. So what was the wise course for the

Sting of the Nettle

sergeant to take? The phrase "pass the buck" wasn't in the sergeant's vocabulary, but nonetheless that is exactly what he intended to do. Let the Inspector decide. Christ, that's what the dithering old sod was there for. Meanwhile keep quiet about your own opinions, and let the young spark hang himself with his own words. And afterwards – come down on him like a ton of bricks!

Derek grinned to himself. He wondered just how close to the Sergeant's actual thoughts were his speculations. Pretty close, he thought.

The Inspector greeted Derek with a bright fatherly smile.

"So, young Martin. Drugs, is it? Gosh. Exciting. Sit down, sit down, tell me all about it."

Derek sat on the edge of an upright chair. The Sergeant hovered in the background.

"Well Sir, to begin with there was the death of the farmer, Tom Williamson."

"Ah yes. Nasty accident, that."

"Well Sir. I'm not sure it was necessarily an accident."

"Now then, Constable." The Inspector managed a blend of gentle admonishment. "The Coroner recorded a verdict of accidental death. I hope you're not presuming to dispute his decision."

"Sir, the evidence would suggest..."

"The evidence, as I recall it, suggested that the farmer had gone into his orchard hoping to shoot a rabbit, had stepped on a rotten apple, and fallen on his loaded gun." Even the inspector couldn't quite hide a note of disbelief in what he was saying. "But go on."

"Well Sir, I was subsequently warned not to pursue

Sting of the Nettle

any enquiries into the death."

"That was me, Sir." The Sergeant broke in. "I considered that any amplification of discussion around poor Mr Thomas would upset both his family and the local community."

"Quite so," said the Inspector.

"Yes Sir," Derek insisted, "but, there were other warnings."

"From whom?"

"Well. There was a man known as Bucky, a local no-good type. He told me to, well, to back off."

"Possibly a friend of the Williamson's? Someone who, like the Sergeant here, didn't want the family unnecessarily upset?"

"Possibly, Sir. But then there was Fergus Bulstock. He too told me to..."

"What? Fergus, Sir Arthur Bulstock's boy? That Fergus?" The Inspector sat up expectantly. "Good heavens. I'm privileged to know that family well, Constable. That young Fergus, he's a bit of a wild one, I'll admit." He laughed indulgently. "Got himself into a bit of trouble at last week's Hunt point-to-point, didn't he, Sergeant."

"Yes Sir." The sergeant was keen to be included in the conversation again. "Excessive use of the whip. But he apologised. And I understand his father has made a significant contribution to the..."

"I don't think we need to go into all that, Sergeant. So, Constable Martin. Any other suspects? What about these dreaded drugs of yours, where do they come into it?"

Sting of the Nettle

Derek took a deep breath. "The source seems to be the German prisoners of war, Sir..."

"Oh them. Well. Nothing would surprise me about them. Scum of the earth. I think we can all agree on that. Constable, you wouldn't believe the atrocities. Ever heard of a place called Malmedy? I don't suppose so, but..."

"Yes Sir." Derek broke in. "Eighty-four American prisoners shot dead by the SS."

"Oh. Yes. It was in the Daily Mirror, wasn't it? Dreadful. You read it there, I presume."

Derek, a News Chronicle reader if anything, said nothing.

"And anyway," the Inspector continued, sitting back in his chair, and twiddling nonchalantly with a stapler, "they're all gone now. All safely back in Hun-land, eating their sauerkraut and their sausages and singing 'I love to go a wandering.' Eh? No need to bother with them."

Derek decided to play a trump card. "I should tell you, Sir, that I have discussed this with a member of the police advisory..."

"What? Who?" Alarm in his voice.

"Colonel George Critchley, Sir, and he takes what I have to say with a certain..."

"Please!" The inspector held up his hand, and there was a certain element of relief in his voice. "Of course I know the Colonel, I respect him. A war hero. A gentleman farmer. Fine man. But the truth is, Constable, and this is confidential, you understand, the Colonel is not a well man. The rigours of combat have, shall we

Sting of the Nettle

say, unsettled his mind. I must tell you, Martin, that there have been several, shall we say, incidents with regard to Colonel Critchley. I'm afraid his wife has felt obliged to leave the family home. it's all very sad. There was some trouble the other day involving a dog, wasn't there, sergeant?"

"Yes Sir," Welbeloved told him. "Sheep worrying. A local farmer thinks that it might have been the Colonel's dog, I gather we may have to take action."

"Oh dear. Yes, well, I think we can leave Colonel Critchley out of this, wouldn't you say, constable? Constable?

Christ! Derek had been trusting that the whole sheep-worrying thing had gone away, that Sally could run free again. No chance.

The inspector cleared his throat. "Constable!"

"Sorry, Sir, I was thinking of something."

"We don't have time to waste on your thinking, Constable," Welbeloved rumbled. "Pay attention!"

"Thank you, Sergeant," the Inspector said. "Leave this to me. Now, Martin, is there anything else you wish to bring to my attention?"

Derek unscrambled his thoughts. The interview was going nowhere. He decided to make one last attempt: "And there's a fifteen-year-old girl in the village who is behaving rather strangely."

"Well! Now there's a turn-up for the book!" The Inspector's sarcasm was palpable, and he and the sergeant exchanged jovial knowing looks. "A fifteen-year-old girl behaving strangely. Well I never."

"That's a new one," said the sergeant in similar vein.

Sting of the Nettle

"Listen, young man," the inspector sighed deeply, then spoke in the manner of someone about to impart the secret of life. "Allow me to explain something to you. All fifteen-year-old girls behave strangely. Why? Who knows? Hormones, they tell us. But act strange they certainly do. And believe me, I should know, I have a fifteen-year-old daughter myself, don't I, sergeant? And does she behave strangely? Does she ever! That girl of mine, sweet little Jennifer as was, these days she's forever flouncing out of the room, or calling me a silly old duffer. Yes, me, a silly old duffer! or being rude to my wife, or wanting to go out on her own with skirts showing her knees." He paused, having run out of breath and things to say.

Derek wondered what he could say in reply, and decided there was nothing. So he said nothing. Nobody said anything for several seconds. Then the inspector sat forward again, put his elbows on his blotter, and made peaks with his fingers. He seemed to make up his mind about something.

"Sergeant.," he said abruptly. "I wonder if you'd mind leaving us, I'd like to have a chat with young Martin on my own.""

"Of course, Sir." The sergeant left the room, no doubt, Derek surmised, to prepare the ton of bricks with which he would come down on him once they were alone.

"Now. Martin." the inspector warmed up his fatherly air which had become a little frayed over the past few minutes. "Derek, isn't it? Yes, Derek, I'd like to give you some sound advice, something I think will be of immense benefit to you in your career as a police officer.

Sting of the Nettle

Okay?"

Derek nodded hopelessly. There was nothing else to do, to say. Not so from the inspector's point of view.

"You see, I've seen lots of young coppers, much like yourself, I've seen them come and go over the years, and some of them have done well, and some have, well, fallen at the first fence, as it were. And the ones who get on, who do well, who reach exalted ranks, like mine, they're the ones who keep their heads down, who don't make wild accusations or run around thinking up conspiracies or exotic crimes. Instead they just get on with the job. You'll find, if you stay with us, that In the force it's best to be known as a solid man who does his duty and otherwise refrains from rattling cages or theorising willy-nilly with absurd notions about conspiracies or corruption or, well, or drug rings. You take my meaning?"

"Yes Sir." What else could he say?

"Now listen," the Inspector rose to his feet, clearly ending the interview. "I like you, Constable Derek Martin. Yes, I do. I think you have the makings of an excellent officer. Now you'll have heard rumours, I daresay, about a reorganisation of policing in Devon and Cornwall, more centralisation, more mobility. About time too, one might think. And it will probably mean the end of the village policeman. If and when that happens, and if I'm still in harness, I'm going to make sure you get a plum reassignment. That is, a front-line position at Exeter. I know you're an Exeter man, and there'll be a police flat for you and your wife. So how about that then?"

Sting of the Nettle

"Thank you very much, Sir."

"Off you go then, son. And remember what I said, eh? Keep your head down. Keep your nose clean."

When Derek emerged from the inspector's office, Sergeant Welbeloved was in the lavatory, enjoying an extensive evacuation of his bowels. By the time he came out, in an almost visible wave of essence, Derek was already puttering away on his motorcycle.

"Damn," the sergeant said to himself. He had that ton of bricks, ready to come down on Derek with.

Fortunately a new woman probationer had joined the station that week. She unwisely asked the Sergeant if she could take an extra half hour off at lunchtime to visit her mum in hospital. She got the whole load.

CHAPTER TWENTY-FOUR

The meeting at the Williamson farm that morning went well. Almost too well.

Mrs Williamson welcomed them warmly. Quantities of tea had been produced, accompanied by a large platter of jam-and-cream scones, of which Derek had taken one before Mary could remind him of their calorie content. They were joined by Peter in his well-worn overalls and his stockinged feet, his crusty wellingtons having been left on the doorstep.

It was some little time before Mrs Williamson finished telling Mary how she'd known her as a little girl, and how pleased she was that she and Derek had chosen to live in the village. Derek could have argued with the word 'chosen'. But he let it go.

Instead he said: "Mrs Williamson, I have some news for you. Good news. I've found Hans."

Her face lit up. "You have? Oh well done, that's wonderful. Where is he?"

"Well, as you thought, in Taunton."

"D'you have his address? A phone number?"

"Yes." Derek was already producing his notebook and taking a slip of paper from it which he'd prepared before leaving home.

"I'm going to ring him now," Mrs Williamson declared. She half got up, then sat back down. "Soon as you've gone, of course."

Sting of the Nettle

Peter broke in to ask: "Is he working? Has he got a job?"

"I'm afraid not."

"Well there's one here for him, any time he likes."

"Now that's a good idea," his mother told him, then turned to Mary. "Since his father went, poor Peter, he's been working like the devil. Look at him, he's wasting away."

With his broad shoulders, bronzed arms and weather-beaten face, and his stomach full of pasties and jam and cream scones, poor Peter was anything but wasting away.

He said, "Well, I think that sounds like a very good idea." He made sure not to catch Mary's eye. It had of course been her very good idea, but.

"He's still married, is he?" Mrs Williamson asked.

"Yes, I met his wife. She's nice. Quiet. And devoted, I'd say"

"That's even better. I could do with some help around the house. So there's a job for her too. Brilliant!"

Mary said hesitantly: "Of course they'll need somewhere to stay."

"No they won't."

"Oh?"

"They'll stay here. They can have Margaret's old room. Perfect."

"But..."

Well! That, thought Derek, was the wind taken well and truly out of their sails. But Mary had thought of another complication, and, while Derek took the opportunity to sneak another scone, she asked: "Are you

Sting of the Nettle

sure, Mrs. Williamson. I mean, if and when Margaret might come home."

"She won't come home." Mrs Williamson's usually mobile face froze into an almost hostile gaze. "She's left. And she won't be back. That's one thing you can be sure of." And then, softening a little towards Mary, "You get to know these things, dear. When you have children of your own. Which, judging from the look of this young man, won't be long either."

Mary laughed. Derek blushed. These Devon women.

They rose to go. Mrs Williamson had Derek's scrap of paper in her red hand, and was clearly waiting for the moment when she could make the call to Hans. But at the door Derek turned to her.

"I'm still looking into the background to your husband's death, Mrs. Williamson," he said. "Hope to have something to tell you soon. I'll keep digging."

"Oh no, dear, I wish you wouldn't."

"I don't mind, really."

"No, I really wish you wouldn't, Derek." She meant it. "He's gone now. I'd really rather not have to think about the whys and wherefores. Won't bring him back, will it? Let it rest, dear."

* * *

"Well that's it. I'm finished with all this messing about. I'm packing it in."

"That'll be the day."

Mary, at the wheel of her car and driving slowly up the slope leading away from the Williamson's farm,

Sting of the Nettle

glanced across at Derek and gave a disbelieving snort. Unfortunately, as she did so, she failed to see the approach of a deep pothole. The car lurched in and out of it like a bucking bronco. "Whoops! Sorry." she exclaimed, and waited for an expected sardonic remark from her husband, which never came.

It nearly came. A withering exposition of women drivers and their uncanny ability to find every pothole in the road hovered on Derek's lips, but manfully, he suppressed it. Marriage, he reminded himself, was an education, like school, and this was a part of the curriculum he had well and truly covered.

Instead he said: "Listen. The inspector told me in so many words to drop it. Or, not in words but in implication, he told me if I didn't, the force would drop me. And now with what Mrs Williamson said. Well, I might as well give up."

"I don't believe you will for a minute," Mary told him. "But if you do find you can drag yourself away from detective-ing there's a small matter of a garden still full to overflowing with weeds, rubbish and nettles back home, which..." She left the rest unsaid.

Derek sighed. What with charging about the country and in and out of Okehampton, the battle against the weeds and nettles had reached a stalemate, and indeed it was a conflict that he was in danger of losing. Many nettles still reared their proud prickly heads to a passing bare arm, and some nettle casualties, previously thought to have been beaten into submission, now seemed to be recovering to sting another day. And if he took Mrs Williamson's kindly-meant advice, he'd have to throw

Sting of the Nettle

himself back into the battle, armed with hoe, spade, fork and every other implement of destruction that his father-in-law supplied so willingly, damn him.

Now in the car, as they crested the first rise to join the minor road from the farm lane, Derek thought over what she had said.

"'Let it rest,', she sounded like she meant it," he commented, a little bitterly. "If I was her, I'd want to know what drove the father of my children to do what he did."

Mary gave him a half glance, then concentrated on steering the car along the narrow lane. "But you're not her," she said. And after a pause, "So, do you mean it? Will you really let it all go?"

"Oh." Derek almost moaned with frustration. "I can't. How can I? It's not just a niggle anymore. Now it's, well, personal." More personal than you know, he thought. Personal courage, that was the issue. That question of the fear he had to face, to conquer.

She didn't reply, and they drove on for a few moments in silence.

Derek felt the need to lighten the atmosphere. "So, what's for supper tonight then? Oh Lord, not pasties. Please God, not again. Have mercy."

Mary giggled. "No, not pasties. Though you've got to get to like them, they're compulsory. No, tonight you'll be glad to hear I've got a couple of pork chops."

"Pork chops! Oh great, I. Christ! Look out!"

It happened in a split second – a cliché, Derek thought later, but accurate, none-the-less. Their car was approaching the point where an even more minor lane

Sting of the Nettle

joined it from the right, and Mary jammed on the breaks as a white sports car flashed out of the opening, just missing her front wing. The driver of the sports car must have glimpsed her, must have realised how close they had come, and over-corrected. His car fish-tailed down the lane, its back swerving from side to side, before the driver lost control entirely. The vehicle mounted what was, for a Devon road, a rare wide verge. It leaped, bumped over a couple of ridges, probably created by some heavy lorry during a wet spell and buried its nose in the hedgerow. Its engine stalled but its horn blasted a continuous ear-splitting honk.

Mary came to a halt. They leaped out. The passenger door of the crashed car swung open, and a girl fell out onto her hands and knees in the weeds. It was Sandy, Landlord John's daughter. Mary ran to her. The girl staggered to her feet and collapsed against her rescuer.

Derek wrenched the driver's door open. A man was slumped over the wheel. There was no sign of blood, but the man wasn't moving. Derek reached through, took the driver by either shoulder, and eased him back. The horn stopped. With a shock he realised he knew the unconscious man. It was Fergus, the arrogant and volatile son of Sir Arthur Bulstock. And Derek also realised with a moment of shock and panic, the man was deathly still, not even breathing. Derek felt his chest. He felt nothing.

"Mary! Come! Quick!" What should he do? He knew that it was dangerous to move people in traumatic moments like this. But he wasn't breathing. Surely, he had to do something. Something. He shook Fergus.

Sting of the Nettle

Nothing. No sign of life. He had to get him out of the vehicle. He caught the man by the shoulders again and pulled. It wasn't easy, Fergus's feet were caught behind the pedals, and the low, narrow shape of the car meant he had to manoeuvre the body both up and out. Two careful pulls failed to shift it. Frantically, he wrapped an arm around the man's torso, pulling and wrenching, and finally the body came free, and they both tumbled backwards onto the ground.

"Is he all right?"

Derek looked up, to see Mary standing over him, her legs astride, and ludicrously he noticed yet again what fine legs she had. Behind her he could see Sandy, sitting half in, half out of the passenger seat of their car, eyes tightly shut.

He scrambled to his feet, allowing Fergus to lie on his back. "He's not breathing," he said.

"Oh God. What do we do?"

"Don't you know?"

"Don't you?"

They stared at each other, aghast that, despite their training, their minds at the critical moment had gone blank.

"Artificial respiration." Mary stuttered. "You know, press his chest, lift his arms..."

"Right!" Vague memories of procedure came back. He began thumping rhythmically on Fergus's chest, then lifting his arms.

"Go on, keep doing it!" Mary told him, and there was desperation in her voice.

Derek leaned over the man's chest, pushing hard on

his chest. "It's not working," he told her. "No air coming out." He tried again, then again, but nothing changed. Fergus lay on the grass like a corpse.

And then Derek remembered something. Something from a distant first aid class. He took Fergus's chin in one hand, his nose in the other, and forced his mouth wide open. He looked in. The tongue was twisted at the back of the throat. Derek braced himself, held the man's chin down with the heel of his hand, and poked in two fingers, coiling them around the tongue and jerking it out.

There was a bursting, choking explosion of air. Fergus's body shook in a violent spasm, and then it took enormous breaths, in like a vacuum cleaner, and then out in a mountain of spray and phlegm. Then, gradually, the breathing steadied, but continued, becoming even and regular.

Derek sat back on his heels and looked up at Mary. "I think he's all right."

"Well done." Her voice was shaky, and there were tears of relief on her cheeks.

"The girl all right?"

"Mmm. In shock, I think. But otherwise... What do we do now?"

Derek got to his feet and looked around. "Well," he said. "It's an RTA."

"What?"

"Road traffic accident. I should take some measurements, write a report."

"Oh, don't be such a policeman!" Shock was evident in her voice. "I mean what do we do about him? And

Sting of the Nettle

her?"

It was a good question. Derek and Mary walked back to Sandy at their car. She was shivering, even in the warm sunshine.

"Sandy, you okay?" Derek asked her.

She stared at him blankly. He recognised the look from his first encounter with her in the pub kitchen.

Then she said: "I want to go home."

Derek looked at Mary and shrugged. "Better take her home. Cup of tea and bed should do the trick."

There was a noise behind them, a cross between a cough and a groan. Fergus was on his feet, leaning unsteadily against his car.

Derek walked back to him, leaving Mary to stow Sandy carefully in the passenger seat of her car, shutting the door to keep her safe. As he got nearer Derek saw Fergus focus bleary eyes on his, and grimace as he noted the uniform.

"A fucking copper!" he said thickly. "Fuck my luck."

Derek ignored the greeting. "How are you feeling, Fergus?"

"How d'you think I'm feeling, copper? I just crashed me wheels in front of a bloody policeman. I suppose you're going to do me for it. Bastard."

"I'm more concerned at this moment with your state of health."

"Fuck off." Fergus gave Derek an extravagant V-sign and turned away.

"He saved your life!" Four simple words which were a shaft of pure steel, the lash of a plaited whip, a kick in the groin with a pointed shoe.

Sting of the Nettle

"Wha..." Startled, Fergus turned back, and stared past Derek, at Mary who strode towards him, her eyes narrow, her face red and furious.

"He saved your stupid life, you idiot," she blazed. "God knows why. But he did! He saved your worthless life."

Fergus stared at Derek: "Did you?"

"You weren't breathing," Derek told him. "You'd virtually swallowed your tongue. I sort of hoicked it out."

"Yes, that's what he did, you ungrateful little shit." Mary was still raging. "I'd have let you die, but not him. No, he put his fingers in your filthy mouth and pulled out your stupid tongue, and that's why you're standing up now talking, instead of lying dead in that ditch."

"Did you?" Fergus asked Derek again. "Actually save my life?"

"We're trained for this sort of thing," Derek told him, forgiving himself for the panicky moments when he had forgotten all training.

Mary wasn't finished: "And you might remember, Mr High and Mighty Bloody Bulstock – and yes, we know who you are all right, you obnoxious little creep, I've had dealings with you in the past – and you might remember you had a passenger in your car. Or don't you care?"

"The girl." Fergus had indeed clearly forgotten. "Is she dead?"

In answer Mary stood aside and gestured at her car. The girl Sandy was sitting up, staring back at them.

"Thank Christ!" Fergus muttered. "We didn't want another one."

"What?"

Sting of the Nettle

"We didn't want another person... nearly dying, to be saved by you. And listen," in a tone of fake righteousness, "this wasn't my fault. You pulled out in front of me. I had to swerve to avoid you. You can't do me for this."

"Oh for God's sake." Mary turned away in disgust. "Charge him, Derek. Dangerous driving."

"Fergus, we were on the main road, remember?" Derek pointed out calmly. "You were on the minor road. Now I know there's not much difference in these country lanes, but there is a sign telling you to give way, isn't there?"

"Didn't see it."

"Too busy showing off to Sandy, I expect," Mary snorted, returning to the fray. "And another thing. You might have the grace to say thank you." And then, as Fergus began to reply, "No, not to me, clot. To him." And now as if speaking to a backward child, "He... saved... your... life."

Fergus looked at Derek, then dropped his eyes. He muttered: "Thanks."

"Wow!" Mary's voice brimmed over with sarcasm. "I never thought I'd see the day. The great Fergus Bulstock, super snob of the county, actually saying thank you to a lowly police constable. Wonders will never..."

But Derek had turned to her. "Okay, love. I think you've made your point."

"Oh, have I?! Very well. Then I'll leave you two best buddies to kiss and make up. I'll go and see Sandy. She might show a spark more intelligence than you, Fergus. Though as she was obviously happy to be in your company, I very much doubt it."

The men watched as she stalked back to her car.

Fergus drew himself up, took a deep breath, and when he spoke now, he was clearly regaining his normal poise.

"Spirited little thing you've got there, constable. Bet she's a handful in bed."

Derek turned on him, a threat in both his voice and his manner. "Listen to me, Fergus. I'm one step away from shoving your filthy tongue back down your throat. Another smart remark from you and I bloody well will."

"Okay. Okay. Sorry and all that." Fergus raised his hands in mock surrender. "Just man talk, you know. Two chaps together and all that. She's a very sweet person, your Mary. Very nice girl. For a villager. I've always said that."

Derek gritted his teeth. The facility with which the man used her name, the implication that he had known her for longer than he had, the slur on her background; he hated it. He hated the man. But...

"Let's take a look at your car, shall we, Fergus?"

To the surprise of both, the collision with the hedge seemed to have caused little or no damage to the MG. It was by no means dent-free, there were scrapes down the side panelling and scars on the back bumper, but that was apparently the result of previous ill-usage. This crash had done little or no harm, presumably because the ferns, docks, weeds and assorted greenery of the bank had cushioned the impact. The car had also rebounded a little, and its front wheels had turned away from the hedge.

Sting of the Nettle

"I think we're going to need one of Daddy's tractors," Fergus suggested.

"I don't know. Let's see if we can push her out. Keep the front wheels turning out."

It was surprisingly easy. Two or three heaves, and the little white sports car stood four-square on the verge.

"Right, mind your back." Derek elbowed Fergus aside and got in behind the wheel. The key was still in the ignition. He turned it, and the engine hummed into well-tuned life. He selected first gear, let out the clutch, and the wheels spun uselessly. "Stupid," he abused himself. He selected second, called to Fergus to bounce the car's boot, and this time the tyres gripped, and the car slid smoothly along and off the verge, and onto the tarmac. A quick inspection of the front revealed nothing more than a cracked headlight.

"You're a lucky man," he told Fergus. "In more ways than one. This could be a write-off. And so could you."

Mary came to join him. Her anger still simmered, but she had clearly decided to behave in a civilised manner. "So, what do we do now?" she asked.

"I think it best if you take Sandy home. Soon as poss," Derek told her.

"John will want to know what happened." She glanced at Fergus, who had wandered slightly unsteadily down the lane. "And who she was with."

"Tell him. I mean..." He grinned. "You and I might think otherwise, but to most people the son and heir to the Bulstock empire is someone worth knowing. Someone to respect. And anyway, this might all be to the good. It might shake a bit of sense into Sandy's bonce."

Sting of the Nettle

"I doubt it. All she's been saying is, 'Is Fergie all right?' 'Fergie' for God's sake."

"John thought it would be Bucky. Anything, anyone, is better than Bucky. What's 'Fergie' up to, anyway? Where's he gone now?"

He looked down the lane, to see Fergus leaning one hand against a tree, and vomiting. Something, some connection, nearly clicked in his mind. And then it was gone.

"I better drive him home," he told Mary. "I'll call you when I know he's all right, you can come and pick me up."

"I better get going." She gave him a quick kiss. "Remember, pork chops tonight!"

"And? Anything for dessert?" Derek put prurient emphasis into the words.

"We'll see."

When she'd gone, Derek and Fergus met at his car. Fergus gestured down the lane. "Sorry about that." His breath stank of vomit. "Something I ate."

Of course! Derek remembered. Welbeloved and the lavender bushes.

He said: "I think you're a little concussed. Come on, I'll drive you home. No, no argument. You're in no fit state."

Fergus didn't argue. He settled in the passenger seat of his car, opened the glove compartment, pulled out a half-bottle of Famous Grouse and took two quick swallows.

"That's not going to help," Derek told him, climbing in behind the wheel. "Drinking and driving was stupid

Sting of the Nettle

in the first place. Drinking on concussion is as bad, if not worse."

"Fuck off."

Fergus slumped in his seat, still holding the bottle, and closed his eyes. They drove in silence for about a mile, then the man seemed to wake up. He straightened in the seat, and when he spoke, he sounded reasonable, even polite.

"See here, Derek. It is Derek, isn't it? Do you mind if I call you Derek?" He didn't wait for a reply but went on: "Look. I was a bit of a bore back there, wasn't I? It was the shock, and, well, I can be an arse on occasions. So my friends tell me."

Thank heaven someone does, Derek thought, but he kept quiet and let Fergus continue.

"So anyway. I want to apologise. And to express my sincere gratitude. If it wasn't for you, it appears I would be a goner. So, thank you. And sorry."

"Forget it."

"I won't forget it. I shall be forever in your debt. I say, can I offer you a...? He held out the whisky bottle to Derek.

"Not for me." Derek said firmly, though in truth he could have murdered a stiff Scotch at that moment."

"Quite right." Fergus shoved the bottle back into the glove compartment and snapped the lid shut. "I'll tell you what I want. What I need, really. And that's a nice cup of tea."

"Be home soon. Perhaps your mother will make you one. Or one of the staff?"

Fergus shook his head. "The parental pair are off in

Sting of the Nettle

Norfolk. Murdering pheasants. And the staff are on their annual hols. Apart from the gardeners, of course. They can't go until the weather turns. No, I shall make the tea myself. I'm rather good at tea-making, believe it or not. I shall make a cup for me. And I shall make a cup for you, Constable Friend."

"Oh no, not for me, I'll need to be..."

"Please." Fergus was insistent. And, in mock cockney: "A quick cuppa Rosie Lee, squire." And then, in a reasonable, even humble tone: "Oh say yes, Derek. Just a small, a very small, token of my gratitude. Yes?"

Well why not? Derek asked himself. Why not indeed?

CHAPTER TWENTY-FIVE

The tea tasted odd.

He and Fergus were in the large drawing room where Sir Arthur and Lady Bulstock had held their charitable reception. The room was littered with expensive-looking antique furniture. Fergus had invited Derek to sit on a low green chair, with a sloping back and short legs. Beautiful to look at, but possibly the most uncomfortable chair he had ever encountered. It took a definite physical effort to avoid sliding off the thing onto the thick rug at his feet. Then Fergus had wandered off presumably to the kitchen and returned five minutes later with two mugs of tea.

"It's Earl Grey tea, old boy." Fergus, half-lying on an ornate sofa, had, it seemed, noticed Derek's first reaction to the taste. "Bit different from your usual brew, I imagine."

Derek felt a familiar sense of social inadequacy. He had no idea who Earl Grey was, or why it was his tea he was drinking.

"Yes." he said. It was ridiculous, he told himself. In the car he had felt on equal if not superior terms with Fergus. Now, in the man's house, surrounded by tokens of wealth and social status, he felt absurdly anxious not to say the wrong thing. "I suppose it's an acquired taste."

"Lots of things are, Sonny-Jim. Lots of things are." Fergus obviously considered this remark humorous, because he laughed long and loud at it.

Derek wanted to leave the rest of the tea, but he couldn't think how to do so without appearing ill-mannered. At home he'd have swilled the rest of the cup into the sink. Here, there was no sink handy – in fact nowhere where, perched as he was on this ridiculous chair, he could put the cup and somehow 'forget' about it. He had no choice. He took two big gulps of the stuff. It didn't get any better.

"Well. Thanks for that," he told Fergus. "Better be getting on."

"No rush, surely, Finish your tea. No, go on. Finish it." Fergus's class accent now carried a sharp edge of authority.

Derek obeyed out of good manners. He swilled the dregs in his mug around and swallowed. There. At least it was gone. He stood up, but Fergus remained lounging languidly on his sofa. Head on one side, he seemed to be studying Derek.

"How are you feeling, my friend?" he asked rather abruptly.

Funny question, Derek thought. "I should be asking you that," he replied. "After all, you're the one who had the crash. Who nearly died."

"So true, laddie. So true. But I feel fine. My question is, how do you feel?"

"Fine. Fine." And it was true. He did feel good. He felt light, clear-headed and in control. And then he had a sudden good thought. Something he should say.

"Listen, about the crash. That girl in the car. That's Sandy Jacob."

Sting of the Nettle

"That's her, constable. Lovely Sandy. Sweet girl."

"Maybe. But what were you doing with her? In your car?"

Fergus laughed his mysterious laugh. "You can't do anything with a girl in a car like that, you know. Gear stick gets in your way." And before Derek could say anything, he held up a hand. "Just kidding, old chap. Pulling your leg."

"Yes, very funny. What were you actually doing?"

"Oh, just taking a drive, you know. Sandy likes being driven around in sports cars. It excites her. Whizzing round these little roads, zipping round the bends. Women like that sort of thing, I've always found. Makes 'em go all weak and wobbly." He laughed again.

"That's not the point. She's very young. Only sixteen. And you, you're..." He didn't know how old Fergus was and decided not to guess. "You're old enough to know better. Any relations you might have with her would be highly illegal."

"Oh, don't worry your little red head on that score, my dear Derek. I know the law - can't stop me thinking about it, though."

Now that was funny, Derek decided. Bloody funny. And he joined in Fergus's laughter.

"Sexy," Fergus added.

"Mmm?"

"I said sexy."

Derek thought about that. It was true, Sandy was ...

"And that body. Wow."

"I mean, get a good look, when you get the chance, old boy." Fergus made some sensuous shapes with his hands. "Don't you think?"

God yes, the man was right. He'd never seen it before. But now he pictured Sandy in his mind. She might be young, but, well, in all honesty Fergus was correct. She had a terrific body. Something a man had to see, couldn't ignore, couldn't pretend he didn't. We're all human. I'm a man

He got up from his chair again, feeling suddenly full of life, full of vitality. The room seemed bigger and brighter than before. He realised he was still holding his tea mug, and he turned to put it down on a slight spindly table covered with tiny ornaments, but he missed the edge of the table, and the empty mug fell to the carpet. But that was all right, that didn't matter.

Fergus was on his feet now, grinning at him.

"How are you feeling, young Martin the policeman? Eh?"

"Great, great." And it was true. He did feel great. He felt splendid. This was the way to feel. Alive. Alert. In control.

"Fancy a stroll?" asked Fergus.

"Right you are, Fergie! Why not?" And he did. He fancied a stroll.

Together they walked out of the main door of the mansion, and down the long line of lavender bushes, those same bushes to which Welbeloved had paid such close inspection to after the Bulstock party. The memory made Derek laugh, long and loud.

For ten minutes or more they strolled around the lawns and flower beds, Derek breathing in the scented air, and gazing in wonder at the beauty of the natural

Sting of the Nettle

world, spread before his eyes.

Then without warning Fergus stopped. Derek realised that they had walked about 100 yards down the drive, towards the entrance to the estate.

"Time to go, I think," Fergus said briskly.

"Right. Yes. Why not?" He had a little trouble collecting his thoughts about going. "Better telephone. Need a car."

"A car? On a day like this?" Fergus scoffed. "Why not walk?"

Fergus was right. He would walk. A great idea. And at once he was walking, long firm strides, eating up the gravel drive. He turned aside after about 50 yards, slightly surprised that Fergus was not walking with him. He looked back and saw the man watching him, and laughing again, though at what, Derek couldn't guess. Not that it mattered. Walking was what mattered.

He strode on, and in no time reached the end of the drive, and the T-junction with the road. Question was, which way to turn. It didn't matter, nothing mattered, the thing to do was just to walk, to go forward. And so he went forward, striding across the road, straddling a ditch, and climbing up and over the bank. There was a line of saplings on the top of the bank, ground elder probably, or hazel, but whatever they were those little trees weren't going to stop Derek. Not today. He burst through them, sliding down the bank on the other side, and stepping neatly over a thin strand of barbed wire, to find himself in a broad sloping meadow. There were cattle in the field, cows with calves, who could be aggressive in defending their offspring, but Derek didn't bother with

Sting of the Nettle

them, he just walked straight through them, and they parted to let him go.

The meadow was divided, he discovered, by a single wire obstacle, supported by a series of short iron rods, with enamel tops. The thing seemed to be ticking. He grasped the wire, and an electrical shock rang up his arm, and down the side of the body. Derek sneered at it, grasped one of the rods, and tore it up, throwing the metal and its wire on the ground. He strode over it and marched on.

One part of his conscious mind told him that the electric fence was designed to keep the cows and their calves on one side of the field, and a big bull on the other, but it didn't seem to matter. And there was the bull, looking at him with all the fury of a gardener watching a pet dog peeing on his lawn. It was a solid, chunky animal, with a pair of formidable, curved horns on its snorting head. Today those horns did not threaten Derek. He plodded on towards the bull, staring it in his eyes, and he wasn't frightened. Of course he wasn't frightened. The bull pawed the ground and lowered its head as if to charge. But then, in the face of Derek's staring eyes and implacable advance, it changed its mind and stepped aside, to let the unstoppable human force advance. Derek didn't bother to consider the bull's next move, whether it would attack him from behind, or take advantage of the gap in the fence and saunter down to meet some of his lady-friends. He moved on. Keeping going, not stopping.

His next obstacle was a gate. No problem there. One foot on the second cross-piece, a leap, and he was over,

Sting of the Nettle

both feet landing in a puddle and spraying mud up his trousers. Which didn't matter. Nothing mattered.

Ahead of him was a broad avenue of splendid trees leading him up a slight slope to the crest of a hill and another gate into a further field. Something made him stop at this second gate, and look up. The view took him across a patchwork of fields and copes, to the distant blue of the Dartmoor hills, and dominating those hills, rising with what seemed almost a physical challenge, the magnificent rocky peak of Yes Tor.

Yes Tor. That would be a good place to walk to. Yes Tor. Yes!

* * *

Mary waited at home for two hours before she began to worry. In the relatively short time she had been a police wife, she had learned to be tolerant of long hours and broken assurances. Part of the job, other wives had informed her, with gleeful candour. "You just have to trust the lying so-and-so's" as one put it.

She'd spent some of the time restoring Sandy to the Dragon and her father. She explained briefly to the landlord that his daughter had been in a car accident, that she was unhurt, but that she was in shock, and just needed a cup of tea and the rest of the day in bed. John asked Mary to wait while he got those needs organised, then returned, anxious to know in whose car Sandy had been a passenger.

"Not that bloody Bucky, pardon my French?" He demanded.

Sting of the Nettle

"No. It was Fergus Bulstock. Sir Arthur's son."

"Him?" John Jacob's face was a picture. Mary could almost read his thoughts. Thank God it wasn't Bucky. But Fergus. Posh family, money there. He was known to be a bit of a lout. And far too old to be a boyfriend. But all the same, better than Bucky.

"Better than Bucky," he told Mary. "But what was she doing with him?"

"You'll have to ask her," Mary said, and then, realising the remark was a little blunt, she said: "Better still, ask Derek. He had to drive Fergus home. I'll get him to call in."

"If he wouldn't mind."

"Call in at the pub? He won't take much persuading," Mary smiled. And she went home. And waited for the phone call, for Derek's request to be picked up. The phone call didn't come.

* * *

Yes Tor! That was where he was going. Gates, field, lanes, even a shallow pond. Derek swept through them in an unstoppable charge, and the Tor came nearer and nearer, and to any other walker it would have looked higher and more formidable at every step. But not to Derek, not today. Today it was his for the taking, and take it he would.

Down a farm lane, then across the main road to the west, the A30. No need to wait or look. A lorry driver leaned on his horn, as he swerved to avoid the now slightly bedraggled figure that blithely crossed the road

Sting of the Nettle

twenty yards in front of him, and his shout of outrage joined the shrill squeal of brakes, the rasp of skidding tyres. Derek heard none of it. There was Yes Tor in front of him. He began the climb.

The Tor wasn't new to him. He and Mary had climbed it together, six months before, when they were enjoying a rare and cost-free day out. But it had been a challenge, even a struggle. They'd parked in Okehampton, and walked up the long steep street that eventually led them over a couple of cattle grids, and finally deposited them on the moor itself. That part had been easy enough. Not so what came next. As the ground under his feet grew steeper, Derek had found to his surprise that just the act of breathing became difficult. He could feel his heart pumping as he grimly pushed one foot in front of the other up the bumpy and grassy slope. It didn't help that he was wearing plimsolls which slipped easily on the springy turf. When he stopped and looked at Mary he had seen, almost with relief, that she was suffering the same symptoms.

That was then. Today, for Derek on his own, it was a piece of cake.

Today he steamed up the slopes with no pauses for rest. Today, he told himself, his heart wouldn't thump in his chest, because he was powerful, he was invincible. And it was a funny thing because he could hear the throbbing in his ears, which meant his heart was thumping, but that didn't matter, it didn't slow him down, nothing was going to slow him down today.

And then there he was, up on the summit, or at least on the saddle of gentle greenery that slid flatly up to the rocks on the very top. And there were other people there, other damn people getting in the way. A couple had spread a rug and were sitting there eating sandwiches. Derek had a brief memory flash of doing much the same with Mary, but then the memory had gone and in its place was this wretched couple, looking up at him with stupid smiles on their faces, almost as if they were inviting him to join them in the pleasure of being up so high in such a beautiful place, but he walked right through them, they were in the way, them and their stupid rug, and then they were sprawling away on the grass, and the damn rug caught in his foot, and he kicked it away, and went on to clamber up the top-most rock and look out over the rolling patchwork of fields and woods before him.

His heart throbbed louder in his ears. A small boy, from another party, in khaki shorts and a holey jumper, came scrambling up the rock to join him, looking up at him, grinning as if his presence was desirable, even welcome.

"Fuck off," he told the kid, who half-fell, half-jumped off the rock and ran wailing to whoever had charge of him, Derek didn't know and didn't care.

Instead, he looked out over the countryside. Where was the village? Where was North Tawe? It had to be somewhere. And that's where he had to be. Mary was there, and he wanted Mary. He had to have her. He jumped down from the rock, and almost ran towards the point here he had climbed up.

Someone shouted after him, and the kid was still crying. It didn't matter. Nothing mattered.

Sting of the Nettle

* * *

Colonel Critchley sat in his upright armchair and stared at the picture of his wife on the mantelpiece. You should not be sitting here, he told himself, and he was right. The corn was in, his men were busy preparing for the threshing machine to arrive next day, he should be out there organising things. But he wasn't. He couldn't.

He picked up the thick glass tumbler and looked at the scarcely touched pool of whisky in it. The liquid shimmered, and the Colonel realised that his hand was shaking. He put the glass down untouched and swore silently.

The phone on the table by his side rang shrilly. What new hell was this? He picked the receiver up, but did not speak, just listened.

"Hello? Colonel?" A woman. Nervous.

"Who's that?" The Colonel tried to keep his voice flat, and not betray his increasing anxiety.

"It's Mary Martin. Constable Martin's wife. From West."

"Yes, yes, of course, Mary." The relief and pleasure in in his voice was clear even to him, and doubtless reassured his caller. "Nice to talk to you again, Mary. What can I do for you?"

"Well, it's about Derek."

"What about him? Not in trouble, I hope."

"Well, I don't know if he said anything to you, but Derek told me that if ever I needed help, and he wasn't around, then I was to call you. He said you'd help, I suppose."

"Of course. Glad to. What's the problem? Not another brick through the window, I trust."

"No, thank goodness. No, it's Derek. I've sort of lost him."

The Colonel listened as, keeping it as brief as possible, Mary gave him an outline of the events of the day: the crash of the sports car, the emergency first aid that saved Fergus's life, the girl Sandy.

"That's Fergus Bulstock, right?" The Colonel interrupted. "Son of The Big Cheese Sir Arthur. Am I correct?"

"That's him."

"Speeding in a fast car with a 16-year-old girl, eh? Typical behaviour, from what I hear. I think the boy's a bit unhinged. Mind you, I can't talk, can I? "

"Oh no, Colonel."

"No, no. That's okay, dear. I'm aware I'm a candidate for the funny farm. And if I wasn't aware there's plenty ready to tell me. But getting back to Fergus?"

"Yes, well, I took the girl Sandy home, and because Fergus was still a bit woozy, we agreed Derek would drive him home in his car and call me when he got there so I could come and pick him up."

"Uh-huh. And then?"

"Well, he didn't. Ring me, I mean. And I tried ringing the Bulstock place, their number's in the book, and no-one answered"

"How long ago was this?"

"Oh Lord. Must be five hours by now. No, more. I'm worried. I know policemen can get caught up in things,

Sting of the Nettle

but it's not like him to leave me in the dark like this."

"Have you tried ringing the police in Okehampton?"

"Well, I would, but he's in their bad books already, over what he's been doing, and that Sergeant, Welbeloved, he's hopeless."

"I know the type. Indeed, I know Welbeloved." the Colonel said dryly. "Listen, I'll come over and we can decide what to do. Ten minutes, okay?"

"All right." And then there was a noise in the background, and Mary's tone of voice changed to one of both relief and anxiety. "Oh, he's here! Derek, where have you. Look at you! No don't. Oh!"

It was a cry of shock, even disgust and horror. The Colonel dropped the phone, grabbed the keys to the Landrover, and ran.

* * *

Mary looked at her husband, as he stood panting in the hallway; as he seized the phone from her and slammed it down; as, with equally ferocity, he slammed the front door shut. She shuddered. She scarcely recognised him. His red hair was a bird's nest, his shirt torn, his trousers soaked in something that, combined with the smell of cold sweat, stank to high heaven. But the worst thing was his stare. He seemed to be gazing at her from a thousand miles away.

"Who you ringing?" he demanded, panting from exertion.

"The Colonel. I thought something was wrong."

"What? Why?"

"You didn't ring. You've been gone so long. What were you doing?"

"Walking."

"Why? "

"Cos I could." He seemed to find the question ridiculous. And then: "Walked to Yes Tor."

"All the way? But that's miles."

"Climbed it, then walked back."

Mary took a deep breath. He's ill, she thought. Or drunk. No smell of drink but... She resolved to act as if nothing was wrong.

"You must be exhausted," she told him.

"No. Could do it again."

"Yes, well, for now, come on into the kitchen, take the weight off your feet."

She led the way through, and somehow got him sitting at the table at his usual place.

"Now, darling, you must be hungry. I..."

"No. Not hungry."

"But you've had nothing all day."

"Not hungry. No food."

Afterwards Mary thought wryly that it would have been wiser to accept that he wasn't going eat. Wise, less expensive, and less messy. But instead, she fussed around the kitchen, finding cutlery and plates, butter and so on.

"You'll want to eat when you see these lovely chops, remember? I told you about them. They've been in the oven, got a bit dry, but I'll give them a quick fry, they'll be lovely."

She pulled the cast iron frying pan onto the heat and

Sting of the Nettle

dropped a chunk of lard into it. She took the well-cooked chops from the warming drawer of the Rayburn and put them to sizzle. She found half a loaf of local-baked crusty white bread and cut two thick slices. She chopped up some tomatoes and washed some lettuce. Hardly a balanced meal, she thought, remembering the lessons spelled out in the book on calories. But it was certainly one of Derek's favourites.

As she worked, she kept up a stream of remarks and questions that grew ever weaker and more pointless. "How did you get so wet? Did you get Fergus home safely? I suppose we should have taken him to hospital. Did you see his parents?"

None of this elicited any response from Derek, who sat stolidly at the table, resting his forehead on his clenched fists.

Finally, Mary loaded a plate with bread and butter, two chops and the salad, and placed it in front of him. "Any sauce?" she asked him.

He looked at her blankly, and didn't speak. Instead, he stood, picked up the plate in both hands and threw it at the sink. The plate – and it had to have been one of their best, a wedding present from an aunt, Mary reflected later - spilled most of its food in the flight, then shattered against the enamel.

"Oh Derek." Mary moaned in despair. "What's the matter? Tell me."

"Nothing," he said thickly. "Everything's great. I feel great."

He got up from his chair and moved towards her. It was strange but he seemed bigger than usual. More

Sting of the Nettle

formidable. He reached out for her, and she backed away.

"Derek, sit down! Please!"

"Shut up!" He now moved quickly, and she found herself backed into a corner of the kitchen between the sink and the back door. He reached for her again, broken crockery crunching under his feet, and this time he caught her by the upper arms. His hands squeezed, and she cried out with the pain.

"No. Derek! Stop it!"

As if obeying, he let go of her arms, but instead he thrust his hips against her violently, and grabbed the front of her blouse, ripping it apart, dragging her brassiere down, then scrabbling at her breasts.

She struggled against him, tried to hit him, slapping him on the side of the head, but he ignored the blows, mauling her and at the same time trying to kiss her. Much later she remembered the stock instructions on how to fight off a rapacious male, the main burden of that advice being to knee the attacker in the groin, do it hard, cripple the bastard, squash his things flat. But at the time the move didn't occur to her, and in retrospect she was glad it didn't.

Meanwhile the assault continued, and she continued to fight back, flailing at him, begging him to stop. He tried to silence her, putting a smelly hand over her mouth, and then thrusting the other hand up under her skirt, grabbing her between the legs. She bit his finger, her mouth came free, and now she abandoned pleading with him, and, on the verge of total panic, screamed as loudly as she could.

Sting of the Nettle

"Help!"

The back door crashed open, and the Colonel took one pace into the room, seized Derek's collar, and jerked him back, sending him reeling against the kitchen table. Derek started forward again, but the Colonel met him halfway and punched him with considerable power on the nose. This time Derek fell to the floor. Mary pulled her clothes together, sobbing, and the Colonel put a fatherly arm around her shoulders.

"You're all right now," he told her. She sobbed the harder.

"But it's Derek!" she said repeatedly. "How could he?"

The Colonel stared at the fallen figure of Derek. He nursed the hand that had connected so briskly with Derek's face, and now hurt like the Devil. He knew how Derek could behave as he had. He had seen the look in the young man's eyes. The faraway stare. He had seen it before. Near Falaise. In the eyes of Wehrmacht infantry as they charged forward in hopeless defiance. The memory was crystal clear, and he wished to God that it wasn't.

. And it was the same look he had seen, and now saw again, in the eyes of the young village policeman staggering to his feet in the humble kitchen in sleepy North Tawe.

And he knew what that look meant. It meant a simple German medical product. It meant Pervitin.

But he also felt a sense of relief. Derek was unarmed. And it seemed he had no intention of fighting back at the Colonel, or of resuming his assault on his wife. Instead, he looked about him, located the back door, and moved with surprising alacrity towards it. The Colonel pulled Mary, still in shock, behind him, to allow Derek to get to the door, which he opened, lurched through, and slammed behind him.

They both heard the clatter of the garden tools that were stacked by the entrance.

CHAPTER TWENTY-SIX

Derek was asleep but dreaming that he was awake. Or maybe he was awake but dreaming that he was asleep. He wanted to be awake because his dreams were formless but nonetheless full of pain and the threat of a dreadful fate. But he also wanted to be asleep because although he could neither name it nor picture it, he knew he faced a burden of shame or guilt in the wide-awake real-life world when he returned to it.

Reality won the battle. He became aware that he was no longer asleep, and that if he opened his eyes he would be back in – well, wherever it was that he was. The thoughts muddled and repeated themselves as he tried to form them into sense. For a long and panicky moment he could not remember who he was or where he was or what was happening in his life. Then the flickers of memory, some sense of it all, came fluttering back into his consciousness like shards of broken glass.

Where was he? What had happened to him? And, my God, what had he done?

He was lying on something cool and slippery. He opened his eyes, but that didn't help much, all he could see was a patch of shiny plastic close against his burning face, and then further on, bare floorboards. His head throbbed with the weight of a cataclysmic hang-over, far worse than he had ever experienced, worse even than the one that followed the only time he had passed out

Sting of the Nettle

due to drink. His eighteenth birthday. He'd been sick then, and he was sick now. Not much, but the result glistened on the plastic as he raised his head to avoid choking.

He sat up. His headache flared, and for some reason his nose ached. He looked around, and at last knew where he was. He was at home. He was in the bare and virtually untouched sitting room, on the dreadful couch bought for them as a wedding present by his mother-in-law; the mother-in-law who believed something could only be tasteful and desirable if it was coloured bright orange or bright green, or both together. The mother-in-law who was so easily offended.

What was he doing, lying and now sitting on this dreadful piece of furniture? What had he done? With a shock he realised that all he was wearing was his dressing gown. Under it he was naked.

He remembered walking, climbing. He remembered shouting, but at what? That remained a mystery. And then he remembered something else, something so dreadful, so culpable, so obscene that his mind fought to avoid thinking about it. A dark dread, that had been hovering on the outskirts of his consciousness, now descended to envelope him. What had he done? What had he done? And then he remembered, just a little, of what he had done, and he groaned aloud.

The door to the kitchen opened. He didn't want to look up, he wanted to rest his face in his hands and close his eyes, and never open them. But then he did look up.

Mary stood in the doorway. She had a hot cup of tea in her hand, he could see the steam rising from it. And

Sting of the Nettle

she was smiling. Yes, glory be, she was smiling, and if Mary was smiling then nothing could be that bad. However grim the truth was, whatever it was that he had done, it couldn't be that awful. Because Mary was smiling.

"Hello," she said.

He tried to say hello back, but his tongue was apparently sticking behind his teeth, and he just grunted as he wrenched it free.

"Thought I heard you coming to life," his wife went on brightly. "You can probably do with this."

Automatically he reached for the cup, but his hand shook so violently that she drew back the cup.

"In a minute, perhaps," she said tactfully, and moved to sit next to him on the couch.

"No, don't" He raised an arm to stop her, his voice croaky. "I've just been a bit sick on it."

"Then let's get you into the kitchen." With the teacup in one hand, and the other holding his arm, she persuaded him first to stand, then to walk unsteadily out to the kitchen.

"It'll wipe off," he croaked. "The plastic. I mean, it won't stain the sofa."

"Pity." She sat him down at the table and put the tea in front of him. "We could have chucked it out."

She could joke. Whatever he'd done, she could still make a joke. Derek used both hands on the cup, and lowered his head to sip the tea. It was very sweet

Mary sat down opposite him. "Feel up to talking? Want to tell me about it?"

He nodded. "I think I better."

Sting of the Nettle

"Okay. But don't say anything for a moment. First, I'm going to ask you a couple of things. The Colonel told me what to ask."

The Colonel! He'd been there. He remembered.

"He hit me!" he said.

"He did. Good thing too. But listen. Questions: first, did you take Fergus home okay, after the accident?"

"Yes. I'm sure I did. He recovered okay. Got quite chatty, invited me in."

"And did you eat anything at his place?"

"No. Had a cup of tea, though. He was very... you know. Thoughtful. You wouldn't credit it."

"Oh yes. How was the tea? Taste okay?"

"No. Bloody weird. 'Cos it was Earl something or other."

"Earl Grey."

"That's it."

"And did it make you feel ill?"

"God, no. Actually, I felt great. Never better. And then I walked. Walked for hours, could have walked for ever."

And now, in a flood, comprehension came: "Jesus, it's that drug, isn't it! The one Hans told me about, the thing the Colonel. Christ! The bastard drugged me. Pervitin! In the tea! Bloody Fergus." The teacup shook in his hand, slopping hot tea over his fingers. He put it down quickly.

"That's what we thought," Mary said calmly. "What we don't know is where you went or what you did, during the next few hours. When you were walking."

"I went to the moor, I think. Don't know why. Nothing mattered, I remember that. Nothing and no-one."

"That's the drug. Whatever you did, you weren't responsible."

"Yes, but what if I did something bad. You know, illegal or something. I could get the sack."

"Well. You weren't in uniform, were you? You were in civvies – which incidentally are in the wash. So even if you did do something, you'd probably get away with it. No-one would report you."

"God, I hope not."

"And it's been a full day or more since, so if someone reported you, we'd probably have heard by now."

"A full day or more?"

"You've been asleep for twenty hours."

"Good grief. Anyway, I should be grateful I got home. I sort of remember coming here, you were here." he paused and felt the blood drain from his face as he began to remember. "Christ, what did I do?"

"Well." She grinned. "You broke a perfectly good plate and ruined two very expensive pork chops!"

He didn't smile. "And then. Oh God." Full memory every detail, of what he had done, streamed back into his consciousness. "Oh no, not..."

Mary pushed his cup aside, and, leaning across the table, gripped his two hands in hers.

"It wasn't you!" she said intently. "It was the drug. It acts on your brain. You were someone else, something else. It wasn't you. "

Derek buried his face in his hands, his shoulders shaking with sobs. "How could I? To you. Like that."

Mary pulled her chair around so she could sit by his

side. She put an arm round his shoulders and waited until he quietened down. "Listen, that's enough for now. We can talk about it later if you like. Or we can never talk about it again. Remember, I'm fine. Nobody got hurt. Nobody died."

Derek muttered something that sounded like agreement. Mary found a tea towel, and he mopped his face with it.

"Was that it then?" He asked eventually. "I passed out then, did I?"

"By no means. Would you like to see what you did then?"

"Oh Christ." he said fearfully. "Have I got to?"

"Come on. "She took him by the hand and led him out into the back garden. "There, that's what you did."

Derek stared in astonishment. The garden had been transformed. The nettles and all the other weeds had gone. Even the thick bunch of nettles under which some poor dead dog might lie, had gone. No, not gone. There they were. They had all been cut down, and now formed a substantial but neat pile, a potential compost heap, in one corner. The earth had been dug over, then thoroughly raked, and it looked clean and fresh, ready for new planting, or even a lawn. A small heap of stones and rubble sat to one side, ready for disposal.

"I did that?"

"You took half the night, but yes. You did that, you did all that."

"God."

They were still in the garden, marvelling at the vision of order, when they heard a car pull up in the front.

Sting of the Nettle

* * *

Sergeant Welbeloved breathed heavily with the effort of first getting out of the car seat and second getting safely up onto his two feet on the tarmac. It was a struggle, even with the car's running board to ease the transition.

By the time he was ready to proceed, Mary had the front door open for him. The Sergeant kept his gaze down and said nothing as he squeezed past her, and into the kitchen, where he sat heavily. There was no other way that Welbeloved could sit, of course, but on this occasion, he seemed to sit even more heavily than usual on the kitchen chair that Mary silently offered him.

At length the Sergeant spoke: "Where is he?"

"He's just coming."

More weighty silence. Then Derek came. Face rinsed. Dressing gown discarded. Basic uniform trousers and shirt pulled on. He sat down opposite the Sergeant.

"Should I?" Mary offered to leave, but the Sergeant shook his head.

"No. Sit down, girl," he said gruffly. "You better hear this as well." Then he turned to Derek. "Well, sonny. You've really done it this time, haven't you?"

"Done what?" Derek knew what. Or at least had a tattered memory of what. But he decided to fight things out to the bitter end.

"Made a damn fool of yourself, that's what. I'm sorry, son, but you were on your last warning, nothing I can do for you now."

Derek asked, perhaps a little too belligerently: "Okay,

Sting of the Nettle

exactly what am I supposed to have done?"

"Not sure where to start," said the Sergeant. "We got reports of unusual and offensive behaviour from across the county."

"But he wasn't in uniform." Mary found herself saying.

"So?"

"Well, how would anyone know it was him?"

"Oh dear, oh dear." The Sergeant heaved an ironic sigh. "And you a village girl yourself, Mary. And he's been here months."

"He was recognised?"

"Course he was, course he was. Everyone round here knows their local bobbies by sight. On top of that you've got his carrot top. Flaming beacon that is. Spot him a mile off. Let's see now." With ponderous deliberation, Welbeloved hauled his notebook out of his uniform pocket, flicked through it, found the right page, and slowly read what he clearly saw as a charge sheet.

"Farmer called Smythe, reckons you left a gate open, some of his sheep got into the bracken. He saw you. Least he saw the back of you, the back of that red hair. Someone else says someone destroyed his new electric fence. They think it was you. Nice couple on top of Yes Tor, with a little boy, remember them? 'Cos they remember you. Especially the hair. You kicked their picnic to bits."

Derek did remember them now that he'd been reminded. He winced at what was to come.

"Made some other little boy cry, apparently." Welbeloved sucked his teeth and tutted loudly. "And

Sting of the Nettle

then there was the incident of the milk lorry."

Mary shot a glance at Derek, asking: What was that? Derek shook his head. Had there been something...?

"Witness says you stopped the lorry, clearly identified yourself, and demanded a drink of milk, and when they said no you went round the back of the truck and pulled a bloody great churn off the thing. Now there's one hell of a row between the farmer and the dairy as to who has to pay, not to mention milk all over the Lewdown road."

He snapped the notebook shut. "There's other sightings too, mostly of you galloping along like a madman and shouting at people. But that's enough to be going on with, don't you think?"

Derek said nothing. Mary ventured: "Yes but there was a reason for his behaviour. This drug thing..."

Welbeloved held up a pudgy hand to stop her. "A word to the wise, young Mary. We've already heard a load of Hank Janson fiction about drugs from him. You try and drag all that into it, and it will only make things worse." He paused and blinked. "Not, mind you, that they could get any worse."

"So, I'm fired, am I?" Derek said dully.

"Technically not yet, but you will be. As of now you're suspended. Let's see, Friday today, Inspector won't be in till Monday, you present yourself at the station at eleven, bring your warrant card and all other police property in your possession, and the charges will be put to you, as the system requires. You'll get a fair hearing, put your side of the story. Then you'll be found guilty of a breach of discipline and formally dismissed from the force."

Sting of the Nettle

"Wonderful," said Mary dryly. "As long as he gets a fair hearing."

Welbeloved either failed to hear or ignored the cutting sarcasm in her voice. "Yes, he'll get a fair hearing. And his dismissal will be fair, too. Come in by your motorbike, too. Police property, that is."

"You're welcome to it," Derek said with a bitterness he couldn't hide. "Useless bloody thing, won't start half the time."

"And of course." Welbeloved looked around the kitchen. "We'll need the house. It'll be two weeks' notice."

"Two weeks!" Mary was shocked, fury showing in her eyes.

"Not starting till Monday," said the Sergeant. "Give you time, eh? We don't want to be... Well, I think that's all for now."

He pushed back his chair noisily and rose to unsteady feet. Mary and Derek remained seated. Welbeloved waited for them to move, to see him out. Derek began to rise, but Mary put a hand on his arm to stop him.

Welbeloved waited just a fraction too long, then said: "Right, I'll see myself out." He turned to go, then, as if the painful moment was too much for even him, he turned back and laid a hand briefly on Derek's shoulder.

"Sorry it's come to this, lad." He said gruffly. "I always liked you, you know. So did the Inspector, we both had high hopes for you. Best of the lot, he used to say. Still, can't be helped."

Mary waited until the sound of the Sergeant's car had faded up the road before speaking.

Sting of the Nettle

Then she squeezed Derek's hand with desperate encouragement. "Could have been worse."

Derek looked at her sideways, the faintest smile on his lips.

"Oh, all right," she went on. "It couldn't have been worse." She sighed. "I'm going to miss this little house."

"Specially now I've done the garden."

Despite everything Mary giggled, a sound that merged into a sob. "Oh Derek, what are we going to do?"

"What's the time?

"Oh, just after five. Why?"

"And what time does the pub open?"

"Seven. We'll have to wait."

"Right. That's what we're going to do now. Wait."

CHAPTER TWENTY-SEVEN

The short walk to the pub had been tense.

"I don't want to leave here," Mary had said, as she closed the front door with a gentle, reluctant click, almost as if she was leaving home for the last time. "This is where I live. Not so much this house, but this village."

"Well, we've got to leave, haven't we? Can't afford to buy anything, there might be somewhere to rent but anyway, I'm going to need a job. And there's nothing round here."

"Couldn't you, I don't know, get a driving job? One of the cattle lorries?"

"Me? A lorry driver? You really think so? That's a great new career for me, is it?"

"But if you hadn't started this whole thing. I told you to be careful, didn't I! Why couldn't you just let it go? Why did you have to get so obsessed with Tom Williamson? And please, don't tell me about your rotten niggle."

"I won't. Ever again, you can be sure of that. I promise I will never say the word niggle, ever again."

"Well thank you for that. If for nothing else."

A few paces in cold silence, and then Derek said with some bitterness: "Actually I'll be glad to get shot of this place. Scruffy little village, full of country bumpkins."

"I'm one of your country bumpkins, may I remind you. Me, my family, we're all country bumpkins, thank

Sting of the Nettle

you very much. Mr Townie."

"I didn't mean... Oh bugger." Derek took a deep breath. "I'm sorry. I'm just... I don't know. You must admit, being a village policeman, out here, well there's not much to do, is there? I don't think I've had a single decent case to investigate in the two years I've been here. I suppose that's why I got in over my head in this Williamson thing."

They were nearly at the Dragon by now, and Mary brought them to a halt. "Have you ever wondered why things are so quiet around here? Why there's nothing much for you to do?"

"Because everyone's half dead?" He tried to make it a joke, but she didn't laugh.

"No. It's because you are quite good at this. You don't throw your weight around, you don't have people up on little things, you keep an eye on them, you say the right things, you stop things before they start. These people, they respect you around here. You're bored because you're good at what you do. Things are quiet because you keep them that way."

"Funny." Derek thought for a moment. "Old Welbeloved said something like that once."

"Well. Even old Welbeloved must get it right sometimes."

They had reached the pub. "You ready for this?" Mary asked him. "It might be a bit rough."

"You think they'll know?"

"This is a village."

Friday night was a big night at the Green Dragon. Some of the regulars even brought their wives. The place

Sting of the Nettle

was always full, even heaving. There was the usual cheerful noise, laughter, banter, coming from behind the pub door. Derek took a deep breath, grabbed Mary's hand, and together they walked in. Into the sudden deafening silence.

And then a single voice: "Aye-aye! Here he is!"

And with that came a babble of shouted remarks, accompanied by vague cheers and clapping. Derek heard "Poor old Sherlock, come a cropper!" and "Who's the laughing policeman then" and for a moment he thought he was being abused. And then he realised the noise, the hubbub, wasn't hostile, it was full-on teasing. And, amazingly, support.

He heard "We're with you, Derek!" and "You're not going anywhere!" and "Give the poor bugger a drink!" And then he was being hustled and backslapped to the bar, where a smiling John was waving a clipboard at him.

"We're getting up a petition, Derek," he shouted over the hubbub. "Get you to keep your job. We're calling it You Can't Sack Our Copper."

Derek looked round for Mary, saw that she was already the centre of a group of wives, all of whom seemed to be talking at once. Someone put a pint of beer in his hand, and he drank quickly, trying to supress a sudden ache in his throat and a stinging in his eyes. Must be the smoke, he told himself.

A face he didn't know pushed through the jostling crowd.

"Constable, my name's Smythe. I don't think we've met."

Sting of the Nettle

Smythe. With a gulp, Derek remembered. The farmer, the one who'd seen him when he'd left a gate open and...

"Oh Lord. Your sheep. I'm so sorry."

"So you should be." The man was smiling, which was odd. "I tell you; I was bloody mad at first. Got on the phone. Then my daughter, she told me about you, when she knocked you off your motorbike."

Derek thought back. Yes, he remembered. It had been dusk and this girl had failed to stop at a junction. He had heard her coming, and stopped the bike, but her car had caught his back wheel and dumped him in the road on his bottom. No harm done. And she'd been a pretty girl.

"I remember," he said. "She'd just passed her test."

"That's right," said Smythe. "You told her everyone's entitled to one mistake. I reckon the same applies to you. Landlord, put him in a pint." And the man shook his hand and left him.

Derek turned back to John. "How did you hear about it so quick?" he asked.

"Your sergeant, Welbeloved. He called in for an after-hours drink this afternoon. He does that, you know. Known for it. Anyway, bit of a blabbermouth, isn't he. Told me they were going to give you the elbow. Course, ten minutes later it was all round the village."

"Was it?" Derek asked ironically. "Thanks to you, I imagine."

"Well." John grinned guiltily. "We don't want to lose you, mate."

A little later, and after a lot more teasing comments

Sting of the Nettle

and assurances of friendship from people he knew and others who seemed to know him, Derek found a corner to talk to Mary.

"Bit overwhelming, this, isn't it."

"Yes." She said archly. "And from all these country bumpkins."

"All right, I'm sorry. I just never realised. Have you seen they're getting up a petition?"

"I've signed it!"

"It won't work you know. Petitions never do. It won't do any good."

"I think it's done you a lot of good already."

A young man in his best suit leaned over them.

"You playing, Derek?"

Derek looked across the bar. A darts match was getting under way.

"Yes, count him in," Mary told him, as Derek hesitated.

He took a long swallow of beer. "Okay," he said. "I'm a convert. Not such a bad place, North Tawe, is it."

"So. What are we going to do?"

"Lord knows. "He grinned and shrugged with mock hopelessness, and it made her laugh.

"But I'll tell you this," he said, growing serious. "I know, I know in my guts, that there's something going on with Bucky and Fergus and the rest of it. Not sure what, but something. I've got two days before they sack me. Two days to sort it out. And I'm bloody well going to try. After what Fergus did to me, I've got to. Listen, do something for me. Have a quick chat with John. Find out about Sandy, how she is, and when he thinks she'll be off out again, going wherever it is she goes. Can you do that?"

"Oh dear." Mary didn't know whether to sound pleased or anxious. "You're your old self again, aren't you. And it's that niggle, isn't it."

A call from the dart board: "Derek, you're up!"

Derek got up. "I promised you I would never say the word Niggle again."

She grinned. "You just did."

CHAPTER TWENTY-EIGHT

Next morning he called a Council of War. He didn't call it that to anyone else, only to himself. The Colonel arrived in his Landrover, accompanied by a highly excitable Sally, who proceeded to christen the pristine back-garden as only a dog can. The Colonel himself, looking bright-eyed and brisk, confirmed that Sally had been exonerated of the charge of sheep worrying, after another dog of similar appearance had been shot in the very act of driving some sheep into a river. Mary fell in love with Sally at first sight and registered an early claim on any pups. John strolled over from the pub, and finally the four of them sat around the kitchen table.

They made a slow start. Derek looked at each of them in turn, and they all looked expectantly back at him. Derek got as far as opening his mouth to speak, but nothing came out.

"Say something man." The Colonel's voice had an almost military rasp to it.

"Spit it out, mate." That was John.

"It's all right, we won't laugh," Mary urged him.

"I don't think you'll laugh. You might think I'm a bit touched."

"I'm the one who's a bit touched around here," said the Colonel with a grin. "But not today. If this is a call to action, then believe me, I'm ready for anything."

Derek grinned back. "Good. Well. Here goes. There's

something I want to do, and I need your help. Or at least, I need you as witnesses. I think you all know some of it already, but I think I better start at the beginning. And that's with the farmer, Tom Williamson."

"Shot himself in his orchard, right? I remember, they rang the pub that day, and I came round and told you." John put in.

"Yes," said the Colonel. "And the coroner brought in a verdict that could only be described as unsatisfactory."

"That's what got me started," Derek told them. "It was clear as day the old boy had shot himself. The evidence was there, and he'd even put all his affairs in order before he did the deed. And I was interested in finding out why. I just felt that, if someone like that decides to end his life, we should know the reason. Right?"

"It's usually depression," the Colonel said. "I should know. And it's not easy to explain."

"That's what I thought," Derek said. "But then I just made a couple of casual enquiries and out of the blue I got warned off. Twice. First by that lout Bucky."

"Him!" said John contemptuously.

"And second by Fergus, son of Sir Arthur Bulstock, squire of this parish."

"Quite the other end of the social scale from your lad Bucky," Mary commented.

"And then we got that brick through the window."

"Disgrace, that was," said John. "I mean, in this village."

Derek continued: "I couldn't think of anyone I'd annoyed sufficiently to be that stroppy, except either Bucky or Fergus. I assumed it was because I ignored their advice."

"And that's when he really got his niggle," said Mary, with a grin.

"His what?" the Colonel queried.

"His niggle." She explained. "It's what he calls it when he suspects something, or wants to sort out something, it's a feeling in what passes for his brain, and it means he won't stop, come hell or high water. Which is why we're here, sitting in my kitchen on a fine Saturday morning. It's his niggle. He's weird, you know. He's a ginger, of course, and they're all a bit strange."

She grinned at Derek and ruffled his hair. He grinned back. "Well thanks very much. For that you can make the coffee."

Then, to the sounds of clinking cups and a boiling kettle, he went on: "I thought I better have a bit of a chat with the widow, with Mrs Williamson. She wasn't too keen to talk at first, but her son Peter helped, and eventually we got on well."

"Nice family," John commented. "Shame about the daughter. Margaret, was it?"

"The one who ran off to London?" Mary asked, pouring water on the black Camp liquid. "She was always a bit, well, flighty."

"What they told me," Derek continued, "was that Williamson had changed over the past couple of years. Once he'd been a normal pleasant man, and then, quite out of the blue, he started behaving oddly. Shouting, raving, full of manic energy. They got quite scared of him sometimes. It didn't get out generally. He wasn't a particularly social man."

Sting of the Nettle

"Never saw him in the pub," John put in.

"So, no-one outside the family noticed, or if they did, they thought nothing of it. And then, a few weeks ago, he suddenly calmed down, became more like his old self, very quiet though, and then that morning, he topped himself. Mrs. W. said it was a surprise, but somehow not a shock. Not really sure what she meant by that but..."

"And then she told you about the German prisoners," Mary interrupted.

"What German prisoners?" John asked.

"Williamson had a couple of POWs working on the farm," Derek explained. "Several local farmers used them. After VE day, of course. Apparently, he got pretty thick with one of them. Anyway, long story short, I tracked down the other one, who decided to stay in England, and he told me about Pervitin."

"What the hell's Pervitin?" John asked.

"A German drug," the Colonel told him. "They gave it to their troops. Gave them courage and endurance. Drove them crackers too."

Mary put steaming coffee cups on the table, together with the milk bottle and the sugar bowl. "We think," she said, "that Fergus doped Derek with some of it, day before yesterday."

"Which accounts for you going do-lally," said John almost triumphantly. "We were wondering what got into you!"

"It did. Anyway, it seems reasonable to assume that Tom Williamson had started using the stuff.".

"Which accounts for his behaviour," the Colonel added.

"But it still doesn't explain why he killed himself," Derek finished.

There was a moment's thoughtful silence. Then, "Oh God!" John exploded. "That Fergus. My Sandy's been riding around the country with that bastard. We know that, from the other day. What if he gives it to her? Bloody hell, she's been acting weird. Derek! We've got to stop it."

"That's why we're here," Derek told him. "I couldn't care less about him and Bucky. They can drug themselves silly. But if they're involving a juvenile..."

"So," the Colonel said, with a military tone once again in his voice. "What do we do? Plan of action! That's what we need."

"Okay. I think I've got one". Derek sipped his coffee. The other three waited. The drink was too hot, and he sucked in air to cool it.

"Well out with it, Sherlock!" Mary told him.

"All right, sorry for the dramatic pause. It's the actor in me." He turned to the Colonel. "How well do you know Sir Arthur, Colonel?"

"Served with him. Nowhere special. Aldershot mostly. But I can tell you, he's a good man. Bit pompous, likes to play Lord of the Manor. But he's pretty sound. And I'll say this – he knows he's got a problem with Fergus. Kid's his son and heir, but Arthur says he gets more difficult to handle every day."

"Well, would you go over there this evening? Just call in for a social chat. Let's face it, you're the only one of us who can do that. And assuming Fergus isn't around, see what the boy's been up to lately. Where he goes,

Sting of the Nettle

who he sees, that sort of thing."

"Is that all?" The Colonel was disappointed. "Okay, if I must. We don't want you, you know, falling off your motorbike again. Do we?"

Derek looked at the Colonel. There was a knowing look his face. Derek looked at his wife, at his friend John. Both had the same expressions.

Mary reached across the table and gave him a friendly punch on the arm. "We're not thick, you know," she said. "You just didn't say anything, so we didn't."

Derek swallowed. He could think of nothing to say. He cleared his throat, feeling himself flushing.

"To continue," he said with an effort, "John thinks that Sandy may be meeting either Bucky or Fergus tonight. I can't think they'll go to the manor house. So John and me will check out Bucky's place."

"I'll kill the bastard. I'll kill both of them if they've laid a finger on Sandy." John's fists were clenched on the table in front of him.

"And I'll be there to arrest you when you do, John," Derek said soothingly. "Okay, can I suggest the three of us meet at the pub at about seven. You got someone to cover for you, John?"

"Yes. My usual chap. And the nurses are coming for Lucy. No problem there."

"Fine. The pub at seven, then we'll go from there."

"Excuse me!" Mary's voice had an edge that surprised the men. "Haven't you forgotten something? Or rather, someone?"

The other two men looked at Derek, then at Mary. Derek said: "No, look, darling, sorry, but you can't be

Sting of the Nettle

involved in this. Bucky and his sort, they could get violent. No, sorry, but really. I've got to say no. You can't come."

Mary smiled sweetly at the other two men. "Doesn't it strike you as strange, I can know a man for five years, be married to him more than two, and yet discover that after all this time, all this togetherness, he still doesn't know a thing about me?"

* * *

"Why are we going this way?" Mary asked, as she steered her car through the narrow lane. "It's not the way to Bucky's place. That's off the Hatherleigh road, surely. And we're heading south."

They were using Mary's car, John's being off the road with mechanical problems of which he had given Derek a full description, and of which Derek had failed to understand a single word. The Colonel had sailed off in his splendid new Land-Rover, promising to do his diplomatic best to find out what Fergus was up to.

"Take the left up here," Derek instructed, and they turned into an even more constricted lane edged by high banks full of foxgloves, and with a strip of grass flourishing down the centre. "Now. This is the road Fergus was using, only coming the other way, when he nearly hit us, remember? Back at that last turning."

"All right, but still..."

"I looked it up on the Ordnance Survey. A couple of miles on there's a turning off to the right, just a field track, but from the look of it, it leads up towards the back of

Sting of the Nettle

Bucky's property. If you ask me, Fergus uses it so no-one notices he goes there. Especially if he's got some girl like Sandy in the car."

"The bastard," John muttered from the back seat. "I'll kill him."

"If it was my daughter, I'd do the same," Derek assured him.

"You haven't got a daughter," Mary said.

"Not yet."

They exchanged glances, and Mary nearly steered into the bank.

"You're sure she met up with him tonight, John?" Derek asked.

"Sure as I can be. She always says the same thing. She's going out for a walk, to clear her head. I've tried following her in the past, but it's difficult to leave the pub, and she gives me the slip. But there's always been his car hanging about, or so people tell me. But I'll catch up with him, don't you worry. And when I do, I've got something for him."

Derek caught a glimpse of a gesture out of the corner of his eye, and he turned in his seat.

"Oh Lord... John, whatever have you got there?"

"Bit of lead piping."

"For God's sake, that's an offensive weapon. And I'm a policeman. Well. I am until Monday. Chuck it out the window."

"But Derek..."

"Chuck it! For Chrissake, I'm still on duty. Look. Full uniform. Helmet and all. We've got to stay legal."

Derek heard John give a loud sigh, and then he felt

the draught as the back window was wound down. There was a reassuring clang of something metallic hitting asphalt. He looked ahead through the soft light of a late summer evening, as they drove on for another five minutes. Then he saw what he was looking for.

"That must be the track I was talking about," he told Mary. "Pull in, just go up fifty yards or so. We'll leg it from here."

The air was cool, now, and Derek was glad he'd worn a sweater under his uniform jacket. He grabbed his helmet, which had been sitting between Mary's feet, and stuck it on his head. Mary had sometimes teased him about the helmet, calling him the Mekon, after the Eagle comic's dome-headed baddie. But he'd witnessed demonstrations of how the thing could endure heavy blows from a truncheon, and, as he told her, he chose safety before beauty.

"Mary," he now told her, "You stay in the car, John and me will take it from here."

"Shut your face!" Mary used an expression she'd picked up from Form 5b. "I'm coming. And don't you 'little woman' me again tonight, or you'll regret it."

Derek looked to John for support but got none. John clearly liked and admired Mary, and he just grinned and shrugged. Derek conceded.

"Right. If you must. Come on then."

The three of them began walking, slowly and quietly, up what proved to be a surprisingly wide track. Derek guessed that once it had been in regular use, possibly by cattle drovers, in the days long before muddy lorries took over. But now the track's old broken-down gates, the

Sting of the Nettle

overgrown verges, the thick encroaching brambles, had turned it into a relic of the past.

He wondered why such a one-time thoroughfare had been left to moulder. Surely a modern farmer could use it, and probably had once upon a time. But no longer. Why? A change in agriculture usage, perhaps. Or the collapse of some tyro farmer's project? Or maybe, and more likely, someone had put in a new and more appropriate access? Whatever the reason, the result was a track that in bright sunshine might have made for a pleasant Sunday morning stroll. But now, in the light of the lowering sun, felt just a little creepy, just a little threatening.

"We could have brought the car up here," Mary commented. "But I'm glad we didn't. Look at these ruts."

"Someone did," he told her. "Some of these tracks are fresh." He thought for a moment, remembering his previous visit to Bucky, remembering the glimpse he had of the white sports car, parked at the far end of the property, beyond the chaotic landscape, half hidden in trees. "Could be Fergus," he said.

"Fergus!" Mary snorted with contempt. "What sort of idiot brings a flash car like his up a place like this?"

"The Fergus sort," said John dryly. "Upper class twit sort. I mean, have you seen the state of that motor of his? Bloody disgrace."

"A present from Daddy, I expect." Mary put in. "You wouldn't treat a car like that if you had to pay for it yourself."

They had walked on for perhaps a quarter of a mile, when John stopped suddenly, and raised a warning hand.

"Listen!"

They listened. Yes, there it was. Music. Something modern, jazzy, Derek thought. Some twenty yards further they stopped again. The music was louder.

In the quiet country the sound carried clearly. It meant people. Bucky? Fergus? He would soon know.

He turned to the other two: "Okay. Here's what's going to happen now. I'm going ahead, to have a first look. You two are going to wait here."

They both started to protest at once, but he stopped them

"No. For God's sake, this is not a sodding democracy!" He felt rather than saw Mary flinch at the adjective, but he didn't care. "I'm the policeman here. I'm the authority. I may need you as witnesses later but you're not official. By all rights you shouldn't even be here. You'll do as I say. I repeat. You two stay here. If I'm not back in 30 minutes, then..."

He hesitated. Mary asked: "Then what?"

"Then..." He didn't know. Shit! He knew he should have thought this out beforehand. "But I will be back. What's the worst that can happen? I'll just have to issue a warning, most likely. And assuming Sandy's with them, I'll bring her back. So, again, listen. You two stay here!"

He was whispering, but Derek tried to give his last words the penetration and command of a sergeant major's parade ground bellow This time there was no reply, just slightly resentful silent acceptance from both of them.

He turned and started walking as quietly as he could

Sting of the Nettle

towards the sound of the music. He soon came to where the track ended with a rough and partly destroyed wire fence, that seemed to mark the limit of Bucky's domain.

He remembered how he'd had a glimpse of the area when he had called using the frontal approach to the cottage. He'd seen a semi-wilderness of discarded junk, broken-down motors, hummocks, ditches and nettles, that now lay between him and the house. And now there was Fergus's car, where he had seen it before, parked carelessly at an angle, its passenger door hanging open, and its scarred bodywork shining palely in the dusk.

He moved on towards the building, carefully avoiding obstacles when he could, on one occasion barking his shin against an abandoned mangle. The music grew ever louder. He recognised it as one of his personal favourites, Stan Kenton and his jazz orchestra. As he listened the tune came to a stop, there was a short pause, and another began. It was Kenton's big hit, The Peanut Vendor, a record Mary had promised to buy him, if and when they could afford a record player. Now he resented hearing it coming from Bucky's place. It was somehow demeaning that he should share a taste for music or anything else with the lout.

Walking more carefully than ever, treading on the sides of his feet in the way he had been instructed in his school's cadet corps training, he reached a corner of the building, where he stopped to consider his options. The music blared on, and with it he could sometimes catch other sounds, voices. But nothing that made any sense.

The only entrance to the cottage, he remembered from his previous visit, was at the side of the building, a

Sting of the Nettle

stable-type door leading into what might be a kitchen. The top half of the door was wide open, swinging in the slight evening breeze. There was no light in the kitchen, which was unoccupied. Nothing to see there.

He reversed his steps, and now crept carefully along the side of the building. There seemed to be two main windows, one covered by what looked like an old blanket, the other with half a yellow curtain hanging loosely, and it was clear from the music and the light that whatever was going on in the cottage was happening behind those windows.

Keeping against the wall, side-stepping through what might once have been a strip of kitchen garden, but was now an overgrown miniature jungle, and still moving as quietly as he could, though with the music blaring there was little chance that anyone would hear him. He reached the first window with its single curtain and edged carefully forward.

For a long, long moment he stared through the glass at the room with its meagre and broken furniture, and the people in it, and what they were doing. Then he ducked back and down into a crouch, and shut his eyes, almost as if to blank out the scene he had just witnessed.

Much later, days later when he came to write a report on the happenings of that night, he would still find it hard to form proper clear sentences, and would resort to clinical, almost medical language. But in his memory, there remained the raw image. There was Sandy. She was almost naked, just a thin blouse hung loosely around her shoulders. She was on her hands and knees, on top of a low wooden table. Her face was flushed and twisted into a grimace. Behind her, Bucky was fully clothed, but his trousers were around his ankles. And he was thrusting himself against the girl, almost pushing her off the table. Standing to one side was Fergus, fully clothed, but grinning at the couple and clapping his hands to Buck's obscene rhythm.

Derek tore his eyes away from the scene, and ducked down, out of sight of anyone in the room. He felt shocked, quite shaken. And yet, he told himself, he wasn't surprised. Ever since he had made the connection between Fergus, Bucky and Sandy he had half expected something of the same.

So what did he do now? Strictly speaking nothing illegal was happening. Sandy was sixteen. The age of consent. He couldn't charge Bucky or Fergus with that offence. And if this frightful drug Pervitin was involved, which seemed likely, well, according to the Colonel the stuff probably wasn't even illegal.

But there had to be something, surely to God. Something he could get the two men on.

One thing was certain. He couldn't allow John to witness what he had just seen. Sandy might not be in any danger, she might even be consenting, be a willing partner. But whatever the truth of it, her father must not see her. Not like this. To see one's much-loved daughter so abused, so corrupted, so blatantly, shamefully degraded. No father should ever see that. So he had to stop John seeing it. If he did, he'd be shattered, destroyed by the sight. What's more, Derek was afraid that even now, back in the lane, his friend would soon lose his patience, he'd ignore Derek's orders, and, fearing justly

Sting of the Nettle

for his daughter's safety, he'd come charging up, he'd stare through the window, and he'd go berserk. Someone might get hurt. Someone. Anyone.

He had to stop John. He was afraid that his friend would soon lose his patience, he'd ignore Derek's orders, and, fearing justly for his daughter's safety, he'd come charging up, he'd stare through the window, and he'd go berserk. Someone might get hurt. Someone. Anyone.

Derek retreated, forgetting any fear of being overheard, and running around the cottage and hurrying as best he could across the waste ground, and finally back into the lane, past Fergus's car and on down to where he had left Mary and John.

Mary was alone. Derek slid to a stop beside her, panting. But after swallowing hard a couple of times, he was able to gasp the question: "Where is he?"

"Don't panic," Mary told him. "He's just gone for a pee."

"Thank Christ. Now listen. I want you to do something."

"What's the matter? Is it Sandy?"

"Shut up and listen. Before he comes back. Sorry but... Do this." He took a deep breath, trying to get the words right. "Tell John I need something from the car. I don't know, a torch! Yes, I need a torch."

"What do you want a torch for? It's not dark. Nowhere near."

"Look, don't argue, tell him I want a torch from the car."

"We haven't got a torch in the car."

Sting of the Nettle

"Doesn't matter. Just pretend. And take him with you to find it."

"And what if he won't come? You know John, he'll want to join you, he just said he was going to, he won't want to mess around with me."

"Tell him you're scared to go on your own."

He half expected her to argue that she wasn't scared, of course she wasn't, but bless her, she didn't. Instead after a moment of thought, she just nodded.

"Good girl," he said, realising as he said it how patronising the phrase sounded, but again she made no protest, when normally she would have bitten his head off for it. "Just keep him away," he said. "Long as you can."

She looked up at him, her face suddenly drawn. "Oh God! Is it Sandy? It is, isn't it! Is she dead or something?"

"No but please. Just keep him away. I'll try and sort it out."

John stumbled into view, buttoning up his fly. "What's happening, Derek?"

"Nothing much." Derek kept his voice as steady as he could. "Listen though. Got a job for you. Mary will tell you. See you in a bit." And he turned, and walked quickly back up the track. After a few yards he looked back. John and Mary were still there, but he could see her pointing, evidently insisting, and John was turning reluctantly in the right direction. He was sure that soon the landlord would lose patience and insist on coming to the cottage, but he hoped he had bought enough time to get things in that awful room looking at least acceptable. And that John would see his daughter in

259

Sting of the Nettle

circumstances that might be dubious but would not be a sordid vision of the girl's degradation.

When he reached the cottage and peered again through the window, the scene was already less shocking. Sandy was now sitting on a dilapidated couch, a coat around her shoulders but otherwise still naked. Bucky had a bottle in one hand – whisky, at first glance – and was offering it to Sandy. As Derek watched she took a drink from the open bottle. She seemed stunned perhaps a little droopy, but otherwise okay. Drugged? he wondered. Pervitin?

Or just drink?

He looked for Fergus. No sign of him.

Well, Derek told himself, it was time to do something, to get the girl dressed for a start, to make her presentable for her father to take home. Then he could begin the business of questioning Bucky and Fergus, warning them of possible prosecution, arresting them for something or other. He wondered vaguely as he walked round to the kitchen door whether what he might achieve this night would save his job, or perhaps even make things worse. The latter, probably. After all, he was hardly following correct procedure. Far from it. But sod it. He'd come this far.

He un-latched the lower half of the kitchen door, and stepped inside, leaving it open. Again, this was hardly normal police procedure. By rights he should have knocked and ask to be admitted. But, he reasoned, he had grounds for suspecting a crime was being committed. Corruption of a minor. That might do it. Okay. In he went.

Sting of the Nettle

The first thing he noticed in the empty room was a double-barrelled shot gun, lying on the kitchen table. He picked it up and snapped it open. Two twelve-bore cartridges automatically half-ejected from the weapon. He held it open and shook it, and the cartridges fell to the floor, their metal parts rattling faintly on the bare boards. Typical Bucky, he thought. No sensible gun owner left a shotgun lying around fully loaded. He closed the now harmless weapon and placed it back on the table.

Right. Time to get on with it. He reached for the knob on the door that led to the main room.

Something exploded on the back and side of his head, and he fell face down onto the sticky surface of Bucky's kitchen floor.

CHAPTER TWENTY-NINE

There are various states of being knocked unconscious. The most significant and final of these is death, involving the crushing of the skull, the trauma of the brain, and the final and definitive answer to the question "Is there an after-life?"

The force of the blow Derek sustained, delivered, as he would eventually find out, by a starting handle from an ancient Fordson tractor, could well have resulted in that end. But the standard police helmet while far from being a fashion statement, did have its uses.

The one on Derek's head absorbed some portion of the impact, thanks to its surprisingly simple construction of cork. He also benefited from the fact that Fergus, who delivered the blow, was by that stage of the evening not functioning at optimum level, physically - or mentally, come to that – and his aim was askew. Thus, Derek narrowly avoided the fatal version of unconsciousness, and instead experienced a version by which he first felt as if an electric shock had run down his spine, and almost immediately after sank into a hazy and painful otherworld where nothing made any sense whatsoever – a state that continued for at least fifteen minutes.

The first of his senses to return was his hearing.

"Christ this is bad!" he heard. He recognised the voice chiefly by its accent. Bucky. Sounding scared.

Sting of the Nettle

"He had it coming." He knew that voice by its accent too. Plum-in-the-mouth Fergus.

"Yeh but hitting him with that. Could have killed him."

"Jumped up little shit, puts a uniform on and thinks he can lecture me," Fergus's voice continued. And then in a silly lecturing voice: "You're old enough to know better. Any relations with her would be highly immoral." And then in his normal voice: "Hear that, Sweetie-pie. Our relationship is highly immoral. Fun though, wouldn't you say?"

If the girl said something, Derek didn't hear it. Instead, it was Bucky's voice again.

"All the same, you didn't have to bloody hit him. Christ, there may be more of them out there. You can't go round hitting policemen, they..." there was a catch, almost a sob, in Bucky's voice, "they don't like it."

"When they meet someone like me, they better get used to it. Ha ha."

"But what are we going to do with him now? You can't smack a copper and just..."

"We'll ditch the dear boy. Properly. Like we did before, with Shaggy Maggie. That'll sort it. As you Devonian peasants say – proper job!"

A savage pain wracked Derek's head, and he opened his eyes. He found that he was sitting on the floor in the cottage main room. His back was against something hard and ridged, probably a chair. His wrists had been fastened behind his head with something he couldn't identify. His ankles were also bound together. He opened his eyes.

Sting of the Nettle

Fergus was standing over him, smiling, holding the shotgun he had seen in the kitchen. Behind Fergus, Bucky was striding from one side of the room to the other, and back again. Derek looked for the girl, for Sandy, but couldn't see her. Then he did. She was still on the couch, sitting hunched over, her head bowed. Her blouse had disappeared, and she was quite naked

The orgy might have stopped but was not necessarily complete. He guessed that, whether or not she'd been a willing participant, Sandy seemed reluctant to witness what was going on now. His head throbbed. He wanted to be sick, but he was equally afraid that, with his head forced back by his arms, if he did vomit, he would choke. He swallowed furiously. The pain in his head came in waves.

"Well, well, sleeping beauty awakes."

Derek felt the hard cold end of the shotgun barrel push up under his chin. The smell was of stale smoke. An uncleaned weapon. Not that it would make much difference.

"Good evening, Mr Redhead. Soon - ha ha - to be Mr Deadhead. Back to life, are we? Well enjoy it while it lasts. Which won't be for long." Fergus now knelt on one knee in front of him, looking up at him, smiling.

Derek tried to say something, but his mouth was dry, his throat felt tight, and no words would come He just groaned.

"You can't just kill him." Bucky came to join Fergus, gazing down at Derek, his face working.

"We can you know. Course we can. And we will. Don't worry, I'll do it. It'll be like shooting a dog. Piece

Sting of the Nettle

of cake."

"Shooting a dog." The phrase echoed in Derek's fuzzy brain. It wasn't a piece of cake. At least not for him. Not with the Colonel's Sally. But maybe for Fergus.

"But you just can't shoot a copper," Bucky insisted. "They top you twice over for that. And what about the body, what are we going to do with that?"

"Same place as the other one. Bit of spade work for you, Bucky."

"What about the others?"

"What others?"

"Other police. They could be all around us now."

"What, for him? Never. Didn't you hear? Everybody else heard. He's being kicked out of the police. They don't want to know him, not after I slipped him the stuff, and he made a damn fool of himself across half the county. Good move that, eh? That reminds me, we're running short. Better send Horst some cash." He straightened up. "Well, let's get on with it."

Derek found he could speak. Just. "Do a deal," he croaked.

"You're a dead man, sonny-boy. I don't do deals with dead men."

"Let me go. With the girl. And I'll say nothing. Not even about the Williamson girl. And even if I did, police, they wouldn't listen. You said yourself."

"Ah, but they might, dear boy. They might." Fergus sounded like a drunken Noel Coward, his vowels and tone a caricature of affected upper-class speech. "And we can't take that chance, can we? Now then."

He looked around the room, calculating. "Better not

do it in here. Not that you'd notice any more mess in here, would you! But all the same, we'll make it an outdoor job. Get him on his feet, would you, Bucky my lad. I'll just check outside, make quite sure none of his fellow fuzz are mucking up the place."

Derek heard the door open to the kitchen. Bucky bent over Derek from behind and began lifting him up.

"For God's sake, Bucky," Derek hissed. "Stop him! It's murder."

"Shut your row!" Bucky told him, but there was a hesitancy in his voice.

"Shooting a copper!" Derek tried again. "They hang you for it, every time."

"I can't stop him. He's high."

"The drug?"

"When he's on it, nothing stops him."

"Undo my ankles." Derek urged.

Bucky shook his shaggy head. "No way. Anyway, they won't hang me, not if he does the shooting."

"Oh yes, they will. They hanged that boy Bentley, remember? He didn't shoot anyone, but they hanged him all the same."

Derek was on his feet now, but his ankles were still fastened by what he now saw to be some kind of thick adhesive tape. Bucky began to push him and together they shuffled towards the door. "Nobody will know we done it," he muttered.

"Everybody will know, Bucky. People know I was coming here. Look, think. That Pervitin stuff, it makes you feel you can get away with anything. I know that., It made me feel like that. But you can't. They'll get you."

Sting of the Nettle

"Shut up." Another push.

Derek felt his stomach lurch. Abruptly realisation came. They were going to do it. They were going to stick a shotgun in his face and pull the trigger. The fear – the same fear he had felt back on the road during the midnight attack – gripped him again, only this time he couldn't run away from the danger.

Then he remembered something. A ray of hope. A question. One he hardly dared to ask himself. It didn't matter, he'd know the answer very soon. Perhaps too soon. Until then, he told himself, until that question was answered, keep talking. He forced himself to sound more reasonable, less desperate, pushing the fear away as he did so.

"Think about it, Bucky. Hanging! Execution! They'll do it at Exeter. They haven't done one there for a while, not since the war, but they still got all the kit. I've seen it. The rope, the trap door. That nice Mr Pierrepoint will be along one cold morning. He's very quick they say. One moment you're standing there, on the trap, the next..."

"I said shut up!" Bucky's voice broke hoarsely.

Fergus looked in from the kitchen. The shotgun was still in his hand. "All clear. As I expected. Come on, let's get him out then."

Together they manhandled Derek through the kitchen, Derek hobbling with his linked ankles, out into the evening air. It was almost sunset now, but still warm and clear. He looked desperately for any sign of John or Mary, but all was quite still, no movement anywhere. So, no rescue. Just as well, he thought bitterly. He sensed

Sting of the Nettle

that once he started, Fergus would shoot anyone who got in his way. Even Mary.

"All right. This'll do," Fergus ordered. Derek found himself standing unsteadily on what seemed to be a surface of uneven and broken brick. Probably the remains of some kind of terrace. Wildly, illogically, he wondered whether the brick that smashed his window came from here. Yes, he thought. It probably did. Bucky turned him round to face Fergus.

"Right. I'm not fucking around." Fergus's voice sounded clear, hard, and in his classy cut glass accent, even more threatening. "Get on the floor."

Derek stared back at him, and didn't move.

"Bucky! Kick him!"

Bucky kicked, and Derek crashed to the ground, his head hitting the brickwork with a sickening thud. He squirmed, wriggled, trying desperately to at least get to his knees, gasping with the effort, but failing. He squinted up at Fergus. The man stood over him, the shotgun held loosely in his hands.

"Get out of the way, Bucky boy. Unless you want some of this too."

Derek sensed rather than saw Bucky stumbling to one side. Fergus put the shotgun to his shoulder, pointing the thing until Derek, twisting his head to one side, could see down deep into the twin barrels.

"No last words from the condemned man?" he managed to say, as if to convince all three of them that this was all a joke. And there was still the question.

"Fuck off." Fergus closed one eye and aimed

The question? Now he would know the answer.

CHAPTER THIRTY

"What the hell does he want a bloody torch for?"

The fact that he used ripe language not only when a lady was present but directly at that lady was an indication of how desperate John the landlord was growing.

"Don't ask me. He just said..." Mary managed.

Both of them were out of breath, with John the landlord leading the way as they rushed back up the track towards Bucky's place.

"I mean, sorry." John remembered his manners. "But what the heck is he up to?"

"I don't know, do I?"

"You're married to him. He's your husband."

"Thank you for reminding me, I'd quite forgotten."

They pushed on for several more stumbling yards, until they reached the spot where Derek had left them.

"So, what did he say to you, when he came back. Not that nonsense about needing a torch. What else? I know there must have been something."

Mary looked at him, saw in the dusky light the agony of a suffering father in his strained face.

"Look," she began, but he over-rode her.

"It's Sandy, right? He's found her, and she's in trouble. Don't say I'm wrong. I'm going after him."

Mary grasped his arm. "No. Please John."

John turned to pull himself free, then stopped, staring

back the way they had come. Mary turned with him, and saw it too.

Lights. Bright lights of an on-coming vehicle.

"Who the hell is that?" John demanded, forgetting his linguistic manners again.

Mary sighed. "I think it's the cavalry."

* * *

Click! Loud and clear and metallic. Click again. And Derek had the answer to his question. It was no.

"Shit!' Fergus turned on Bucky. "I thought I told you to load the thing."

"I did. I loaded it. Both barrels."

"No. You forgot. You stupid thick peasant."

"But I did!" Bucky wailed. "I did, I put the cartridges in, and then I put the gun on the kitchen table. Honest, I did!"

There was something in the man's voice that changed Fergus's mind. "Did you now? In that case, someone took them out."

Derek managed to roll over onto his back and looked up to see both the men staring down at him.

"Of course," said Fergus languidly. "It was you, Copper-top, wasn't it! Before I came in behind you and dotted you one. You unloaded the gun. Well done. Your perceptive action has bought you a few minutes more of your pathetic existence. Bucky, go and get two more cartridges."

"I can't."

"God save me, do it!"

Sting of the Nettle

"Them was the last two. I told you we was running out."

"Jesus wept. Then find the two he ejected. They'll be in the kitchen somewhere, he didn't have time to throw them out or anything, I'd have seen. Go on, find them!"

Bucky scurried away past Derek and disappeared into the cottage. Derek tried to gather some strength from somewhere. With a contorted struggle and feeling that perhaps the tape around his ankles had loosened slightly, he managed to roll over and pull himself to his knees. Fergus watched him silently, then lowered the shotgun, reversed it in his hands, and jammed the butt hard into Derek's ribcage.

Derek had seen the blow coming and braced his muscles, but it still knocked the wind out of him, and he fell face down, again cracking his temples on the old brickwork. The ache in his head redoubled. Bloody bricks, he thought vaguely. Bricks in the back garden, bricks through the window, and now Bucky's brick.

"Found them?" he heard Fergus shout.

"I'm looking." Bucky's voice was muffled.

Fergus stared down at Derek, who once again had tried to roll a little onto one side and look up.

"This is your fault," Fergus told him. "You asked for it."

"Why?" Derek managed.

"Making your special enquiries," Fergus sneered." I told you to stop it, didn't I! I instructed you to pack it in, that day of the party when you were treading your size twelve police boots across our dining room carpet. Remember? Ring a bell, does it?"

Sting of the Nettle

"Yes but..." Derek tried to think clearly, as the pain in his stomach and his head receded a little.

"That's the trouble with oiks like you. Won't do what you're told by your betters."

"All I wanted to know was why that old boy Williamson wanted to top himself."

"Well, you'll never know now, will you!"

Derek sighed. "Have it your own way, Fergus." He closed his eyes for a moment. Was there still a chance? Some hopes! Bucky would find those cartridges. They were on the floor of the kitchen., where he had ejected them. They had to be lying there. Even Bucky would his hands on them, sooner or later.

Fergus echoed his thoughts loudly: "Bucky! I'm not waiting here all night. Find the bloody things!"

Bucky shouted something back, but Derek couldn't make it out. However it seemed to satisfy Fergus for a moment, who just muttered "peasant" under his breath.

Derek managed to get some semblance of thought together. "That's what I don't get," he told Fergus. "You and Bucky. I wouldn't have said you two had much in common. I mean, what do you talk about with each other? Palace garden parties? Henley Regatta? The price of turnips?"

"Wouldn't you like to know!" Fergus turned away, looking around in the half light, then abruptly turning back to Derek. "Actually, I suppose I might as well enlighten your foggy police mind. After all, you're not going to be able to tell anyone, are you?"

Keep him talking, Derek told himself. Fight back the fear. You never know. "What is it, between you two

Sting of the Nettle

then? I mean, do you fancy each other or something?"

Fergus shaped to kick him but stopped himself. "Ha. Some policeman you are! If we were queers, what do you think we're doing with that little tramp in there?"

"Okay, so it's women. Or rather, teenage girls, eh? School uniforms do it for you, do they?"

"You're disgusting. I'm not a pervert. Or a rapist, if that's what you're thinking. They love it. Once you work on them a bit. Some vodka, couple of pills, and they're up for it."

He seemed pleased with that remark and smiled to himself.

"I know." Derek said. "I saw."

"What?"

"Early on. I looked through the window."

"You sneaky little toad. So, what did you think you saw?"

"I know exactly what I saw, Fergus."

"And you were shocked, I suppose. You would be. Someone of your type, your background, you tend to think of sex as a bit of rumpy-pumpy on a Saturday night, marrieds only, straight up and down, missionary position. But some of us prefer a more sophisticated approach."

"What? You prefer doing it with a slob like Bucky and some little kid in a dump like this? Oh yes. Very sophisticated."

"Well people get upset if you do it in the Co-op window with the Mayor's wife, you know." Fergus hesitated. "All right. You've got a point about Bucky. But this place is private, and anyway it was him who got us,

Sting of the Nettle

well, started, as it were, in the first place."

"What, him?"

"Well, getting the women, yes." Fergus smiled to himself. "Land girls it was, at first."

"Land girls?"

"You know. The women working on the farms, during the war. Smelly old cows, most of them. But gagging for it."

"With Bucky?"

"Well, he was about the only young bloke around. Reserved occupation, you see. Farmer – would you credit that? I was the same. Estate manager. All right, in the normal course of things I wouldn't waste my time with someone like him, but, well, we met in the pub one night, he was going on about this particular girl he'd met up with, some sort of raver, and he invited me to come along. To join in, as it were."

"And you did."

"Nothing else to do. And then of course Horst turned up on the scene, with his magic pills, and things really got cracking."

"Horst the POW?" Derek prompted.

"Yes. Only it was '46 by then, they weren't prisoners exactly, just waiting to be sent back. They could go anywhere they fancied. He met up with Bucky, and that made the three of us. The three musketeers, Bucky called us. Twit."

"And Horst supplied the Pervitin?"

Fergus looked at him in faint surprise. "Oh. Worked that out for yourself, did you, Copper-top? There's a clever boy. Of course, you know all about our happy

Sting of the Nettle

pills now, don't you! They really worked on you, didn't they"

"Bastard. It got me the sack. But listen, where did Old Tom Williamson come into all this?"

"Him? The interfering old fool." Fergus turned to shout: "Bucky! For God's sake..."

"Hang about. Just putting another record on." As if to confirm this, another blast of Stan Kenton surged through the evening air.

Fergus raised his voice almost to a scream: "Find the fucking cartridges!"

"I'm looking!" Bucky sounded uncertain.

My God. Hope surged in Derek's heart. Bucky must have found the cartridges by now, – unless he wasn't really looking. That must be it. Bucky didn't want him killed, he was wasting time, he was pretending, hoping that Fergus would change his mind. Fergus couldn't shoot him without the cartridges. Bucky was going to say he couldn't find them!

"Found them!" Here came Bucky, triumphantly appearing, holding a cartridge aloft in either hand.

"Splendid. Well done." Derek guessed that Bucky wouldn't hear the irony in Fergus's voice. "Give them to me, dear boy. And then we can conclude tonight's entertainment."

He broke open the gun, took the cartridges from Bucky, and began loading, sliding the red tubes easily into place, and clicking the weapon shut.

"You were asking about our Mr Tom Williamson," he said casually. "The chap who got you into trouble in the first place, eh? Think about it - If it wasn't for old Tom,

Sting of the Nettle

you wouldn't be here. Or, ha ha, dead."

"I just wanted to know..."

"You just wanted to know why the old boy topped himself. Well. I'll tell you. And you can take the information with you to the grave. Which Bucky will shortly be digging for you."

Bucky started to say something, possibly to argue in Derek's defence, but Fergus raised a hand, and he stopped.

"Yes," he went on, almost conversationally, "Horst felt sorry for the old chap, seeing him working himself to death on his scruffy little farm. So he slipped him some P's."

"Peas?" Derek queried.

"P's. Pervitins. for God's sake. Anyway, they worked like a charm. The old feller nearly went berserk. Worked all day and all night. Never seen anyone react so strongly. And then of course he came back for more. Paid for it, mind you. But he had to have it. The way you do, with that stuff. You always come back for more."

"Not always. Not me."

"No, not you. You're a policeman, you wouldn't. You're so far up your own arse. Anyway. Tom loved it. That's why everything began to go a bit pear-shaped. You follow?"

"I'm fascinated."

"So. One night Bucky and I had this girl up here, she was gagging for it."

"And she was getting it!" Bucky put in, then stopped at a look from Fergus.

"Quite. But old Tom Williamson chose that night to

Sting of the Nettle

run out of Pervitin, he wanted more, and I don't blame him, he was paying for much of it by then. So anyway, up he comes, out of nowhere, crashes through the kitchen. The door's open and he sees us with the girl. And in a bit of a threesome, too. Now, Mr. policeman, can you guess who the girl was?"

It was hardly a guess. "His daughter. Margaret."

"Indeed. Now there was a raver, if there ever was one. Anyway, Old Tom goes berserk. Rants and raves, while we untangle ourselves. He reckons he's going to kill us, grabs the shotgun, marches into the room, points the thing at me and pulls the trigger. Bang!"

"And?"

"And I'm not an idiot. Threw myself flat. Thing is, little naked Margaret had run to hide herself behind me. Copped both barrels."

"My God. "

"Yep. You should have seen his face. Come to that, you should have seen hers."

The music blared. Bucky must have turned up the volume.

So that was it. The niggle was over. Now he knew why Old Tom Williamson had done what he'd done. He had shot his own daughter. And the shame, the guilt, had been too great a burden to bear.

Bucky spoke, sounding subdued. "He helped us bury her. No-one really missed her. She had a bit of a reputation around here. Then I told someone I'd seen her at Exeter St. David's with a man, and that was her. Gone."

Derek hardly heard him. He felt a surge of pity for

Sting of the Nettle

Old Tom. He could almost feel the shame the farmer must have felt. The shame, remorse, self-hate, self-disgust, had overwhelmed him. He'd tried but he couldn't live with the memory. He couldn't live with himself. So he didn't.

"Course, we didn't want people asking about it. Which is why you were warned off in the first place." Fergus said calmly.

"But you hadn't actually committed a crime," Derek protested." Technically you were innocent."

"Perhaps. But I was on a big warning. The pater has let me know that if I fucked up again, he'd disown me. Fire me. Cancel my inheritance. I couldn't have that. So now you know. Even you can see why you've got to go as well." Derek felt the same old surge of fear, strong, keen, irresistible.

"Anyway," said Fergus with frightening matter-of-factness. "Here goes."

He raised the gun back to his shoulder. The barrels pointed.

Derek rolled himself sideways, squirming, somehow wrestling himself up and onto his knees.

"Keep still!" Fergus's voice was shrill.

Derek ignored him, struggling, swaying from side to side.

"For God's sake." Fergus waved the gun one way, then the other.

"I'm getting up!" Derek told him.

"It won't be clean, not if you keep moving!"

"Fuck you, I'm getting up."

Derek rocked from side to side, sensing the barrels

following his movement, and then, once again, with a titanic clenching of his stomach muscles, and with a determination born of almost manic desperation, he did it. Somehow, he struggled to his feet.

He stood. Swayed a little, then caught his balance.

His head cleared. The pain left him. He felt strong, ridiculously he felt free. He faced Fergus. He faced the gun, as the barrels steadied their aim on his face. And the fear had gone. The fear he had known from that time he'd run down the road, hidden under the bridge, it was no more

"To hell with you, Fergus. Go fuck yourself."

CHAPTER THIRTY-ONE

Fergus stared back at him. For a few seconds they held each other's gaze. And then Fergus, blinked, looked away, hesitated for a fraction of time. His face changed. He seemed to forget where he was or what he intended to do. The gun barrel lowered, drifted to one side.

And Derek knew that the moment of his death had passed. Fergus couldn't do it. Not face to face, one man standing against another. While Derek had been squirming at his feet, like a dog, like Sally had squirmed, he could have pulled the trigger. He did pull the trigger. But now, eyeball to eyeball, for all his threats and bravado, with the gun fully loaded, he couldn't. And Derek would live.

"Fucking hell!" Bucky's ragged shout shocked both of them out of their mutual trance. "Look!"

From where the man stood, he could see past the cottage wall, and he was staring at the wasteland behind the building.

"What now?" Fergus began – then stopped, turned from Derek, and ran to Bucky's side. "Jesus. What's that?"

Derek at first could see nothing. Then he could – and he could hear it. A roaring engine, bucketing towards the cottage, coming - was it possible - across the broken junk-ridden impassable ground.

Fergus swore again, then ran back to line up the shotgun with Derek's face again.

Sting of the Nettle

The Colonel's Land Rover skidded to a juddering stop. The figure of the Colonel leapt from it, gripping what looked like a pistol in his hand, holding it out in front of him as he strode forward, then stopping as he took in the sight of Fergus, Derek and the shotgun.

Other figures emerged from the vehicle. Mary, running through the kitchen door into the cottage, John joining the Colonel.

Then a scream from Mary, a cry of distress and horror. "John! It's Sandy!"

John disappeared. A door banged violently, and a male voice shouted something indecipherable. There was a crash, and the music stopped.

The twin barrels of Fergus's gun were steady again, close up against Derek's face. The Colonel was standing five yards away, legs braced, both hands on his revolver, which pointed relentlessly at Fergus.

Fergus shouted: "Fuck off or I'll kill him. It's loaded."

"Then I will kill you." The Colonel's voice was icy cold. "This is a Webley MkVI .455 calibre service revolver. And it too is loaded."

"You won't shoot," Fergus tried to sneer, but there was a wobble in his voice.

"Try me."

Fergus looked wildly around and saw Bucky standing frozen with shock and fear.

"Bucky! Get the bastard!" he screamed.

Whether Bucky would have 'got' the Colonel or not Derek would never know. Because now John burst out of the cottage, the iron starting handle in his hand, and ran at the man.

Sting of the Nettle

"Bucky, you bastard! I'm going to kill you."

Bucky took one look, turned, and ran. John sprinted after him, straight through the eye-lines, the firing lines, and then pursuer and pursued disappeared into the growing gloom.

The Colonel spoke as if nothing had happened. "Drop the gun, Fergus. Now."

Fergus waited for a moment, then seemed to shrug, and threw the gun down violently on the broken brick surface.

It fired on impact. And Derek pitched forward, once again to crash face down on the brick flooring.

CHAPTER THIRTY-TWO

"I've got a pressie for you! In fact, I've got two pressies for you!" Mary stood at the foot of his bed in the private hospital room, holding up a light-weight crutch in each hand.

"I can go home then?"

"So they say. If you take it easy."

Derek grinned at her. "Brilliant. So. What's been happening? Bring me up to date."

"What do you know? What do you remember?"

"Not a lot. Well. I remember my feet hurting like hell when the gun went off. And then not much more. I think the ambulance men must have given me a shot, 'cos next thing I knew, I was in Emergency and they were sticking a mask over my face. Then I suppose I had an operation."

"Operation indeed!" Mary scoffed. "They just dug out a few pellets. I've had worse, squeezing blackheads."

"Are you going to tell me what's been going on or do I have to throw a bedpan at you?"

"All right. Listen carefully" She grinned." I don't want you to be, um, *mizzled*. Or even, *devasted.*"

"A full bedpan?" he threatened.

"Okay. Pin back your ears." Mary sat down on the side of the bed and started ticking off points on her fingers. "First, Sandy's okay, which is the important thing. She's safe."

"Wait, go back a bit. Where did the Colonel come

from? I told him to..."

"Yes, and thank goodness he took no notice of you. He'd followed us, we met up with him when me and John went back for your fictional torch. He said he was disobeying orders, so you could have him on something called a whizzer?"

"A fizzer."

"What's a fizzer?"

"It doesn't matter. Go on."

"Well, then we waited like you said, but it was obvious something was wrong, and in the end the Colonel said it was a case of Action This Day. And it was. We piled into the Land Rover and came charging in like the Seventh Cavalry, didn't we! Through the fence, over the bumps."

"Thank goodness you did. What happened after I got shot?"

"Well, the Colonel told me to take the Land Rover and fetch help. Which I did. Oh, and Derek, we've got to get ourselves one of those. It goes anywhere, like a tractor only at sixty miles an hour. I found a phone box and summoned your lot and the ambulance. When I got back, John had collared Bucky, who'd got a big bruise on his jaw and a sprained wrist. John said he fell over, and we pretended to believe him." She giggled at the memory.

"What about Sandy?"

"She'd almost passed out, bless her. John got her to hospital in my car, and they say she's addicted, but there are places she can go to get cured. If she's lucky."

Derek swung his legs off the bed, wincing at the pain.

Sting of the Nettle

He was mildly surprised that it wasn't worse.

"And I assume," he went on, "that Fergus and Bucky are under arrest."

"Mmm. Threatening behaviour, assault with a deadly weapon, and something about corrupting a minor."

"And drugs?

"Apparently, that stuff, what is it? Methamphetamine, it's quite legal."

"Then that'll have to change, before the whole country goes barmy. Okay, go on."

"Yeah, well, the good news is, I spoke to your Inspector, and to Welbeloved, and they say well done. The Inspector, he's a nice old boy, isn't he? He seems to think you're Devon's version of Dan Dare, with all the derring-do that you've been derring-doing. Anyway, they say you can keep your job. And that's it. Happy?"

Derek stared at her in disbelief. Not at what she was saying, but at what she wasn't saying. Mary stared back, puzzled.

"Oh God, you're not happy, are you! What's up now?"

"What about the girl?"

"I told you. Sandy..."

"No, no. Not Sandy. The other girl. Margaret Williamson."

"Her? The Williamson girl? But she's in London, or..."

"She's dead. And those two were there, they buried her. She's up there at Bucky's place. Somewhere."

* * *

Sting of the Nettle

In the fresh light of day, a busload of constables came from Exeter, bearing spades. Carloads of ranking officers turned up. A pathologist and a dog crew arrived. A superintendent remarked that there hadn't been such a major police operation since Rubber Bones escaped. The man had not been collared until he got to Soho and then the superintendent rather wished he hadn't mentioned such a resounding local police failure, at least not in the hearing of the Chief Constable, who also turned up.

Derek, pale but gallant, was of course present, leaning on his crutches in bandaged feet and soft slippers, and surveying the search operation. Sergeant Welbeloved himself personally found a suitable chair in Bucky's cottage, carried it out himself, and placed it on that dodgy brickwork that had once been a terrace, after which Derek could sit in comfort.

Mary fetched her own chair and sat with him. John was at the hospital with Sandy, but the Colonel turned up trying to look steadfast, an image rather spoiled by the presence of Sally, for whom he unbent and petted frequently.

Finally, Fergus and Bucky arrived in the back of a police van, giving Derek dirty looks but otherwise expressing themselves willing to co-operate with the authorities. When challenged about the death of Margaret Williamson and the subsequent concealment of her body, they expressed disbelief, denial and innocent astonishment.

A distinguished detective, his sergeant, and two burly constables took both of them to stand in front of Derek on his chair.

Sting of the Nettle

"Hello Fergus," Derek said implacably. "You told me about Margaret, how she was shot, didn't you? How you buried her." A woman P.C. took assiduous notes. "You told me all about it. Just before you were going to shoot me."

"My dear man!" Fergus adopted his painful cut-glass accent. "I wasn't going to shoot you. We were just having a little fun. Weren't we, Bucky?"

Bucky, looking frightened to death, nodded as vigorously as his bruised face would let him. "Having a little fun."

Derek pointed at his feet. "And that," said Fergus, "was, as you well know, a complete accident."

"You were going to shoot him," the Colonel said dryly. "And then I was going to shoot you."

"I'd advise you, Sir, not to admit to threatening behaviour at this time," the distinguished detective told the Colonel. Then he turned back to Fergus.

"Now, as to the allegation concerning Miss Margaret Williamson..."

"He told me!" Derek insisted, then turned to Fergus: "It might have been accidental, but you buried her somewhere here..."

Fergus smiled his most benevolent smile, adopted his most aristocratic tone, and focussed his most supercilious charm on the distinguished detective.

"Your young constables do have vivid imaginations, don't they, Superintendent! The young lady as I understand it was reported missing at some stage, but then I heard she'd run off to London with some man or other."

Sting of the Nettle

The detective raised an eyebrow to his sergeant, who replied: "Er, yes Guv. If memory serves."

The searchers did their best. Bits of old machinery, galvanised sheets, anything large enough to cover anything else was moved. Soft ground was prodded. In two places men with spades dug carefully and found nothing but old cattle bones and more abandoned ironmongery.

Welbeloved sidled up to Derek where he sat in the chair that the sergeant had personally provided for him. "Are you quite sure about this, young Martin?"

"He's quite sure," the Colonel told him.

"Are you, Constable?" Welbeloved insisted.

"Of course I'm sure. I'm damned sure. "

"Well. I hope so. For your sake. And there's no cause to be impertinent."

Fuck you, Derek thought, and came close to saying it, before a glance from Mary held him back.

The dog unit had a sniff around, and the two police dogs peed extensively on various parts of Bucky's little acre, but neither showed any particular interest in any specific site. One dog did pay keen attention to Derek's bandaged feet and had to be shooed away by Mary before it dampened the slippers. Sally growled ineffectually.

The Inspector said something about overtime payments, and anyway he had an important meeting. The Chief Constable said he too had an important meeting, and the Chief Superintendent breathed a silent sigh of relief and told the Inspector the same thing. Impending important meetings were suddenly all the

Sting of the Nettle

rage within the Devonshire constabulary, and inevitably and eventually the order went out. "Okay lads, pack it in." Little groups of blue uniforms began to trickle towards their vehicles. Spades and other implements were stowed away. Lunch beckoned. The search was over.

Bucky looked deeply relieved and allowed himself to be led away towards a waiting police car. Fergus gave Derek a long look that promised much, none of it pleasant, then turned away in the same direction.

Mary squeezed her husband's shoulder.

"She's here somewhere," he told her, sounding plaintive even to his own ears. "Somewhere out there, under the docks and the thistles and the nettles, and..."

"Nettles!" They both breathed the word at each other, almost simultaneously.

"Over there!" Mary had pointed, in their garden, so long ago it seemed. A patch of nettles, deep green, thriving, outgrowing everything else. "Could be a dead dog under there," she'd said.

"Inspector!" Derek bellowed, nearly falling off his chair with the effort. The Inspector, perhaps the one person who might still take a paternal interest in what his young constable might have to say, stopped with his hand on his car door.

"What?"

"The nettles, the patch of nettles, over there. They grow big on dead things. She's under those nettles!"

As he spoke, Derek knew that he wouldn't be listened to, that his claim, his theory, would be dismissed, that it was the longest of long shots. The Inspector paused,

Sting of the Nettle

hesitated.

And then, thank God for Bucky! Obligingly the man saved the day. He was about to be ushered into the van he arrived in when he heard Derek's exclamation, heard what he said, saw what he was pointing at, and made a break for it. He wrenched himself free from the casual grip of a constable and ran like a stag.

Which was a mistake when you come to think about it. Dogs do a lot of chasing down stags in the west country. It's in their make-up, their DNA. The dog unit ran down Bucky within a minute. Sally arrived late and loud, but the Colonel claimed some of the credit.

Fergus saw all this, sagged at the inevitable result, and launched a vicious kick at Derek's slippers. He missed.

The police had only dug down a foot deep in the nettle bed when they found what remained of the late Margaret Williamson. She was wrapped in an old yellow curtain.

CHAPTER THIRTY-THREE

A much-used expression in West Devon, and possibly elsewhere in 1952, was 'It'll all be the same in a hundred years', an echo, if you like, of the philosopher's dictum 'This too shall pass.' But in North Tawe it would have been more appropriate to say, 'It'll all be the same in a hundred days.' Because, remarkably after such dramatic and traumatic events, involving residents of the village, it practically was. Almost.

Poor Margaret's body inevitably suffered the indignity of a postmortem, with the obvious result. The elderly coroner, who had pronounced so misguidedly on the fate of Old Tom Williamson, found himself revelling in a choice of possible verdicts. He whittled the list down to either death by misadventure or his favourite, accidental death. When this was queried by someone a little higher up the chain of legal authority, he protested that whatever way you looked at it, the death was indeed an accident, as it could not be described as having been caused deliberately And, annoyingly, he was right.

Mrs Williamson and her son Peter were then able to lay Margaret to rest, opting first for cremation, and then burial of the ashes. The elderly parish vicar provided a site in a secluded corner of the churchyard, and a small flat headstone was laid on the spot of the internment.

This practice not only freed up space, but also led other bereaved families to follow suit, and in due course the site became a small enclosure specifically for the

Sting of the Nettle

burial of ashes. So, in a nuanced fashion, the plot became a positive memory of Margaret's short time on earth.

The proposed centralisation of the police was called off for the time being. Sergeant Welbeloved claimed that it was his advice that did the trick. But actually it was the bumbling mistake of an Exeter civilian clerk that led to the matter being left off the appropriate agenda of a critical meeting.

In the Okehampton police office some clumsy constable broke the Sergeant's lipstick-inscribed mug. But Mrs. Welbeloved, demonstrating a hitherto unsuspected talent for both forgiveness and humour, gave him a new one, inscribing it, in a new shade of lippy, with the one word "His!"

The Colonel's health remained fragile. His wife returned home but marital harmony was not helped by her frequently expressed opinion that he thought more of that damn dog than he did of her. Sally thrived. So did the Williamson's farm under the joint management of Hans and Peter.

Bucky and Fergus served out their short jail terms for concealing a death and perverting the cause of justice. Fergus's father found his errant son a job on a coffee farm in Kenya. Bucky, barred from the pub for ever, sold his placed to a would-be gentleman small holder from Bath, and did what so many in his position would do. He moved to Cornwall.

Sandy spent three months in a sanitorium in Barnstable and returned a normal bright-eyed teenager. For John and his stricken wife Lucy, it was a small but valued compensation for an otherwise bleak future.

Inevitably after such trauma Constable Derek Martin had to cope with flashbacks and nightmares and should have commanded the attention of a police mental therapist. But there wasn't one. Mary helped drive away some of the demons. But even so there were bad dreams, bad nights

That March it rained on North Tawe for twenty days. It washed away a ton or more of mud and cattle droppings from the road surfaces, and some might have hoped that it would wash away memories of shotguns and suicides and drugs and corruption and the click of a shotgun mechanism. But it never rains that hard. Not even in West Devon.

END

Printed and Bound in the UK by CMP Books, Dorset

DIAMOND CRIME

Passionate about the crime/mystery/thriller books it publishes

Follow
Facebook:
@diamondcrimepublishing

Instagram
@diamond_crime_publishing

Web
diamondbooks.co.uk

DIAMOND BOOKS

Printed in Great Britain
by Amazon